# My Husband's Child

by

Allison Lee

Copyright © August 2025

I, Allison Lee, hereby assert and
give notice of my rights under section 77 of the
Copyright, Design and Patents Act, 1988
to be identified as the author of this work.

All Rights Reserved. No part of this publication
may be reproduced, stored in a retrieval system
or transmitted at any time by any means
electronic, mechanical, photocopying, recording or
otherwise, without prior permission of the publisher.

All characters in this publication are fictitious and
any resemblance to real persons, living or dead,
is purely coincidental.

Cover design by Castenzio Cusumano
Cusumano Designs Ltd

Interior design by BAD PRESS iNK

ISBN: 978-1-0687203-3-8

published by www.badpress.ink

Dedicated to my husband, Mark,
for his unwavering love and support.

# Chapter One

It hit me hard when my husband died. Very hard. Not least because I didn't really know how I was supposed to feel. Was I devastated, distraught, bereft? Yes, I was probably all of these, at least to a certain extent. However, I was also relieved, detached, and somewhat dispassionate about the whole thing. I knew these were feelings I had to keep hidden, certainly for the time being, but they were feelings I experienced nonetheless. The truth was, although Miles was still technically my husband, I hadn't seen him for years, and whilst I loved the man that I thought he was and had hoped he was, I despised the person he had become.

Miles was ten years older than me, and when I first met him just after leaving school, he seemed worldly and well-read. To my schoolgirl awkwardness, he was sophisticated. I fell for his charms immediately. After dating for just a few months, Miles asked me to marry him. In hindsight, I was far too young, but at the time, it felt right. I had no parents to guide me; both my parents had died in a car accident when I was just sixteen, so I had to grow up quickly and learn how to care for myself. Miles was my knight in shining armour, the father figure I so desperately missed, and I believed him when he told me how much he loved me. I had just had my twenty-first birthday when we got married. It was a simple ceremony with very few guests. I had no family to speak of except for a couple of elderly relatives dotted around the country who I wouldn't recognise if I walked past them in the street. Miles was an only child with few relatives and even fewer friends. We kept everything simple. It was Miles's idea not to make a fuss; after all, a wedding is about the people getting married, not the guests, he had told me. Although I had always dreamed of a fairy tale wedding, with the flowing gown and the horse-drawn carriage, I relented easily and went along with his ideas rather than hoping to realise my own. I smile now as I recall how I believed everything he said in those early days, how I hung on to his every word. What a fool I had been.

Married life with Miles was good at the beginning. The first few years were happy; at least, I thought they were. Then again, if Miles had been happy, then we wouldn't have ended up like we did, so perhaps I was just kidding myself, and our marriage had never been good, not even in those early days. Miles was a successful lawyer, and I didn't have to go to work. We had a beautiful house; it wasn't big by any means, but it was quaint and pretty, and I was free to do what I pleased. He was a good husband, and he provided well for me. I felt safe and loved, and I was truly grateful for my life in the beginning anyway. We both wanted children and, looking back, I knew this was when the problems first surfaced. It wasn't really a case of who was at fault; it never really crossed my mind that it was anyone's 'fault', but the cracks started to appear as we remained childless as the years passed. After about three years, I think I consoled myself with the fact that we simply weren't destined to become parents. Miles had suggested that we seek medical help and find out what the 'problem' was, but I had been reluctant.

'What difference does it make?' I asked him one

morning when he broached the subject again. 'It's not a blame game; it doesn't matter who can't have children; we are in this together,' I remember looking at Miles and seeing him wince at my comment, but he simply said nothing, nodded and left for work. I have often wondered what would have happened if I had agreed to seek medical assistance or, indeed, whether Miles had done so without me and was therefore certain that it was my fault that we were unable to have children. He never admitted if he had sought advice, but then how could he? That would well and truly be laying the blame at my door, and I don't think even Miles was that cruel.

We had drifted apart. It happened slowly, as it often does in marriages that go stale. Neither of us saw it coming, and if we did, we chose to turn a blind eye, cover up the cracks, paint on a smile, and carry on. Miles started working longer hours at the office. He spent nights away, which eventually led to a week at a time until I no longer expected him to come home. When he showed his face, it was usually for fresh clothes or a certain suit he needed for a conference. He always seemed to say the right things even when he hadn't been home for days, but I knew even then that he had left me in his heart, if not through the divorce courts. To be fair to Miles, he never did ask me for a divorce. I don't think he wanted one, and I certainly didn't. He just spent less and less time with me and more and more time with someone else. I had no idea who he was seeing, but I wasn't naïve enough to think he lived a single life away from me. I certainly didn't think he was spending nights away from home alone. Although I wanted to hear him tell me it was all over, the truth of the matter was I simply wasn't strong enough to listen, so I ignored the obvious, although the signs were there. To a stranger, it would be obvious my husband was having an affair, but I refused to believe it. Until Miles told me he was leaving me for another woman, I would remain defensive. Miles never asked me for a divorce, so although we hadn't seen each other for years, he was still my husband. My dead husband, and I had a funeral to organise.

# Chapter Two

In a funny sort of way, I was glad we had a small family and few friends. At times like these, people usually take comfort in friends and family, but I didn't need comfort. I needed this to be over quickly so I could return to my normal, sedate life. I wasn't used to hiding my emotions. I had lived on my own for years, and if I wanted to cry, I would; if I wanted to play loud music and dance around the house like a lunatic, I could. There was no one to watch me, ridicule me or berate me. I didn't need anyone. I wasn't looking for another relationship; heaven forbid, the last thing I wanted to do was tie myself down to another man and get into another loveless marriage.

The house and, I suppose, everything else that Miles owned, whatever that may be, now belonged to me, so the sooner I sorted the funeral and necessary death procedures, the better. I could continue living the life I loved, only this time as a widow instead of a wife. *Widow*, I said the word over and over to myself. It had a special kind of ring to it, and I quite liked being seen as the grieving widow. Only I wasn't grieving, was I? That was the difficult part of it all. Everyone expected to see me red-eyed from crying, dishevelled and distressed. I found acting quite difficult despite the fact that I had spent my entire married life acting the happy wife; playing the bereaved widow seemed so much more difficult.

## My Husband's Child

As it turned out, I didn't have to worry too much, and I didn't have to act for very long. The funeral was professional, efficient and, above all else, quick. I was eternally grateful to the funeral director as he took care of everything. Unsurprisingly, he thought I was too upset to deal with the arrangements when, in fact, I didn't actually know my husband, so it would have been pointless sharing my input. I know what he liked years ago when he lived with me, but now, who knows? Had his taste in music changed? Did he even want a burial? Would a cremation have been more appropriate? I had to admit I had absolutely no idea, so I simply followed the funeral director's suggestions and hoped that no one would see through my charade.

I felt guilty, and yet I hadn't done anything wrong. It wasn't like I was pretending to be his widow. It wasn't even as if I didn't have some feelings for Miles, although it would be a hard stretch in anyone's imagination to say I actually loved him. I did have feelings for him, that much was true, but the feelings were mixed: a small dollop of affection from years ago mixed with a huge wedge of resentment for a life I could have had. Miles's actions had put my life on hold for years, and I found it difficult to forgive him for that. I didn't really know why I hadn't moved on. Did I think he might come back to me? Ask to start again? Take up where we left off? I honestly didn't know, although I had thought about it so many times. What would I have done if Miles had returned with his tail between his legs? Would I have taken him back, no questions asked? Maybe at the beginning, when I was still young and naïve, but not now. Now, I was glad he was gone. I no longer needed to think about him, consider his next move, and wonder when the divorce papers might drop through the letter box.

## My Husband's Child

I was alone but not lonely. I had never felt lonely. Well, maybe that was a lie. To begin with, when Miles started working longer hours, I felt lonely. We bought the house together, with his money admittedly, but as his wife, it is as much mine as it is his; it is beautiful, but it is also remote. It lies in the countryside, surrounded by meadows. We have a pretty south-facing cottage garden with a stream running through it. It is serene, and I love it, but in the early days, when Miles started coming home after I had retired to bed, I began to feel isolated. As the years went by and Miles increased the time he spent away from me, I grew more and more used to being on my own, and instead of feeling lonely, I felt free. The house was my saviour, not my downfall. If I needed company, I could find it, but when I needed solace, which I often did, I had it in abundance right here in my home. I would never leave this house. Miles knew how much I loved living here, and, to be fair to him, he left me in peace to enjoy it. Wherever he chose to live when he wasn't with me made no difference as long as I could continue to enjoy the tranquillity that was mine. If Miles had asked me for a divorce, I would have relented. I would have had no choice. It wasn't like we were living as man and wife and no court would refuse to grant him a divorce, but he never asked, and for that, I was truly grateful. Maybe he was thinking about returning to me? I will never know. The answer to that question died when Miles did.

There were just a handful of people at the funeral. I recognised a couple of faces as being old friends of Miles from his university days, but I didn't recognise any of the others. It wasn't surprising as I hadn't been a part of Miles's life for many years. I was comforted to see that there was just one woman at the graveside, and I was certain she wasn't Miles's mistress. She was much younger than Miles. Although I myself was ten years younger than him, this woman was much younger than me too, so I doubted she would be having a relationship with my now dead husband. Still, I couldn't help myself from watching her closely. I scrutinised her every move. Did she look upset? Was she a friend, a work colleague? Despite the age gap, I found myself wondering if she was his lover. She was slim, and I guess I would put her in her early twenties. She was dressed in a black coat, with sunglasses to shade her eyes, making it impossible for me to tell if she was crying. I hadn't arranged a wake; I couldn't bring myself to swap stories with strangers and pretend I knew the man I had just buried, so after the short service, everyone left quickly. The funeral director swapped pleasantries with me, but I wanted to tell him to shut up so I could speak to the young woman. I was intrigued. I felt an irrational need to know who she was and how she knew Miles. By the time the funeral director had done being nice, she had gone. I looked frantically around, but the churchyard was empty. I turned and walked towards my car, parked under a huge oak tree at the entrance to the churchyard. I looked around one last time to satisfy myself that the young woman was nowhere to be seen, and then I drove the short distance home, my mind spinning with endless possibilities about who she might be.

# Chapter Three

I let myself into the house and put the kettle on. I had left an empty glass and a bottle of Miles's favourite whisky on the kitchen table, and I looked at it wistfully. Listening to the kettle boil, I walked over and poured myself a drink from the bottle. I put the glass to my lips and gulped the liquid down. It burned my throat as I swallowed, but I willed myself to take another gulp. I drained the glass and replaced it on the kitchen table.

'To Miles,' I said sarcastically, 'every woman should have an absent husband.' Well, he was most certainly absent now, I thought, as I busied myself making coffee. I cut a slice of cake and took my plate and mug into the conservatory. The area was small, but it gave me a full view of the garden, and the scenery was beautiful. I watched as the birds flew from branch to branch and a couple of squirrels scurried in the undergrowth.

I let my mind wander back to when I first found out that Miles was dead. I received a telephone call from his solicitor. I don't know who informed him I was Miles's wife or how he knew my contact details, and I never thought to ask. The call had taken me by complete surprise, and when the man on the telephone introduced himself, I honestly thought the time had arrived when Miles was seeking a divorce, and he had instructed this man to contact me to get the ball rolling. I was prepared for that, but I most certainly wasn't prepared for what he did tell me.

I remembered how my blood ran cold as the solicitor told me Miles was dead. I can't remember when I stopped listening and started crying, but it had been somewhere after I was notified that Miles had suffered a heart attack.

'Mrs Jameson, are you still there?' I heard the solicitor say, jolting me back to my senses. Through tears and shock, I acknowledged what the solicitor said before ending the call. I had arranged to go into the solicitor's office the next day to review Miles's will and other paperwork. Thankfully, I wasn't asked to identify the body. I wondered who this task had been afforded to, but as it wasn't something I wanted to do, I didn't ask.

The next day, I had driven the twenty miles or so to the nearest town. There was a village closer, but it was tiny, and other than a pub and a village store, there were no amenities. I was surprised that Miles hadn't changed solicitors. I expected he would want someone nearer to where he lived, wherever that might have been, but I was also grateful that I didn't have far to travel. I was still in shock, and the news of Miles's death hadn't fully sunk in. Whilst we didn't live together, he was still my husband, and I wasn't entirely sure how I felt about his untimely passing.

My appointment with the solicitor went quickly. I was informed that, as my husband's next of kin, everything had been left to me. His estate was sizeable, and I was shocked to find out that I was now a rather wealthy woman in my own right. I hadn't needed to work even after Miles had left. He had always provided a healthy allowance for me, and I knew the house was mortgage-free. However, I didn't know that Miles had also purchased another house, a large, detached Victorian residence not far from where we had lived together at the start of our married life. Had Miles been living within a ten-mile radius of me all this time, and I hadn't had a clue?

I left the solicitor's office and wandered around the town in a daze. I stopped at a small café and ordered a coffee whilst pondering the conversation I had just had with the solicitor. I took the envelope from my handbag that I had been given earlier in the meeting and tore it open. It contained a couple of sets of keys, the address to the property Miles had purchased without my knowledge and a copy of Miles's will. I had been informed that both properties were mortgage-free and that the deeds to both were kept at the solicitor's should I wish to sell either or both of the houses. Sell? Well, I certainly didn't need two houses, but I hadn't any intentions of selling my own home. I didn't need to move away. My memories of Miles might not be great, but the house held nothing but happiness for me, and I intended to continue living there. I was, however, intrigued by the house that Miles had bought after he had moved out.

Although I never had any proof and Miles never admitted to having an affair, deep down, I did believe he had left me for another woman and that he had gone to live with her. Was it in this house? If so, where was she now? I looked at the address on the tag attached to one of the sets of keys and decided to take a look at the property. I would sell it, I knew that, but for now, I wanted to see it for myself, see where Miles had lived in the latter years of his life. I drained my coffee cup, replaced it on the table and headed back to my car. Turning on the engine, the SatNav sprang to life, and I quickly tapped in the address. Putting the car in gear, I pulled out of the parking space and followed the SatNav's instructions.

I was both curious and nervous as I neared the house. I turned slowly along a tree-lined avenue and followed it to the very end. A huge electric gate faced me, and I fumbled as I entered the code written on the piece of paper supplied by the solicitor. As soon as I had punched in the last digit, the gates swung open effortlessly, allowing me access. I followed the sweeping gravel driveway and stopped outside the vast wooden door. I turned off the engine and climbed slowly out of the car. I looked up at the huge house in front of me. It was the complete opposite of the tranquil cottage we had bought together and, at first, I thought I had got the wrong address. This house, although enormous, was a monstrosity. Ugly in its entirety, I couldn't imagine Miles living here. But then, I couldn't really image Miles living anywhere other than with me, but he had led another life, and I was oblivious to how and where. Until now. I was no nearer to knowing how he lived his new life. I was hoping I was about to find out, but I certainly now knew where he lived.

I walked up to the huge door and rang the bell. Laughing as I did so. Who did I expect would answer it? The mistress? The housekeeper? Miles's ghost? In all honesty, although I laughed at the idea of all three, I don't think I would have been in the slightest bit surprised if any of them had answered the door. Such was the fanciful situation I found myself in. Still, I waited a few minutes before taking a set of keys from my pocket and fumbling with the lock, heard it ping. I turned the handle and swung open the door. I remained where I was on the doorstep a little while longer, taking deep breaths of fresh air and willing myself to walk inside.

I took a few tentative steps inside the house and stopped in the hallway. The alarm on the wall beeped furiously as I walked towards it and entered the code that had been scribbled on the same piece of paper as the code for the gates. The bleeping stopped immediately. I looked around the colossal space with its sweeping staircase and vast marble floor, polished to within an inch of its life so that it gleamed in the sunlight pouring through the stained-glass window on the landing above.

I pushed the door closed and leaned against it, taking in the sight before me. There were six heavy oak doors off the hallway, each one closed. I walked over to the first one and pushed it open. It revealed an expansive drawing room with an enormous bay window surrounded by heavy drapes. The room was lavishly furnished with beautiful sofas and tables and a deep plush carpet. Sunlight streamed through the window, giving the room a warm homely feel despite its size, and I was surprised to find myself actually liking it. I moved slowly from room to room, searching for signs of Miles. I found none. From the sitting room to the games room to the orangery, and the kitchen, there were no personal artefacts to show who lived in this house.

There were fabulous paintings adorning the walls and other works of art stylishly arranged around the house, but not a single photograph or a piece of personal memorabilia. Perhaps it's all been cleared out, I thought to myself as I wandered around the downstairs rooms. I knew this was impossible as Miles had only just died, and I was the sole beneficiary of his will; therefore, no one else had access to the property. I moved around the kitchen aimlessly. It was spotless. I could see no sign that anyone had lived here only a few days before; there were no cups in the sink or plates in the dishwasher. I opened the fridge. It was bare. Not so much as a can of beer or a bottle of ketchup. It all felt strange to me.

I left the kitchen and headed back into the hall, seeking out the staircase. I felt like Scarlett O'Hara in *Gone With The Wind*, as I slowly ascended the stairs, running my hand along the smooth banister as I went. At the top of the staircase, the landing branched into two with three more oak doors on each side. I turned right along the hallway and opened the first door, which revealed a simple but beautiful bedroom with a strikingly modern bathroom and dressing room. I moved from one door to the next; each room was identical in size and shape, the only differences being the colour and design of the bedding and drapes at the window. The bedrooms, like the downstairs rooms, were beautiful but soulless.

Had Miles really lived here? Has anyone ever lived here? I couldn't image this house having been lived in. It was immaculate, not just tidy but flawless. There was absolutely no sign of anyone having lived here, ever.

I opened the wardrobe before me and found coat hangers but no clothes. I pulled open drawers in dressing tables, bedside cabinets, and chests, but each one was empty. There wasn't a single item of clothing in any of the bedrooms. If Miles had bought this house to live in, then he must have moved out a long time ago. He hadn't just packed to go on a holiday. He had packed and left. I couldn't understand why he would keep the property if he didn't intend to live there. It was huge, and its upkeep alone would have been costly. It was obvious that someone was cleaning it, and judging by the immaculate lawns and flower beds, he must have employed a gardener. Had been employing, I quickly corrected myself, because now that had been left to me to sort out.

Satisfying myself that the house held no answers, I retraced my steps, reset the alarm and let myself back out into the glorious sunshine. I pulled the door behind me and locked it, trying the handle to check before climbing back into my car. The gravel under the car's wheels made a satisfying crunch as I headed towards the gate. I was in a trance, my mind wandering back to the house and the lack of any reminders of Miles having ever been there. I was disappointed. I had hoped to get a glimpse of Miles's life without me. It would have been painful; I was aware of that, but I was also prepared for it. I wanted to see for myself where he had lived; I needed to see everything. But there had been nothing to discover. No answers to my questions. So, if he wasn't living here, where was he living?

A screech of brakes brought me back to my senses, and I swerved quickly to avoid the Mini coming down the drive in the opposite direction. Climbing out of my car, I saw a middle-aged woman and two younger men. The woman smiled at me and offered her outstretched hand.

'You must be Mrs Jameson,' the woman said, smiling. 'I am so sorry about your loss,' she continued, without giving me a chance to respond. 'I'm Jean, the housekeeper, and these two are James and John, my sons, and also the gardeners.' I reached to shake Jean's outstretched hand, smiling as I did so. I wanted to ask her so many questions, but I knew they would sound ridiculous to someone who didn't know our predicament. But then Jean must be aware that I didn't live here; otherwise, she wouldn't just be introducing herself. Then again, as I had just discovered,

Miles didn't appear to live here either, but I was reluctant to admit that this woman, the housekeeper, obviously knew more about my dead husband's whereabouts than I did. I didn't have to wonder for long.

'I know Mr Jameson had intended selling the house, but if you decide to keep it now that...' Jean's voice trailed off, and she lowered her eyes, embarrassed. She was obviously trying hard to keep her job but didn't want to sound heartless after the death of Miles. 'We would be more than happy to stay on Mrs Jameson; myself and the boys are hard workers, and we would keep the house and gardens pristine, just as we always have.' I didn't doubt that she and her sons wouldn't keep their promise, but I had no intention of living in this house. I decided to swallow my pride and dig a little deeper.

'When exactly did my husband say he would sell this house?' I asked, studying the woman carefully.

'Well, let me see, it would be about seven or eight weeks ago when he moved out and asked me to clear the house of all his belongings. He took them all with him down to the south coast. Said he'd be putting the house on the market at some point but that we were to carry on looking after it until he did. I hoped he might change his mind; he always seemed happy living here and said he liked the fact that you were nearby.'

I almost choked when she said that. I opened my mouth to speak, but no words came out. I stood there staring at the housekeeper as if she had just said the most ridiculous thing. Well, in my mind, she had. Why on earth would Miles be happy living so close to me when he had chosen to leave in the first place? I quickly pulled myself together.

'He said that?' I asked incredulously.

'Oh yes, Mrs Jameson, he always said he was happiest when you and he were together. He never went into a lot of detail, and it's not my place to ask, but I do know he loved you very much.'

I continued to stare at Jean. This stupid woman seemed to genuinely believe what she had just said. What on earth did she think? Why would Miles pretend to her that he loved me when he had moved out and we hadn't seen each other for years? I felt my chest tighten; this didn't make sense. I wanted to ask Jean if she knew where Miles had moved to. Did she have an address on the south coast for him? Who had he left with? I didn't dare ask; I was absolutely terrified of the answers. I simply climbed back into my car. I pressed a button, and the window opened. I leaned out.

'Thank you, Jean. I am afraid I won't be keeping the house, but I would be more than happy to retain your services and those of your sons until the house is sold,' I said. Jean nodded, and I put the car into gear and continued my journey home.

# Chapter Four

Once home, I poured myself a glass of wine and went to sit in the garden. It was a bit early in the day to drink wine, but I needed the alcohol to steady my nerves. I sat on the lover's seat by the stream, remembering how Miles and I used to sit here together in the early days of our marriage when we had our whole lives ahead of us. This was how I remembered Miles. He used to enjoy the peacefulness of this garden and the house, although it wasn't on the scale of the house I had just visited where he spent the final years of his life; I believed he was happy here with me, at least at the beginning.

I still had a lot of questions, and I needed answers. The problem was that I had no one to ask. For the past forty years, I had been married to a man who, in truth, I hardly knew.

I was now a very wealthy woman in her early sixties, and I had just buried my husband. I knew it didn't help to dwell on things, and, in all honesty, nothing I could do would alter the fact that Miles was dead, but it would help me to try to understand what had happened to our marriage and come to terms with how I had ended up in this situation. It wasn't that I was distraught and needed consoling; the opposite was probably true. Without Miles alive, I didn't have to spend the rest of my life tied to a loveless marriage, waiting for the inevitable divorce papers to land on the mat. Still, then again, Miles had never given me any reason to believe that he intended to divorce me. I guess nothing he did really made much sense to me, and as I hadn't had the courage to ask Miles the questions I needed answers to when he was alive, I didn't really know who I could turn to now.

When Miles was alive, I didn't need to know anything. I was afraid to ask; I thought I wouldn't like the answers. I suppose deep down I really wanted to believe what Jean had told me, that Miles was comforted by the fact that he lived close to me because he still loved me. But then, what did she know? She was the bloody housekeeper. I doubted very much that Miles would open up to her and confess everything. Hell, he never opened up to me or confessed his feelings, so I was pretty sure he wouldn't tell the housekeeper. Maybe she wasn't just the housekeeper? Even I had to laugh at this idea. I was starting to get paranoid now. I drank my wine, my mind racing unhealthily. I tried to clear my thoughts and concentrate on the birds in the trees. I watched the flowers blow gently in the breeze and spotted a dragonfly hovering over the stream.

I tried to make a plan in my mind for all the things I needed to do. Tomorrow, I will call the estate agent and get the big house valued and put up for sale. There was no point in prolonging things. The house was huge and costly. I would need to pay Jean and her sons to maintain the place and pay bills until it was sold. As I had no intention of living there myself, and it was already empty of personal belongings, I saw no reason to hang on to it longer than necessary. I had decided I would also contact the solicitor again. Maybe he could shed some light on Miles's last whereabouts. He must have an address for him. I would ask him what he knew about Miles's last movements. Somehow, it felt less intimidating for the solicitor to know I was unaware of Miles's predicament than to admit to Jean that I didn't know anything about my husband in his final years. Part of me longed to know what Miles had divulged to her, what she knew about our marriage, but I didn't want to ask her. To ask her would be admitting my marriage was a sham, and I wasn't prepared to do that to a total stranger.

My mind wandered back to the funeral and the young woman I had seen at the graveside. Did Jean know who she was? Jean, I figured, probably knew a lot. I didn't even know how long Miles had lived in the huge house, but I guessed it was when he had first moved out of our home. Jean, I surmised, would have been employed shortly after, as I doubted Miles would be able to keep up with a house of that size without any help, although her sons wouldn't have been old enough to help out in the garden then as I would put them in their mid-twenties now.

So many unanswered questions. My mind continued to race. Did I really need to know the answers to things that had never concerned me in the first place? This was a part of Miles's life that I had not been privy to; therefore, I felt like an intruder delving into things that didn't concern me. Perhaps it would be better to let sleeping dogs lie, not ask questions, sell the house, and simply move on.

Wishing something in the past hadn't happened was a fool's game, and I was no fool.

# Chapter Five

The next morning I rose early. I had slept well despite the questions which I kept going over again and again in my mind. Today, I was determined to get some answers. I might not have been a part of Miles's life when he had bought the house, but it was a part of my life now, and I had every right to know about it. I made myself some toast and coffee and took it out on the patio. Despite the early hour, the sun was already high in the sky, and it had the promise of being a beautiful day. I love rising early.

I have no immediate neighbours, but everything still appears even more peaceful and quiet in the early morning. I have time to think more clearly before most of the population has woken. Today, though, rather than thinking clearly, my mind raced. What did I need to know? Who held the answers to all my questions? Did I really need to find the answers, or was I simply tormenting myself? Why couldn't I just let things lie? Why couldn't I be content that Miles had loved me? Jean had said so, hadn't she? Why wasn't this enough? Because none of it made any sense, that's why, my brain screamed back at me in defiance. If Miles loved me, why hadn't he come back to me? Why had he bought a house less than ten miles away when he could have come back here to me? I probably wouldn't ever find out the answers. After all, the only person who could tell me truthfully was Miles, and he was dead. Even then, I didn't really believe that he would have told me the truth even if he had been alive and kicking. He certainly didn't tell me the truth when he lived with me, so why change the habit of a lifetime?

I showered and dressed and was ready to leave the house just before eight-thirty. I knew the drive back to the solicitors would be busy with commuters leaving town to work, so I decided to set off. In fact, I think I made this decision because if I had held back any longer, I might never have ventured out. I was beginning to lose my nerve. All the hours spent planning what I was going to say and all the questions I was going to ask were quickly becoming a lost cause as I began to bottle out. I didn't need to find the answers to any of my questions. I could just put the house on the market, take the money and live happily ever after; end of. No reasoning, no questions, no recriminations, no regrets. Just me in the here and now with enough money to enjoy life to the full.

I thought back to a life lost. One where I was happily married. Where my husband came home every night after work. A life without children but one that was happy all the same. Don't they say you never miss what you never had? Well, that had been us. We might have wanted children, but we weren't lucky enough to have them, so we could and should have accepted that and moved on with our lives. Only we didn't. The realisation drove us apart, and we blamed each other even if we had never actually said it out loud. Miles had badgered me to seek medical advice at first, but I had refused. I think deep down, I didn't want to know. I didn't want a doctor confirming I was the problem. That I was barren and couldn't have children. I didn't want to know if it was my fault that we couldn't conceive. I had been weak. I should have faced the music. Owned up to having a faulty, infertile body. Instead, I had pushed Miles into seeking answers by himself, and I was pretty sure the doctor had confirmed that everything was working well in his department. It was obvious that was why he had left me. To find another woman to bear his children. One who could. So why didn't he divorce me and have the family he craved? Maybe he did. Well, no, he didn't divorce me, obviously, but maybe he did have the family he wanted. Just because I wasn't aware that he had children didn't mean they didn't exist. After all, he was hardly going to give me a call and let me know he had fathered a child to another woman, was he? Surely, if he had children, they would have been at his funeral? I thought again about the young woman. Was she the right age to be his daughter? I pushed the thought to the back of my mind. It was too awful to think about, and anyway, it was all just speculation. If Miles had had children, surely he would have provided for them in his will. The solicitor had said I was the sole beneficiary to Miles's estate; therefore, no one else mattered enough in his life for him to leave them anything.

I pressed ahead before I could lose my nerve completely and climbed into the driver's seat of my car. I turned the radio on and drove slowly along the lane. I knew there would be no traffic to contend with along the lane, but there was always the odd rabbit or squirrel dicing with death when I drove along the track leading down to my cottage. Funny how I had started to refer to it as *my* cottage rather than *our* cottage so soon after Miles's death. He wasn't even cold in the ground, and I had already taken ownership. I laughed at my own thoughts. I had taken ownership when he left me all those years ago, I thought defiantly when I had to sort out the leaking roof and fix the dripping tap.

I reached the solicitor's office in less time than I anticipated, leaving me with time to spare, so I popped into the nearest estate agent to enquire about putting the big house on the market.

The sales negotiator was very professional, and when I told her the house was in my late husband's estate left to me, she proceeded to give her condolences, much to my chagrin, as I certainly didn't need her sympathy. Instead, I smiled sweetly and continued to answer her questions. She looked at me strangely as I struggled to recall how many bedrooms and bathrooms the property had, whether it was double-glazed or what kind of heating system it had. Finally, I admitted I had only visited the property once, but I would be more than happy to show a valuer around so they could see for themselves what was on offer. An appointment was made for later in the day, giving me time to keep my scheduled meeting with the solicitor first.

I left the estate agents and made my way to Connor & Son. Mr Connor greeted me warmly as I opened the door.

'Mrs Jameson, it's so lovely to see you again so soon,' he said, as he offered his hand, and I genuinely think he meant it. I shook his hand and followed him into his office, which was now more familiar to me than the second house I owned, courtesy of my dead husband. Now, what can I do for you?' Mr Connor continued. I coughed quietly while trying to choose the right words.

'Well,' I began. 'I'm not really sure where to start.' Mr Connor looked at me, and I could see an unfeigned glimmer of pity in his eyes. I tried to ignore it and pushed forward for the answers I needed. 'I went to the house on Wentworth Drive, the one my husband bought without my knowledge,' I blurted out the words. Mr Connor nodded and waited for me to carry on. 'Well, there's nothing there,' I continued. Realising how confusing this last statement sounded, I rephrased my words. 'Well, of course, the house is there, but there is nothing of Miles's there, no clothes, personal possessions, or anything at all.' I finished feeling drained but content that I had the courage to say it out loud.

'That's because he never actually lived at the property, Mrs Jameson,' the solicitor stated matter-of-factly. My mouth dropped open. Before I could say anything, Mr Connor continued. 'I believe Mr Jameson bought the house as an investment about twenty years ago.'

'So, where did he live?' I asked without thinking. I didn't care what Mr Connor thought at this point. Clearly, he knew Miles and I didn't live together, and it was none of his damn business why. I just needed answers.

'He lived somewhere in Lymington, Mrs Jameson. I believe he had lived on the south coast for many years.' I didn't know what to say. Despite the well-rehearsed questions, I felt winded. I hadn't expected Mr Connor to tell me that Miles had never lived in the house. It was the opposite of what Jean had told me the previous day. One of them was clearly lying, but who and why? I had no idea. I stood to leave.

'Do you have the address?' I asked hopefully. Mr Connor shook his head, a look of sadness on his face. 'Did he live alone?' I asked before I could stop myself.

'I'm afraid I can't answer that question, Mrs Jameson. I have no idea whether your husband lived alone or not.

'I've instructed an agent to sell the house,' I said, not really knowing why I was telling the solicitor. Mr Connor nodded.

'Good luck with the sale. I would be more than happy to act on your behalf when you find a buyer,' he said professionally. I thanked him for his time and left.

Once outside on the pavement with the sun's heat on my face, I felt calmer. The solicitor's office had been hot and stuffy, and I had found breathing difficult. Or was it because I found it difficult to take in what Mr Connor told me? I glanced at my watch and noticed I still had an hour to kill before my appointment with the selling agent. I decided to get a coffee and consider the exchange I had just had with Mr Connor. I was even more confused than I had been before I met with him. I found a table on the pavement outside a little bistro café and sat down in the sunshine. Within a few minutes, a middle-aged woman in a red and white checked apron holding a small notepad and pencil came to take my order.

'Just a latte, please,' I requested, smiling. The waitress put her notebook in the pocket of her apron, turned, and went back inside the café. I guess she could remember my order, I thought sarcastically, and hadn't needed to scribble it down.

As I waited for my coffee, I pondered what Mr Connor had said. So, Miles had bought that bloody huge house, furnished it, and employed a housekeeper and gardeners but never actually lived in it? Was I really supposed to believe that? Well, I didn't! I might be naïve, but I am not that bloody gullible. But why would Mr Connor lie to me? What had he to gain by pretending that Miles lived on the south coast and not ten miles from me?

## My Husband's Child

The waitress brought my latte, and this time, she offered me a smile. Hoping for a tip I imagine, I thought cynically, as she walked away. I drank my coffee as I watched people passing by. They were all in their own little bubbles. A world they had created for themselves in which I imagine they all think they are safe and happy, but I wonder how many of them are like me, living a lie, not knowing who to trust and who to avoid. How many of them had husbands who cheated on them? How many turned a blind eye because the truth was too painful to acknowledge?

I had become cynical. I knew that. Living as I had all these years had made me that way. I was happy. In a twisted, strange, surreal kind of way, Miles had made me happy simply by leaving me alone. He had abandoned me in every sense of the word, that was true, but he hadn't cast me adrift. He had, in his own way, cared for me, looked after me and given me a life I had enjoyed. It could have been better, granted. I wasn't denying that for a second, but it also could have been worse, much worse. He could have left me with nothing, and I would have had to return to working in a dingy office on a low wage, scrimping and scraping to keep my head above water. Instead, here I was, living in a gorgeous house with another one to sell, with a healthy bank balance, my health, and, hopefully, many years of life ahead of me. Yes, things could definitely be worse.

I shuddered as I thought of Miles, six feet under with no one who had genuinely mourned him. Even I couldn't bring myself to be that much of a hypocrite. I could take his money, his houses, and his assets, but mourning him was a little too out of my reach. I convinced myself I had earned the inheritance. I was his wife, after all. I had let him walk all over me, leave me, and make a fool of me; I deserved this happiness now.

I finished my coffee and left the money, along with a healthy tip, on the table. I was in a good mood, and if I wanted the waitress to benefit from that, I would. I was in control. It had been a long time since I had felt in control, and it felt good.

I returned to my car and headed to the big house that Miles had left me. Despite the fact that this was only the second time I had travelled to it, it felt strangely familiar, and I didn't need to set the SatNav this time; the directions were stored in my memory, whether I had wanted them to be or not. I got to the house just as the valuer was pulling up. He waited whilst I opened the electric gates and followed me up the gravel drive. I had hoped that Jean or the boys might be around as I wanted to ask her some questions, mainly about why she had said that Miles lived here when he didn't. To my disappointment, there were no other cars on the drive, and Jean was nowhere to be seen.

I introduced myself to the valuer and let him into the house. I instructed him to view the property at his own leisure and then to come and find me when he was finished. There didn't seem much point in me following him around like a faithful Labrador, as I knew as much about this house as he did, so I wouldn't be much help answering any questions he might have. I told him my solicitor would be able to assist. I was sure that Mr Connor would have acted on behalf of Miles when he purchased the property, and I would be instructing him again on its sale. It took the valuer almost an hour and a half to walk around the property and its grounds before he came to find me sitting in the kitchen. I had been reminiscing, and he startled me when he came through the doorway.

'Mrs Jameson, I think I have all the facts I need about the property in order to value it, and if you are in agreement, I can arrange to have measurements and photographs done at a later date and get the house on the market. I imagine we can get around the two-and-a-half million-pound mark for this property.

I almost fainted on the spot. I knew it was a big house, but I had no idea it was worth that kind of money. Miles had already left me in excess of five million pounds in his will, in addition to the cottage I lived in and some jewellery that had belonged to his mother, but this was another huge slice of the pie I hadn't bargained for.

It really was turning out to be a good day, a very good day. I didn't need any more valuations; two-and-a-half million quid was fine by me, and I instructed the valuer to get things moving. I entrusted him with a set of keys and told him he could arrange to get the measurements and photographs done at his convenience; I wouldn't be accompanying him again, and I didn't wish to show any prospective purchasers around the property. The valuer nodded in agreement and informed me everything would be taken care of and the contracts would be sent by email for my signature. I also told him about Jean and the gardeners so that whoever did the viewings wouldn't be surprised if they were here at the same time. It then dawned on me that I didn't have Jean's contact number, so I would have to return to the house if I wanted to speak with her. Maybe Mr Connor had a number for her, I thought, as I showed the valuer out and thanked him for his time. As I bid him farewell, I fished my mobile out of my handbag and called Mr Connor. His secretary answered immediately.

'How can I help you?' she asked professionally. She informed me that Mr Connor was with a client but that she would pass my message on and get back to me as soon as she could if they held any contact details for my housekeeper. I thanked her and hung up.

I decided to hang around the property a bit longer until either Mr Connor's secretary called back or Jean turned up. After about an hour, when no one had called or shown their faces, I decided to head back home. I had walked around the house again, trying to picture Miles here, but no matter how hard I tried, I simply couldn't imagine him living in this house.

I locked the door and retreated to my car. I drove slowly towards the gates, not wanting another near miss should Jean be coming the other way again, but this time I met with no one. I doubt she would come to the house daily if no one lived here. It would be pointless paying a housekeeper to clean every day when surely once a week would suffice. It was Thursday today, and as I met Jean yesterday, I surmised that her day for cleaning the house would be Wednesday. If all else failed, I would simply turn up again next Wednesday when Jean was scheduled to clean, and I could speak to her then.

With this decision firmly in my mind, I headed back home. It had been a fruitful day, and it appeared my bank balance would be swelling again in the very near future. Although Miles had a successful career, much of his estate had been inherited from his own wealthy parents, inflating his worth on a grand scale. I smiled as I drove along the country lanes back to my humble little cottage and the peace and tranquillity it afforded me.

# Chapter Six

Although I had set off this morning with a clear itinerary and a list of questions that I needed answers to, I returned home just as much in the dark as when I had left. Granted, I had accomplished some of the things I needed to do, like getting the house valued, which was a real eye-opener. I had placed it in the hands of an agent, but I still had no idea why Miles had bought the house in the first place and why Jean or Mr Connor had different stories to tell about whether Miles had actually lived in the house. I mulled things over whilst busying myself in the kitchen and making dinner. My phone rang, and I reached into my pocket to retrieve it. Mr Connor's secretary was on the line.

'Hello, Mrs Jameson. I have spoken with Mr Connor, but unfortunately, we do not hold any details for your late husband's housekeeper or the gardeners,' she said.

I wasn't surprised. Mr Connor was Miles's solicitor, not his personal assistant, and I felt a little foolish at having bothered him in the first place; a clear indication of how completely out of my depth I actually felt. I thanked Mr Connor's secretary and apologised for having bothered her.

'Not at all, Mrs Jameson; if I can be of any further help, please don't hesitate to call,' she responded, churning out a well-rehearsed line that I was pretty sure she said to everyone regardless of whether she felt they were wasting her time or not.

I returned my attention to the meal I was preparing, satisfying myself that I could speak to Jean again the following Wednesday, the day I had figured out was her regular cleaning day. I knew absolutely nothing about this woman, not even her surname or address, and yet she had a key to a house worth millions of pounds. My house. I felt uneasy that I had to wait almost a week before I could speak with her again. I berated myself for undermining the woman. Miles had trusted her after all, and the house was immaculate; there was nothing amiss that I could see, and Jean and her sons were taking good care of the property, so why did I feel so protective towards the house? I sat at the kitchen island and ate my meal in silence. Usually, I would have the radio or the television on, but today, I simply sat silently, pondering the day's events, lost in my own thoughts.

The following few days passed quickly and uneventfully. I received the paperwork from the estate agent, and the house was scheduled to go on the market the following week. I requested the agent to wait until the weekend to arrange any viewings so that I would have a chance to speak to Jean beforehand and tell her personally that the house was up for sale. I figured I owed her that much. I would, of course, pass her details on to whoever purchased the property, and hopefully, they would retain her services along with those of her sons.

Finally, Wednesday arrived, and I got ready to visit the house on Wentworth Drive and hopefully see Jean again. I decided to take some provisions with me in case Jean arrived at a different time, and I had to wait at the house for her. I made a flask of coffee and popped a couple of slices of ginger cake into an airtight container. I figured coffee and cake might be just what was needed to loosen Jean up and get her talking. I went to Wentworth Drive at just after ten, and pulled up outside the huge gates. I pressed the code and waited for the gates to open. As I waited, I looked around me at the neighbouring houses, each with its own high gates, security lights and unscalable walls. This really was a millionaires' row, and the houses were reminiscent of fortresses. What a shame that those with money felt they had to lock themselves away, terrified of being robbed. It reminded me of a bird in a golden cage. People who had everything and yet had nothing, certainly they didn't have freedom. Is this how Miles had felt in the end? I drove through the gates, the familiar sound of the gravel crunching under the tyres, and pulled up outside the house. Jean's car wasn't there, and I sighed. I had been so sure that she would be here. I climbed out of the car and went to unlock the door. I would wait a few hours to see if she turned up later. I put my key in the lock, but it refused to turn; slowly, I turned the handle and pushed gently against the heavy door; it opened with ease. Had I forgotten to lock it the last time I came? I was horrified at the thought, and then I remembered the valuer had been here after me to take measurements and photographs. I reached into my jacket pocket for my phone. I was livid, and the estate agent would be getting a piece of my mind. Could they not be trusted to lock the house after they had been? As I entered the hallway, I noticed that the alarm hadn't been set either, and my anger rose even higher. Whilst all the other houses on the street were armed like Fort Knox, mine had been left unlocked and without the alarm set!

Noises. I could hear noises coming from upstairs.

I froze, suddenly listening to the sounds. Someone was scurrying around in one of the bedrooms. It looks like someone thinks they've won the lottery, I thought, as I listened intently. Surely, no one would rob a house without a car or a van to load things into? Should I call the police or confront them? Before I could decide, Jean came rushing to the top of the stairs. She was just as startled to see me as I was relieved to see her.

'Mrs Jameson, I wasn't expecting to see you today,' she said, rushing down the stairs to greet me.

'Where's your car?' I asked dismissively, wondering how she had gotten here.

'Oh, it's in the garage for servicing; the boys and I got a lift today.' I felt myself begin to relax as I smiled at her. 'I'm so sorry if I startled you. We always come on a Wednesday, me and the boys,' she continued. 'Mr Jameson was never at home on Wednesdays, so he preferred us to come then so we wouldn't be in his way.' She seemed so confident telling me this that I began to think it was Mr Connor who was lying about where Miles lived and not the housekeeper. This seemed like a good time to offer Jean coffee and cake and hear what she had to say.

'Coffee?' I asked, pulling the flask from my bag. Jean looked a little unsure. Clearly, she had a job to do, and she didn't want me to think she was slacking. 'Please,' I continued, 'I would love the company.' I headed for the kitchen, leaving Jean with little option but to follow me. I opened and shut cupboards, hoping to find some mugs that hadn't been packed away with everything else. After looking in half a dozen cupboards, I eventually found a few mismatched mugs that looked completely out of place in the house. Jean laughed as I reached for a couple of the mugs.

'I brought those a few weeks ago so we could have a drink of water,' Jean said as I poured the coffee into the mugs. 'It can be thirsty work when the weather is hot, especially for the boys,' she continued. I smiled, nodded and handed her a mug of coffee.

'Cake?' I offered Jean a piece of ginger cake on the lid of the container I had brought it in, as I was pretty sure I wouldn't find any plates as well as mugs. Jean took the cake and thanked me.

'Not used to this kind of service,' she said, as she bit into the cake. 'Mm, it's delicious. Did you make it yourself?' I nodded as I, too, took a mouthful of cake. Ginger cake had been Miles's favourite, but I didn't dare voice this in case Jean knew differently. I sensed that the woman sharing my coffee and cake knew my husband better than I did, certainly in the final years of his life. I wanted to ask her so much, but I wasn't sure where to begin. What if she had a sense of duty to Miles even though he was dead? What if she didn't think it was right to share her feelings and thoughts with me, even if I was his wife? She knew Miles and I didn't share a house or a life, so I figured she would be very guarded with anything she had to say.

I decided to take things slowly and ask about her and the boys before moving on to Miles. They say people like to talk about themselves, and I hoped this was the case with Jean. Mothers were usually proud of their children and would open up freely to talk about them; I hoped Jean was one of those mothers.

'So,' I began, wiping crumbs from my mouth. 'How

long have you and the boys been working here?' I asked matter-of-factly, or at least as a matter-of-factly as I could muster, given I was bursting with questions but reluctant to bombard the poor housekeeper the minute I had her undivided attention.

'Years,' Jean said non-committedly. 'Obviously, I have worked here longer than the boys because they were too young when Mr Jameson first bought the house. When my husband died, I struggled for money, and that's when Mr Jameson suggested the boys help out. He was very generous, and they did odd jobs and kept the grounds tidy, but to begin with, they didn't know much about gardening, and he was very patient, allowing them to learn, and now, well, they are just a great asset to the place,' she said, beaming with pride.

Jean had mentioned that her husband had died as if I should be aware of it, but of course, I wasn't. Until last week, I didn't even know Jean and her boys or, in fact, the house existed, but I wasn't sure I needed Jean to know that, at least not yet. I waited, hoping she would continue talking, but she didn't. She simply proceeded to eat her cake and drink her coffee, obviously waiting for me to speak. I tried to keep the conversation light. The last thing I wanted to do was pressurise her into saying anything she was uncomfortable about.

'Do you enjoy the work?' I asked. Jean nodded as she swallowed the cake in her mouth.

'Oh, yes, I love this house. I have other jobs, of course, but I have always enjoyed coming here.'

'Perhaps that's because Miles was never at home,' I stated without thinking. Jean shot me a stern look, and I quickly corrected myself. 'I mean, it must be easier to clean the house when the occupants aren't in; I wasn't necessarily referring to Miles.' Jean seemed to relax a little after I had hurriedly explained myself.

'Well, yes, there is that, I suppose. Some people can be critical, and it makes the job much harder if you have to keep out of the way of people, especially if they work from home, but Mr Jameson was very rarely around anyway.'

'How often did you see him?' I asked. Jean thought for a while and then admitted she hadn't actually seen Miles for a long time.

'We spoke on the telephone often,' she stated, as if this made up for not seeing him in person. I guess in her line of work, that was perfectly acceptable. She was here to clean the house, nothing more, nothing less. I decided to take the bull by the horns.

'Could he have moved out some time ago, then? Without you actually knowing?' I asked quickly. Jean pondered this question for a while, and I thought she would refuse to answer it.

'Now that you come to mention it, yes, I suppose that was the natural explanation for it.'

'For what?' I urged.

'The state of the house,' Jean said as if it were obvious. 'There was less and less for me to do each week. Never any laundry or beds to change. Yes, maybe that's the answer; maybe Mr Jameson wasn't living here in the end.' Jean seemed lost in thought, as if she had never considered this before.

'How long had the house been like that?' I asked tentatively, hoping to discover when Miles might have actually moved out of the house.

'Years,' Jean responded sadly. I figured this was her

go-to response when she didn't have an accurate answer.

She moved to the sink and started to wash the mugs and the container in which I had brought the cake. She was lost in thought, and her eyes looked sad and haunted. I had upset her talking about Miles; that was obvious, and I felt a little guilty, but she had supplied me with the answer I needed. Neither she nor Mr Connor had lied. Miles had obviously lived here initially, but then, at some point, God knows when, he moved out without telling Jean. Why would he? As long as she continued to keep the house clean and tidy and he continued to pay her for her services, then she didn't need to be privy to his whereabouts. Taking me by surprise, Jean opened the conversation up again.

'It doesn't have to be Wednesday,' she began. 'I can come to the house any day that suits you.'

'Wednesdays are just fine,' I replied, as I got to my feet. I didn't see much point in hanging around any longer. Jean clearly didn't know where Miles lived or when he moved out, and I didn't want to waste any more of her time. I resigned myself to travelling to Lymington if I wanted to see for myself where Miles had spent the final years of his life. Right now, I wasn't sure I even needed to know. 'Thank you for your time,' I said before adding, 'I have put the house on the market, and the agent will do the viewings. I will inform them that you are here on Wednesdays. Could I have your telephone number, just in case I need to contact you about anything?' I pushed a piece of paper and a pen towards Jean. She dried her hands on her apron and scribbled the number on the paper I had handed her. 'Thank you,' I said as I shoved the piece of paper and the pen back into my handbag.

Mr Connor had informed me that Jean was paid by

standing order, which would continue for as long as I needed it to, so I didn't need any further information from the housekeeper at this moment in time. I said my goodbyes and let myself out into the fresh air, leaving the door slightly ajar to allow some of the air to penetrate the house. It had been shut up for too long, and the stale air was a testament to this. I shuddered as I climbed back into my car and headed back home.

# Chapter Seven

I was kept up to date frequently by the estate agent regarding the house sale. They had arranged a number of viewings in the first few weeks of the house going on the market, and I was optimistic that it would sell quickly, although nothing was certain in the housing market, and the house was expensive. After less than a month, I received an offer of the full asking price, provided all the furniture would be left. I had no need for any of the furniture, and as none of it was remotely personal to Miles, I was happy to let it go with the house. I confirmed my acceptance of the offer and instructed Mr Connor to act on my behalf.

While the sale was going through, I busied myself with other more mundane tasks and decided I would travel down to Lymington as soon as the house had been sold. I knew I had to find an address before even thinking about a trip to the south coast, but I had no idea where to begin. I tried property searches on Zoopla and Rightmove hoping it might give me an idea of when Miles had actually decided to move down south, but again, I drew a blank. I would have to drive down and see for myself. Or I could just walk away, let bygones be bygones, accept that Miles didn't want me, wasn't moving back in with me and had begun a new life elsewhere, probably with someone new. I couldn't. I tried to resist the temptation, telling myself it was his life, he could do as he wished, just as I had been doing these past twenty years, but there was still a nagging doubt in the back of my mind, and I knew the answers to my questions lay in Lymington, and I needed to find them out.

Things appeared to be moving quite quickly with the sale of the house. I learned from the estate agent that a young couple were buying it. As they had only just got married, this was their first home, and therefore, as I wasn't buying anything, there was no chain involved.

'It should be very straightforward,' Mr Connor had said to me. 'As soon as the mortgage has been approved, we can set a completion date.' I couldn't believe how quickly things had happened. The house had sold almost straight away to the perfect couple with nothing to drag things out. I wondered how they could afford a house at over two million pounds. Good jobs, inheritance or stupidity, stretching themselves so thin they may live to regret it? More questions, although these were questions I only fleetingly dwelled upon. As long as they came up with the cash, I didn't care how they got it, and selling the house would be one less thing for me to worry about.

I popped in once or twice to check on things, always when Jean and her sons would be around so that I could keep her updated with developments on the sale. I felt a little mean because selling the house could put them out of work, but it couldn't be helped. Although I had never actually asked her outright, I was pretty sure I remembered Jean saying that she had other jobs during one of our previous conversations. Surely, she wouldn't have a problem finding more housekeeping jobs, and if the new buyers didn't want to keep her on, I would gladly give her a reference.

Jean was always polite and seemed pleased to see me, but I couldn't help but feel she thought I should keep the house and live in it by myself. She had no more bombshells to tell me, like the one when she had told me that Miles loved me, and I was beginning to think this was a figment of her imagination. Had she said it to try to soften me up so I would feel some kind of pull towards the house? Did she think if I lived in the house, I might feel close to Miles and, therefore, no longer want to give it up? If this was her intention, she couldn't have been more wrong. Nothing about the house drew me in. It was an ugly Victorian property which felt cold both inside and out, even when the sun shone brightly in the sky. It held no memories of Miles, and there was certainly no hidden nostalgia or sentimentality within its walls.

It came as a shock to me when Mr Connor called me one morning to tell me that the sale had fallen through. There had been no indication that the buyers were having second thoughts. No queries had been raised that had resulted in unfavourable answers, and no reasons were given.

'I am afraid sometimes these things happen, Mrs Jameson,' Mr Connor said, when delivering the unwanted news. 'Not all offers result in a sale going through.'

'Yes, I am aware of that,' I said a little too harshly, my patience thinning. 'But at what stage did they start to give you a reason they might back out?' What did they say, exactly?' I pushed, hoping for answers. 'Are they trying to get a reduction in the price?' This had been my first thought. I had heard of this happening before to people when house sales had moved along fairly smoothly, and then, at the last minute, the purchaser threatened to pull out unless the price was renegotiated. I wasn't averse to a discussion about the price; I just wished it had come up sooner before solicitors had been instructed and time had been wasted.

'No, no, nothing like that, I can assure you,' Mr Connor answered. 'If I am honest, they didn't really say why; they just had second thoughts and decided to proceed with purchasing another property.' I was livid, and my frustration was palpable over the telephone line. I decided to end the call before I said something I might regret. It wasn't Mr Connor's fault, after all, and alienating him wouldn't help my case.

'Thank you for your time,' I said, as I cut the call dead.

I slumped into the chair at the kitchen table and held my head in my hands. It wasn't the end of the world, I told myself. It wasn't as if I was buying somewhere else, and now that dream had been shattered. To all intents and purposes, my life hadn't changed at all because of the news Mr Connor had just delivered. It just meant I had to keep the house a little longer, Miles's house. Miles's house that was now costing me money. I concluded irritably. I reached for my phone again and scrolled down to the estate agent's number. I waited patiently until a voice at the other end said breathlessly.

'Good afternoon, Alice speaking; how may I help you?' *You can sell my bloody house*, I thought as I wondered why she was out of breath. Had she been busily making coffee or messing about with some other meaningless task when she should have been at her desk?

'It's Mrs Jameson,' I snapped curtly. 'I want to know why my buyers have pulled out at this stage?'

'Just one moment,' Alice replied, clearly expecting my call. I heard her whisper something, and then the phone passed over to someone else.

'Mrs Jameson, how lovely to hear from you!' It was Thomas Gibbon, the senior director of the company. His voice was smarmy, and I could picture the supercilious look on his face as I pictured him in the estate agent's office surrounded by glossy photographs of overpriced houses, one of them mine, all waiting to be sold so he could cash in his fee. I remained silent, listening to him squirm on the other end of the telephone. 'Such a shame about the house sale. I honestly couldn't believe it when I found out,' he continued, realising I wasn't going to help him here and that he had a lot of explaining to do. 'Don't you worry, though, Mrs Jameson, we will find another buyer in no time at all. It's such a beautiful house we will have people queueing up to buy it.'

*Beautiful house? Where had he been looking?* The bloody house was ugly from top to bottom with its drab architectural features, or was this just how I saw it? It was a part of Miles that I had not been privy to. I pulled myself together. Alienating the estate agent wasn't going to sell my house. I breathed deeply.

'Did they give you any reason why they were pulling out?' I asked, not really expecting an answer because if there had been one, Mr Connor would have told me.

'They didn't, I'm afraid, just that after the last viewing, they called the office to say they were withdrawing their offer.'

Last viewing? How many viewings had they had?

As if reading my mind, Mr Gibbon continued, 'They'd viewed the property three or four times so they could measure up and the like, but after last Wednesday, they just seemed to change their minds. It was all a bit sudden, but sometimes these things happen,' he said hesitantly, echoing Mr Connor's sentiments. We will re-market the house immediately, though, and contact those who were initially interested to see if they would like to take things forward.

I thanked Mr Gibbon and hung up. Last Wednesday? I mulled things over in my mind. Had Jean been there at the viewing? Had she said something to put the buyers off? It seemed ridiculous, and what reason would Jean have to jeopardise my sale? Still, it seemed a little too convenient that after she met them, they pulled out. I pushed the thoughts to the back of my mind, thinking I would broach the subject with Jean when I saw her next.

The next few days went relatively quickly. I heard nothing else from Mr Gibbon, so I assumed those who had first shown an interest in the house had either found something else or decided not to pursue things for other reasons. I accepted that things had perhaps been a little too good to be true, and I was back to square one: like it or leave it.

A sharp knock on the front door brought me to my senses. I don't normally use the front door, always preferring to go through the porch and into the garden. I scrambled for the key, which I kept in a key box on the wall in arm's reach of the front door. Unlocking the door, I could see a young woman standing on the doorstep. She looked vaguely familiar, but I couldn't put a name to her face. She smiled broadly as I opened the door. She was dressed in a pretty floral dress, which was fitted at the waist and then flowed into a full skirt; it had short puffed sleeves and was tied at the waist with a bow. The dress fitted her perfectly, accentuating her slim figure. She had long dark hair and the most piercing blue eyes I had ever seen. Her smile was warm and lit up her face entirely. I looked at her in awe as she held her hand out to greet me.

'Mrs Jameson,' she said, and I was stunned that she knew my name. 'My name is Amelia.'

I shook her hand, not really understanding why, as I had no idea who this woman was; despite her vague familiarity initially, her name meant nothing to me. She must have noticed my uncertain expression as she quickly apologised.

'I'm so sorry. I didn't mean to take you by surprise. I saw you at the funeral, and I felt I needed to come and see you.'

The funeral! That was where I had seen her. I knew she looked familiar, but until she mentioned the funeral, I couldn't picture where I had seen her. I wondered who she was. My curiosity overtook my caution, and I stepped aside without thinking to let her into the house. I led the way into the kitchen.

'Can I offer you a drink?' I asked. 'Tea, coffee, lemonade?'

'Lemonade would be lovely,' she replied, looking around my kitchen without trying to hide the fact that she was doing so. I didn't know whether she was being rude or nosey or just being appreciative. 'What a beautiful home you have, Mrs Jameson,' she added as if reading my thoughts.

'Thank you, I like it,' I replied non-committedly whilst I poured two glasses of lemonade and added crushed ice. I put the glasses on a tray and suggested we sit in the

## My Husband's Child

garden. I suddenly felt quite uncomfortable having this stranger in my home, and I didn't know why.

I led the way through the conservatory into the garden and placed the tray on the table, offering Amelia a chair. I sat opposite her and took a sip of my lemonade. The tangy taste helped to ease the dryness in my mouth as I waited for Amelia to tell me why she had called on me. She appeared to be in no rush, and I could feel myself becoming agitated. She obviously knew Miles, but in what capacity, I had no idea. I hoped she would get a move on and explain herself. I wasn't sure how I felt about another conversation with someone about Miles, knowing my knowledge of him was remote, to say the least. My conversations with Jean had always been strained when we touched on the topic of Miles, and she was much more approachable than the young woman sitting opposite me while I was drinking my lemonade. This young woman had an air of aloofness. She was self-assured, and I imagine she knew how to handle herself.

I coughed quietly, hoping to usher her along so that she would instigate a conversation and tell me why she was here. She didn't take the hint, and after a few minutes of polite exchanges about my pretty garden, an abundance of wildlife and the peaceful countryside, I turned the conversation to her.

'So, Amelia, what brings you here?' I asked, as politely as I could.

'I told you; I was at the funeral and thought I should call in on you,' she replied, as if the answer had been obvious all along. I could no longer suppress myself.

'Why?' I asked. 'I don't know you, do I?'

Amelia laughed – a quiet, feminine laugh, nothing

guttural or loud. I felt slightly embarrassed. Was I supposed to know this woman? Had I met her before and forgotten? I wracked my brains, but I could think of no occasion when I had come across her in the past. The first time I had ever seen her was at my husband's funeral.

'No, I don't suppose you do.' She said matter-of-factly. But I do know you.'

I was starting to get bored of this conversation now. Amelia had come into my home, accepted my lemonade and was now being nonchalant. Was I supposed to guess who she was and what she wanted? I felt her presence begin to suffocate me. Was she laughing at me? Clearly, she knew something I didn't. Was this due to the house sale falling through? Had she instigated that? I'd had enough.

'What do you want, Amelia?' I asked the question, leaving it hanging in the air. She looked at me as if I had sworn at her. She was hurt. Had I been rude? Was I rushing her? No, I didn't think so. How long was she prepared to accept my hospitality whilst refusing to tell me who she was? She pushed her hair back from her face and leaned forward.

'I'm Amelia,' she said again. 'Your husband's child.'

# Chapter Eight

The words stung as if Amelia had stood up and slapped me across the face physically. The shock of her admission reverberated despite our sitting in the open air outside in my country cottage garden. Her words were cruel, nasty, and untrue.

I got to my feet, felt myself go dizzy and promptly sat back down again. I wanted to run, to escape this awful encounter. I glanced at Amelia; her expression was non-committal. She had just dealt me the cruellest blow but remained aloof as if it were my fault that she had somehow found herself here telling me the most disgusting lies.

I didn't know how to respond. My first instinct was to throw Amelia out of my home. How dare she come here spouting her lies when Miles wasn't around to defend himself? I needed space. Time to think. A chance to process what she had said. It wouldn't be difficult to find out if she was lying. There would be records of whether Miles had fathered a child. I could check her story out. I needed her to leave. I couldn't concentrate with her here, staring at me as if I were the devil himself. The situation was undignified and irrational, and I was on the defensive immediately.

'Please go,' I said quietly. Amelia stood, placed her glass on the table and walked back through the house to the front door. I knew I should follow her to ensure she had left, but I was rooted in the spot. My legs had turned to jelly, and I didn't have the strength to haul myself out of the chair. I heard the door slam as Amelia left and wondered if she had slammed it for effect so that I knew she had gone. That I asked her to leave. My husband's child had been told to leave. My dead husband's child.

After she had gone, I sat in the garden for what felt like hours, going over and over what she had said. In fact, she hadn't said very much, but what she had said had completely floored me. I felt drained, empty, bereft. Could Miles really have been so cruel that he had fathered a child and not told me? Maybe he thought the truth would have been too hard for me to accept. It would have been the proof that our childless marriage had been my fault and obviously not his. Perhaps he had hoped that I would never find out. Amelia certainly wasn't a child; he had kept it from me for a long time, so I doubted he would ever let me on in his little secret. *We were still married! I had a right to know!* I heard the words screaming in my head. I had so many questions. It felt like that was all I ever did at the moment: conjure up questions. They all had one thing in common: Miles. He was absent when he was alive, but hey presto, the minute he dies, he springs to life with endless bombshells and secrets.

I thought about Amelia again. She didn't look like Miles. But then why would she? Not all children looked like their parents. In fact, I could never see the similarity of parents in small children when others cooed over them and said the stupidest things like ooh, he's got his mother's eyes; of course, he bloody well hadn't; otherwise, his mother wouldn't be able to see. Children were not replicas of their parents. Just because Amelia didn't look like Miles didn't mean he wasn't her father. I wanted to tear her lies apart. I knew that. I was looking for any shred of evidence to discount what she had said. I wanted to dismiss her, make her go away.

I wished I had never answered the door. But I had. I had met her and spoken to her, and now I needed to know what she wanted. She must want something; otherwise, why would she come to see me after all this time? I bet she knows Miles has left everything to me, and she will contest the will. I need to speak to Mr Connor and make sure everything is watertight. But what if she isn't lying? What if she really is Miles's child? Surely, she is entitled to something? So why didn't he provide for her in his will? So many questions, over and over they went until I felt myself going crazy.

I picked the empty glasses off the table, holding Amelia's at arm's length as if it might poison me if I held it too close. I could see the faint imprint of her soft pink lipstick on the rim, and tears pricked my eyes. I took the glasses back to the kitchen and turned on the tap. I put the plug in the sink, squirted some washing-up liquid in and swirled the water around with my hand, watching as the soap suds grew in size. I dipped the glasses into the warm water and swilled them in the suds. When I pulled them out, they glistened in the sunlight. Spotless, all traces of Amelia's lipstick were gone. I couldn't bear to dry the glasses and return them to the cupboard. The thought of drinking from the glass she had used filled me with horror, and I strode over to the dustbin and shoved them both inside. The bin was empty, and I heard them smash together as they hit the bottom. I needed her gone; every trace of Amelia had to go.

I found my phone and called Mr Connor. As expected,

his secretary answered again in her polite, helpful voice. This time, I didn't tell her what I needed to know. I couldn't. I didn't know how to say the words, so I simply asked her if she would get Mr Connor to call me back when he was free. She assured me she would, and I ended the call. I waited for Mr Connor to call me back, mentally preparing what I would say. There was no easy way to ask if Miles had a child, so when my phone rang shrilly and I saw Mr Connor's number on the screen, I simply took the bull by the horns and blurted out my question.

'Did Miles father a child?' I asked, before Mr Connor had even finished his polite introduction. The line went dead, and I heard him take a deep breath.

'I believe he did, yes.' He said with conviction. 'However, I am afraid I have absolutely no other information. I never heard it from Mr Jameson; it was just a passing comment that was made by someone many years ago.' I opened my mouth to ask more questions despite having just been told that this was the only information Mr Connor had; however, he cut me dead. 'I really do have to go, Mrs Jameson; my next client is waiting for me.' He hung up. I was stunned.

I didn't know whether to laugh or cry. Was I really supposed to accept that Mr Connor knew nothing about Miles's child? Surely, he would have asked questions when he drew up the will? Would he not have asked why he was leaving everything to me and nothing to his child or the mother of his child, for that matter? Maybe those aren't the sort of questions that a solicitor sees fit to ask, particularly if the wife is still very much alive and kicking and kept in the dark about the birth of a child with the mistress.

Mr Connor had been rushing to get off the phone; that

much had been obvious. Well, I would make an appointment to see him in person. He wouldn't be able to brush me aside then; he would have to answer my questions.

# Chapter Nine

I strode into Mr Connor's office with a confidence I didn't feel. I was determined to find out what he knew about Amelia, and I was certain he knew something; he was just not prepared to tell me. Yet. Before I could settle in a seat in the reception area, Mr Connor came out of his office. Clearly, he had been waiting for me. If I felt nervous, he looked it. He knew I wasn't happy and, whilst he clearly didn't want to betray Miles, neither did he want to lose my confidence. He had a lot of money riding on keeping me happy, so I was dying to find out exactly where his allegiance lay.

'Good morning,' he said, striding toward me. I shook his outstretched hand, determined that things would go my way in this meeting. I followed him into his office. 'Coffee?' he offered. Usually, I would have declined. I like to get meetings over and done with and prefer to drink my coffee alone and in peace, but today, I thought better of it. I wanted this meeting to last as long as I needed it to so that I could grill Mr Connor.

'That would be lovely, thank you, white, no sugar,' I said with a beguiling smile. I could tell by the look on Mr Connor's face that he had been hoping that I would decline, and I am pretty sure he now wished he hadn't offered me anything. I sat down in a chair opposite him, my hands folded loosely in my lap. I took a deep breath and looked him straight in the eye.

'It came as quite a shock,' I said. 'When Amelia knocked on my door yesterday, introducing herself as Miles's daughter.' I could feel my eyes widen as I frantically blinked back the tears. I would not cry, not here, not in front of this man.

'I can imagine, and I am very sorry.' Mr Connor, in his defence, sounded quite upset seeing me so distraught.

'It would have been nice to have had the heads-up,' I continued, ignoring his look of sympathy. At least then, I might have been prepared for her visit.'

'I do understand Mrs Jameson, but honestly, it never crossed my mind. Miles never told me personally that he had a child, and I never asked him. It wasn't my business, and it was such a long time ago. Then, when there was no mention of offspring in his will, I assumed he didn't have a relationship with his children, so it slipped my mind to tell you about it.'

*Children, did he have more than Amelia? Slipped his mind! Slipped his bloody mind, this was my husband's family, and he didn't think to tell me about it.* I could feel the blood rising in my cheeks. I was flustered, caught off balance. It hadn't occurred to me that Amelia might not be his only child. I guess if Miles had fathered one child, he could have had several.

'Did he have more than one child?' I asked in a quiet voice.

'I really don't know Mrs Jameson. As I said on the telephone yesterday, I have no information about any of Miles's children. I never intended to keep you in the dark; I simply have nothing to tell you.

I stared at the coffee on the desk in front of me. I

hadn't realised that Mr Connor's secretary had brought it in, but, looking at the scum starting to form on the top, I imagine it had been some time ago. I picked the cup up and brought it to my lips, testing it gently to see if it was still hot. It wasn't. It was lukewarm, but then perhaps it had only been tepid when she brought it in. I like my coffee hot, piping hot so that I can feel it burn my throat as it goes down. I replaced the cup on the desk, repulsed by its contents. I didn't see much point in dragging out this conversation. I could tell by Mr Connor's expression that he really was lost for words. I got to my feet and walked towards the door. Mr Connor was following me like a dutiful puppy, hot on my heels, wanting to please but not knowing how. I reached the door and turned the handle. I stopped and turned around, almost knocking the solicitor off balance.

'One more thing,' I said assertively, my confidence having resumed. 'Who informed you that Miles had a child?'

'What?' Mr Connor looked flustered for the first time during the meeting.

'You said my husband didn't tell you he had fathered a child. If he didn't, then who did?' Mr Connor could tell by my demeanour that I wouldn't take any nonsense.

'I can't remember; it was a long time ago.' He tried to fob me off, but I was having none of it.

'Rubbish, think. There can't be that many people privy to the knowledge if I had never found out. So, who told you?' My voice boomed loud, and I could see his secretary squirming in her chair in the reception, not knowing what to do.

'Jean,' he said in a small voice, looking at his feet.

Jean! The bloody housekeeper knew!

Trying to hide my anger, I replied firmly. 'Thank you, some honesty at last.' I strode out of the office.

The fresh air hit me immediately, and I breathed deeply. I had hoped that Mr Connor could have given me more information, but a small part of me was pleased that he didn't have anything to divulge; at least he hadn't been lying to me. I did wonder, however, when Jean had confessed her thoughts to Mr Connor. I wouldn't have considered them to have moved in the same circles, but then I guess Mr Connor might have been a guest at the old house whilst Jean was there, and she had been unable to help herself, sharing gossip and hoping for more information in return.

I wasn't sure what my next move should be. Should I consult Jean and find out what she knew? Yes, that seemed like the logical next step. It was Monday, and I would have to wait two more days before seeing Jean. I had her telephone number, but this was a conversation I wanted to have with her face-to-face. People often give much more away in gestures and facial expressions in these circumstances than in their words, and I wanted to see how Jean handled herself when I questioned her.

I wondered where Amelia was now. She must live locally as it had been four or five weeks since the funeral, and if she had travelled to pay her last respects, surely she would have confronted me much sooner rather than make a return trip. Maybe Jean knew where she lived? I decided to make my way back to the old house. Jean wouldn't be there, but I wanted to have another look around. Knowing about Amelia might shed some light on things I hadn't noticed before. Knowing Miles had a child would make me see the house through different eyes, from a different perspective.

I got into my car and drove to the big house. Going through the now familiar process of dialling the gate code and deactivating the alarm no longer felt strange. Although I didn't have any of these security measures at my own little cottage, I didn't deem them necessary; it felt strange how easily everything came to me. I let myself into the house, feeling the temperature drop as I moved out of the sunshine into the cold marble hallway. With my back against the door, I looked around the hallway for the umpteenth time. This time, I tried to think of it as my first time here. I tried to see things from a different perspective; through the eyes of a child. Was the house more homely? Could this have once been a happy place with children's laughter? I still had my doubts.

This was a rich man's house. A house to be respected and envied. It was ostentatious, pretentious. It wasn't a house where children could run freely, slide down the banister, make a mess in the rooms, or spill flour in the kitchen while baking. No, I simply couldn't see Amelia growing up here with all its grandeur and pretence.

I wandered aimlessly through the downstairs rooms. I wasn't sure what I was looking for, a clue maybe, something to make me feel someone had actually lived here, but I still felt nothing. I took the stairs slowly, looking again at the huge stained-glass window on the landing. It really was beautiful in an egotistical kind of way. The sun cast colours all around me. It felt as if I was in a kaleidoscope. I spun around and around, enjoying the reflection of the sun bouncing off the window. Would Amelia have done this as a child? Probably not. If she had lived here, I would imagine she would be told not to play on the stairs in case she fell. I might not have had the chance to be a mother, but I wasn't completely clueless about caring for children.

I moved to the first bedroom and then the second one until I wandered through all the upstairs rooms. Nothing made me feel any different. The rooms were all the same. I wasn't sure what I was expecting. A cot, maybe? Children's toys? Ridiculous. Even if Amelia had lived here as a child years ago, why would there still be a cot and toys around? Everything had been packed up and moved out a long time ago, and Amelia was no longer a child. She was a grown woman with a story of her own to tell.

I suddenly felt bereft. Why hadn't I asked her about her childhood and her recollections of Miles? I shouldn't have told her to leave. I shouldn't have been so impulsive. I had to find Amelia again. I needed to speak to her to find out everything she knew. I was certain now that it wasn't Jean who had the answers, or Mr Connor; it was Amelia.

# Chapter Ten

Amelia might have the answers I needed, but had to find her to ask her the questions, and I was pinning all my hopes on Jean.

On Wednesday morning, I rose early. I knew there wasn't much point in getting to the house before ten because Jean rarely arrived before then. I don't know how many hours she was paid to work, and I didn't care. She could do as many or as few hours as needed as long as the house was clean and in good order and the garden was well kept. I busied myself in the kitchen baking fruit scones before showering and getting ready to visit Jean. I packed a flask, some picnic plates and mugs, a jar of jam and some clotted cream. I was going to push the boat out a little today. Get Jean on my side; get her to open up. Jean had given me the impression of being a bit of a gossip, certainly after Mr Connor had revealed that she had informed him about Miles having a child. However, I found it difficult to get Jean to loosen her tongue on the occasions I met her. She simply didn't seem keen on divulging information, at least not to me. Either that or she didn't know anything. I felt sure she did. I could feel it in my bones; I just needed to get her to trust me.

The morning seemed to last forever; getting up so early hadn't helped, but finally, at around nine-thirty I climbed behind the steering wheel and headed for the

## My Husband's Child

house. I let myself in through the electric gates, holding my breath, hoping to see Jean's car parked in front of the house. I let out a huge sigh of relief when I spotted the familiar colour of the paintwork, and I pulled my own car up beside it. Retrieving the picnic basket, I waved at Jean's sons, who were weeding the borders. They waved back, but I could feel their reluctance, or was it embarrassment? I had never really spoken to them. They had always been in the garden when I popped by, but today I was in a good mood, so perhaps I took them by surprise by showing the jovial side of my personality. I pushed the heavy front door open and stepped inside.

'Hello!' I shouted, as I walked through to the kitchen, the heavy picnic basket weighing me down. There was no response. Jean was most probably upstairs and hadn't heard me. I put the basket on the kitchen counter and headed for the stairs just as Jean came out of the orangery.

'Mrs Jameson!' she exclaimed. 'I didn't hear you arrive.' She smiled at me warmly, and I immediately felt confident that today would be the day she would open up to me.

'Hi,' I said. 'Coffee's ready if you fancy one?' I said hopefully. Jean shook her head.

'I'm so sorry, I can't,' Jean said, and my heart sank. 'I got here early today because I have to leave a little earlier than normal.' Jean shifted her gaze and looked at the floor, avoiding eye contact with me. 'I have an appointment,' she offered.

'Oh,' I said, 'That's a shame. I've baked fresh scones.'

'Sorry,' she said again. I do hope it's OK for me to leave a little earlier,' she asked suddenly, aware that I might have a problem with that.

'Yes, yes, of course, that's fine. Is everything alright?'

'I'm fine. It's just a routine check-up at the doctor, but it can be quite difficult getting an appointment, so I didn't want to turn this one down.' Jean continued her work, scuttling around like a mouse, dusting the banister, mopping the floor, and vacuuming the carpets. I tried to talk to her whilst she worked, but it was hopeless. She wasn't in a talkative mood, and I wondered if it had anything to do with her appointment, so I reluctantly decided to let things go for the time being. I would just have to wait another week.

I left the scones on the kitchen counter, along with the jam and cream and told Jean she and her sons could enjoy them at a more convenient time. Jean smiled and thanked me. I could see that her thanks were genuine and heartfelt, but I couldn't help but notice that she was rather distant. Not in a rude way; her mind just didn't seem to be focused on anything. She seemed distracted by something, and I really did hope her doctor's appointment was nothing more serious than a check-up. I felt a sense of relief on Jean's part when I departed.

Having left the house, I drove into town. I needed a few supplies, and now that I had travelled this far, I thought I might as well get the things I needed. Although my local village store stocked all the basics, it was nice to venture further afield every now and again to browse the artisan bread shops and fancy cake shops. I enjoyed baking, but I was also quite partial to an indulgent treat that someone else had made every now and again. I also liked a good bottle of wine. Usually, a bottle would last me a few days, but I had indulged in a glass or two most nights since I had discovered that Miles had fathered a child, and my wine stock was getting quite low. I spent a couple of hours browsing and shopping before deciding to stop for lunch before returning home.

I was annoyed and frustrated that the morning hadn't gone to plan and that I hadn't been able to quiz Jean about Amelia, so the thought of lunch cheered me up a little. I found a little bistro in the square, which overlooked the shops and other eateries, and I chose a seat by the window to watch people as I ate. I love people-watching. It is probably one of my favourite pastimes, and I know how lucky I am to be able to spend time away from others rushing about frantically going about their business, never having enough hours in a day. I, on the other hand, had all the time in the world. I was alone, but I wasn't lonely. I had time on my hands, but it wasn't often wasted. I had an extraordinary, wonderful life, and I hadn't always appreciated it. In the beginning, when Miles left, I felt lonely. I suppose because things happened over time, I got used to being alone bit by bit. It wasn't as if I woke up one day, and he was gone. No, Miles had been nicer than that, more caring. The end result was the same, of course, but the journey had been easier than most people's when their marriages broke down. I scanned the menu. It was basic but more than acceptable, and I found my mouth watering as I considered one or two of the dishes. When the waitress caught my eye, she smiled and, taking her notepad and pencil from her apron pocket, promptly jotted down my order before leaving me to my thoughts.

As I waited for my lunch, I thought about Jean and wondered what the doctor's appointment would reveal. I hoped it was just a check-up and that Jean was OK.

I had been lost in thought, gazing through the window

at the erstwhile shoppers, when the waitress arrived with my lunch. The food smelled inviting, and I could feel my stomach turn with hunger pangs. I had skipped breakfast that morning, hoping to be sharing scones with Jean, but when she declined my offer, I had felt it only appropriate to leave the scones at the house, resulting in me having not eaten at all so far today. I paused, trying not to show my impatience, whilst the waitress arranged my plate, placed my coffee down and sorted the cutlery. I thanked her and then promptly dived into my dish of fresh pasta, ham and parmesan. It was delicious and well worth the wait. I concentrated on my lunch, momentarily ignoring the passers-by until my hunger pangs dissipated, and I felt I could slow down a little. I looked around sheepishly, hoping no one had seen me devouring my food.

I finished my meal and sat back in the chair, savouring the last mouthful, when my eye caught someone familiar outside. I looked again, straining to see if I was right, and as they moved closer, I could see that it was Jean. Before I could raise my hand to wave, I noticed that she wasn't alone, and I suddenly felt a sharp pang. Had she brought someone with her to see the doctor in case it was bad news? That was when I realised who she was with. Striding by her side, in a pink jacket and jeans, was Amelia. I looked away quickly, not wanting them to see me, but I had to be sure that I hadn't been mistaken, so I picked up the menu and peeped from behind it. It was definitely Amelia. Her eyes were hidden behind large sunglasses, but her hair, her manner, her body shape, everything screamed Amelia. She had the same air of sophistication about her. A look that was unmistakable and blared out a privately educated woman, confident, demure, assured. She looked comfortable walking beside Jean, and yet their stance, dress code and demeanours were worlds apart. I could feel the pasta rising in my throat, and I swallowed hard to stop it from spilling onto my plate. I felt sick to my stomach. My mind raced, and I struggled to breathe. I wanted to run outside and fill my lungs with fresh air, but I couldn't do so in case Jean and Amelia saw me. The waitress saw my anguish and rushed over, clearly concerned.

'Are you alright?' she asked. 'Do you need a glass of water?' I nodded, unable to speak. I had calmed down a little when she returned with my water, and I apologised.

'I'm so sorry, I just felt a little light-headed,' I said by way of an explanation. The waitress smiled, clearly relieved to see that the food she had served me hadn't in any way been to blame for my current disposition. 'Would you mind fetching me my bill, please? I think I could do with some fresh air?'

'Yes, of course, one minute,' she replied, rushing over to the counter and returning with my tab.

I left the money on the table, along with a healthy tip, collected my bags and headed for the door. I had left ample time for Jean and Amelia to depart the square, so I was sure I wouldn't bump into them on my way to the car. It was funny how earlier in the day I had wanted to speak to both of them and still did, but not like this. Not together. It hadn't crossed my mind that they might still be in touch with each other. As Jean hadn't offered any information on Amelia, I hadn't even known until this morning that she was aware of her existence. I kept my head down as I walked towards my car, praying that Jean and Amelia had gone. I needed to get my head together and think things through before tackling either of them. I was confident that they hadn't seen me, and that was a good thing. The fact that I had seen them together and they didn't know gave me the advantage. I drove home in silence, my mind working overtime with irrational thoughts that threatened to spill over.

# Chapter Eleven

It was dark when I woke. I shivered and pulled the throw over my shoulders.

I had arrived home, put away my shopping and poured myself a glass of wine. And then another and another until I had fallen asleep on the sofa. It was a long time since I had done that. Not since Miles had left me had I felt so low that all I wanted to do was drink away my woes. The wasted years, the unhealthy lifestyle, the constant feeling of worthlessness, the pitying looks. I had experienced them all, and I didn't want to go back there. I couldn't go back there. I wasn't that person anymore. I was stronger now. I had a purpose. I was a survivor. Miles had taken a lot from me, too much, but I wouldn't let him have the rest of my life. I wouldn't let him or Jean or Amelia ruin what I had left. I had to sell the house, and then I wouldn't have to see Jean again. Yes, that's what I needed to do, I told myself through my drunken haze.

I would call the agent in the morning and reduce the price. I wanted to get rid of the house as quickly as I could. But what about Amelia? How could I make her go away? Right now, I wasn't sure I wanted to make her go away, well, not entirely anyway. The drink had made me feel less guarded, and I wondered what it might be like to meet her properly. Get to know her, talk to her. Not in the way I had the other day, that had been a surprise, an awful admission, and I had been ill-prepared. Now that I knew who she was, I could cope. I could handle her confessions. I needed to speak to her. Tomorrow was another day. I would have to wait another week to speak to Jean.

I knew I needed to go to bed. It was almost midnight, and the sofa, with just the throw, was cold. Despite the fact that it had been a glorious summer's day, once the sun had set and the alcohol had got to work, my body began to shiver. I had no energy to haul myself off the sofa and into bed. I laid back on the cushions, feeling the tears of self-pity roll down my cheeks and allowed myself to drift back to sleep.

The next time I opened my eyes, the sun was up and streaming through the windows, making me blink as I tried to focus. My head felt heavy, pounding with pain, and my stomach was churning. The pasta from the day before mixed with a couple of bottles of wine last night had been a bad idea. I needed to vomit. I could feel the bile rising as I ran to the bathroom and leaned over the toilet bowl, wrenching the entire contents of my stomach into the pan. There wasn't much, to be fair. A small dish of pasta looked relatively pathetic when mixed with an awful lot of wine. The putrid smell filled the air, and I could taste the acrid vomit in my mouth. I stripped out of my clothes and reached for my toothbrush, scrubbing vigorously at my teeth, trying to erase the taste and smell of the bile. I stood under the shower for almost twenty minutes, willing the water to wash away how I felt. I wanted the steam to lift my emotions, pound the uncertainty from my limbs, and make me strong again. I had to be strong and get through this next phase of my life. I had to deal with things, sort them out or ignore them, but not let them bring me down.

I had already surmised that I couldn't ignore what I had discovered. Certainly not Amelia, anyway. I had to have one chance to speak with her, then, if I felt she had nothing to offer or anything worth listening to, I could walk away. Only then, not before.

The bathroom was filled with steam when I finally turned off the shower, and I pushed open the window to allow the fresh air to penetrate the space and dry it out. I dressed and applied a little make-up. I stared at myself in the mirror. I looked dreadful, or was it all in my mind? Did I look dreadful or just feel dreadful? My head was still pounding, and my stomach was churning. I headed downstairs and made myself some toast; the smell filled the kitchen and made me feel hungry. It's funny how the smell of toast always evokes hunger pangs in me, even if I have just thrown up. I force the buttered toast down and swallow a couple of paracetamol washed down with large gulps of fresh coffee. Slowly, I began to feel human again.

The rest of the week passed uneventfully. I willed myself to keep off the alcohol, reminding myself of how important it was to keep my wits about me if I wanted to deal with Amelia and all the invasive, distasteful thoughts she had provoked within me. Wednesday came around soon enough, and it was time for me to go to the house and speak to Jean again. This time, I could get her to tell me where Amelia lived, and I could pay her a little visit and see how she liked it.

I got in the car and headed to the old house to speak with Jean. I didn't bother with a flask of coffee or homemade cakes. This time, Jean would speak with me whether she liked it or not, at least if she wanted to continue to work for me. I didn't need bribes.

## My Husband's Child

The gates swung open, and I slowly drove along the gravel, half expecting to see an empty space where Jean usually parked her car. I was wrong; Jean had turned up for work this morning. Reassuring myself that she was unaware that I had seen her with Amelia last week, I entered the house ready for a confrontation. Jean was in the kitchen, busy wiping down the surfaces and cleaning the sink. I found it quite unnecessary, given that no one had used the kitchen in the last week, but she was paid to do the job, so I let her get on with it.

'Morning,' I said in as friendly a voice as I could muster, trying to overcome the betrayal I felt. Jean looked over and smiled in the way of reply. She didn't say a word. 'How did your appointment with the doctor last week go?' I asked, hoping to get Jean to open up a little before I asked about Amelia.

'It was fine, nothing to worry about,' Jean replied, keeping her eyes on the sink, which she was still cleaning.

'Did you take anyone with you? To the doctors, I mean?' I asked. Jean stopped cleaning and looked up, surprised by the question.

'No, why?' she replied non-committedly.

'Oh, it's just that I saw you with someone and wondered if she was giving you a little moral support.' Jean suddenly became wary of me.

'Oh, I met up with a friend afterwards,' Jean said.

'Really? How nice.' I continued to watch as Jean turned her attention to the kitchen floor. I could tell that I was in her way as she tried to mop around me, but she wouldn't get rid of me that easily. 'You're not rushing off today, are you?' I asked.

'No, Mrs Jameson, I am doing my usual hours today.'

'Good, please put the mop down and come with me; I want to talk to you,' I said, and walked out of the kitchen before Jean could protest.

I led the way into the drawing room, and Jean followed me like a scolded child. I sat down on one of the plush sofas, not knowing whether Jean had already cleaned the room and not caring in the slightest whether I had spoiled her newly plumped cushions, *my* newly plumped cushions. I patted the sofa next to me, indicating that Jean should sit down. She did, but she chose the armchair opposite me, clearly wanting to keep her distance.

I cleared my throat, but before I could speak, Jean blurted out, 'It was Amelia.'

I closed my mouth, shocked that she had admitted this without any prompting from me. 'I met up with Amelia yesterday. She called me out of the blue; I didn't even know that she had my number. I hadn't seen her in years, but then she called me and asked if I would meet up with her. I couldn't really say no,' Jean finished, looking down at her hands clasped in her lap.

Well, you could if you had wanted, I thought to myself as I looked at the wretched woman in front of me.

'What did she want?' I asked without admitting that I knew who Amelia was, although it was clear that Jean already knew I was aware.

'Nothing really, just a catch-up after the funeral, ask how I was, that kind of thing.'

I knew that Jean was lying, but I couldn't quite pinpoint why. What was she keeping from me, and why?

'Did she tell you she had been to visit me?' Jean nodded. 'Do you know how she found me?' Jean shook her head. She was starting to irritate me now. Someone had told her where I lived, and I wanted to know if it was Jean. 'Did you give her my address?' I asked more forcefully. Jean turned and looked at me.

'No,' she said with clarity, the tone of which I neither liked nor appreciated.

Jean was being utterly unhelpful and downright disrespectful. I was her employer, and she had met up with my dead husband's child behind my back, and I didn't like it. I listened to myself and shook my head in disbelief. What didn't I like? Why is it so unacceptable for Jean to meet someone I didn't approve of? It was none of my damn business. Jean appeared to read my thoughts.

'With all due respect, Mrs Jameson, what I do in my time is none of your business.' I felt as though Jean had slapped me across the face.

'Well, technically,' I said defiantly, 'It was my time; I was paying you to clean the house when you met Amelia.' I knew my words sounded petulant and unfair. Jean had asked permission to leave early, and I had agreed.

'As I explained to you beforehand, I had come into work early and made up my time so that I could leave for a doctor's appointment.'

'But you didn't see the doctor, did you?' I snapped. To my amazement, Jean stood up.

'I have work to do, Mrs Jameson, so if you will excuse me, I would like to get back to doing what you pay me to do.' Jean returned to the kitchen, leaving me aghast on the sofa. I could hear her clattering about with the mop and bucket. I strode into the kitchen.

'What did you say to the buyers to make them change their minds?' I demanded. 'Why did you delay the sale of

## My Husband's Child

this house?' Jean put the mop down and looked me squarely in the eyes.

'Now listen here, Mrs Jameson, I am more than happy to continue to be your housekeeper until you sell this house, but I do not like being accused of things I haven't done nor told who I can and cannot meet up with. You pay my wages for one day's work a week, and that is the only time I will be accountable to you. I did nothing to make the sale fall through. I didn't even speak with the buyers.' Her voice was calm but stern.

Her attitude towards me took me aback, and I suddenly wondered if I had spoken out of turn. What she was saying was true. She wasn't answerable to me. Just because she cleaned the house didn't mean she felt anything towards me. Miles had employed her, not me. Until recently, I had never met the woman, and here I was, demanding that she answer to me. I felt my cheeks flush. I was embarrassed. I needed to apologise to her, but something stopped me. There was a look of hatred in her eyes as she glared at me. I wouldn't apologise to this woman. She had no right to talk to me like that. If she weren't so bloody cagey all the time, I wouldn't need to reprimand her.

At that moment, the door swung open, and one of her two sons, I can't remember which one, came into the kitchen. He looked from me to his mother, beads of sweat pooling on his forehead, his T-shirt tucked in the waistband of his jeans, revealing a toned, lean torso. He stopped instantly sensing the atmosphere between Jean and me.

'Is everything OK?' he asked awkwardly.

'Fine,' I said, and seeing this as the perfect moment to leave, I turned on my heels and almost ran back to my car.

That was an absolute disaster, I thought, as I turned on the engine and headed back down the driveway. I had achieved absolutely nothing productive but simply managed to alienate Jean even further.

I drove home slowly, parked up and let myself into the house. Fighting the urge to reach for the wine bottle, I flicked the switch on the kettle and waited for it to boil. In the corner of my eye, I noticed something on the mat at the front door, and I walked aimlessly towards it. I bent down and retrieved a piece of pale pink paper folded in half. It wasn't in an envelope and had clearly been pushed through the letterbox rather than posted by Royal Mail. I unfolded the piece of paper and immediately smelt the floral scent engulfing me. Captivating scents of rose, jasmine and lilies filled my nostrils as I slowly opened the paper. The writing was neat. Rounded letters scrawled across the paper in straight lines. The message was clear and to the point.

> It must have come as a huge shock meeting me the other day, and for that, I am truly sorry. I just wanted to meet you and see for myself the woman my father had loved. If you change your mind and would like to meet again, my number is...

I read the note again over and over. *The woman my father had loved.* I heard Jean's words echoing in my head. Hadn't she said the same thing? Didn't Jean believe that Miles loved me? Now, his daughter was telling me as well. Why did they feel this way? Had Miles told them? If it was true, why hadn't he come back to me? I felt the tears fall down my cheek and tasted them on my lips as they fell in salty droplets. One of the tears splashed onto the pink paper in my hand, and I tried to brush it away; it left a smear underneath Amelia's signature. She had wanted to meet me. Just, as I imagine, she had wanted to see Jean again. Was there any harm in seeing her? I was more aware now and not as easily shocked. I knew everything; there would be no more nasty surprises, would there? Surely, it wouldn't do any harm to meet Amelia and hear what she had to say. It would be much fairer than badgering Jean, and anyway, Amelia had the answers, not Jean.

I stared at the note, the neat handwriting and floral scent, which, although initially sweet, was now becoming overpowering, the acrid smell lodged deep in my nostrils. I turned the note over in my hands and placed it back on the kitchen table. I was at a loss. I knew I needed to speak to Amelia, but equally, I felt the longer I remained in the dark, the longer I would feel protected. Amelia held the key to everything I didn't want to know about Miles. Although I had accepted that Miles and I were no longer married in the real sense of the word, and we were husband and wife in name only, his betrayal, even after all these years, cut deep. Discovering he had fathered a child and not told me was the most hurtful thing he had ever done to me.

I spent the next couple of hours busying myself around the house. I didn't really have much to do, but the longer I could put off making any decisions as far as Amelia was concerned, the happier I felt. The day was hot, and I opened all the windows and the patio doors to allow fresh air to penetrate the house, but still, I could not escape the heady scent of the pink notepaper. I tried to push it to the back of my mind, concentrating on mopping floors that didn't need mopping and wiping cupboards that didn't need wiping, anything to avoid the inevitable.

The afternoon passed slowly, and by three-thirty, I had tired myself out. The sun's heat was still burning, sapping what little energy I had. I reached for the bottle of wine chilling in the fridge and took a glass from the cupboard. I headed to the garden, the pink notepaper fluttering in the slight breeze on the kitchen counter. I ignored the note and carried the bottle to the lover's seat. I didn't need to bring the note with me; I knew exactly what it said, word for word.

I sat in the lover's seat, my mind still focused on the note. I unscrewed the cap on the wine bottle; I have never been great with corks. Miles always dealt with them. I poured myself a large glass of Pinot. I took a deep sip, enjoying the cool liquid on my tongue and relishing the warm sensation as I swallowed. I blinked back the tears that were starting to well up in my eyes and visualised the note. What could Amelia say to me that would have any effect on my life now? Probably nothing, but I felt I needed to give her a chance, hear her out. It wasn't her fault that Miles had a wife who he never bothered to divorce. I still had a niggling doubt in the back of my mind, and I wasn't sure what was holding me back from contacting Amelia. Was it because I was scared of what she might tell me, or was it because I was worried that she might contest the will? I shook the thought from my mind. This wasn't about money, I scolded myself. Or was it? Was that what was really concerning me? Was I scared Amelia had a right to some of Miles's estate and my rich life would be brought to an abrupt end by a woman who had shared more of my husband's life than I had? I was annoyed with myself for having these thoughts, but the truth of the matter was that these thoughts, fuelled by sadness and a little alcohol, had hit a nerve; they were closer to the truth than I dared to admit.

I headed back into the house and snatched up the note from the kitchen table, along with my mobile phone. I didn't need the note; I knew Amelia's number by heart. I started to punch the number into my phone and then stopped, cancelled the call and headed back outside to where the bottle of wine was waiting for me. I needed some Dutch courage I told myself as I poured another glass and took a deep gulp, almost choking as I swallowed the cool liquid. I decided to text Amelia instead of calling her. I didn't want her to hear the sadness in my voice, I didn't want to say anything I would regret, and I certainly didn't want to get into a long conversation over the telephone. I hated speaking to anyone on the telephone. Yes, a text would be better. To the point, blunt, emotionless.

I added Amelia's number to my phone and saved it. I hit the text button and quickly typed my message. I suggested meeting with Amelia the next day, in a café in town. I didn't want her to visit me at home again. It somehow felt disrespectful to me when she had turned up here unannounced. This was my home, my sanctuary, and I didn't want strangers popping in when they felt like it. Strangers, is that how I saw Amelia? Yes, that is exactly what she is. She might be Miles's daughter, but to me, she is a stranger. Someone I didn't even know existed until a few days ago. I pressed send and sat back in my chair. Seconds later, the familiar ping of a message received filled my ears. Reluctantly, I glanced at the screen of my phone.

'Perfect, I will look forward to it! X' As with the note on the pink-scented paper, I read Amelia's reply repeatedly, dissecting the seven words, looking for ulterior motives in her reply. She had typed the words using an exclamation mark and a kiss, like an excited child who was eager to meet up. I, on the other hand, had suddenly turned cold, the summer sun no longer burning in the sky, my arms were covered in goosebumps, and I wasn't sure whether the sudden chill I felt had come from the drop in air temperature or the reply from Amelia confirming our meeting tomorrow.

I scooped up my wine glass and the almost empty wine bottle and headed inside. Closing the patio doors behind me did nothing to eradicate the goosebumps, which still stood on end, making the skin on my arms resemble sandpaper. I decided a long soak and an early night was the answer. I toyed with replacing the contents of the wine bottle in the fridge but decided it wasn't worth saving, and topping up my glass; I headed upstairs.

# Chapter Twelve

It was another beautiful morning as I woke and glanced at my phone on the bedside table. The screen showed the time to be just after eight. Despite retiring to bed early, I still slept for a long time. I obviously needed the rest. I was surprised that I didn't have a headache, considering I had drunk a bottle of wine last night, but I thought I had probably slept off any sign of a hangover, having been in bed for over eleven hours. The sun streamed through the windows as I pulled back the curtains. I was beginning to regret sending the text to Amelia last night and pondered reneging on the arrangement we had made. I could tell her I wasn't feeling well. My mind went over and over different scenarios of how I could put off meeting Amelia but each one came back to the fact that Amelia would simply want to rearrange. Or she might just turn up here again unannounced. I shuddered at the thought and decided today was the day. I could meet her, listen to what she had to say and then walk away. I wouldn't have to see her again, ever, if I didn't want to.

I went downstairs and put the kettle on, popping a couple of slices of bread in the toaster simultaneously. As I waited for the kettle to boil and the toaster to pop, my eyes flickered to the pink notepaper on the kitchen counter, still where I had left it the night before. The smell of the bread toasting made my stomach rumble, and I realised I didn't eat much yesterday; my mind had been occupied with thoughts of Amelia. I opened the fridge and reached for the milk, butter and marmalade.

I sat at the kitchen counter with my coffee and toast, staring at Amelia's note. The scent from the paper was still as powerful as it had been yesterday, and mixed with the tangy oranges from the marmalade, I could feel myself starting to feel queasy. I gulped down a mouthful of coffee and wiped the crumbs from my mouth. It was nine-thirty, and I had arranged to meet with Amelia at ten-thirty. I didn't fancy having lunch with her. I had always been a little self-conscious about eating in front of strangers, and I didn't know whether I could stomach food when talking with Amelia anyway. I was pleased that I had stuck with this decision. Coffee would be fine. A quick coffee, a chat and then I could leave. What harm could that possibly do? I washed the breakfast things, and after retrieving my handbag and cardigan from the hallway, headed to my car. I hoped the drive would help to clear my mind, but I didn't hold out much certainty about that.

The roads were quiet. They always were. My cottage was in the countryside, remote and peaceful, just the way I liked it. The only traffic jams I usually encountered happened when the local farmer moved his cows or sheep to another field. I smiled at the thought. I loved living here. I knew I would remain here for the rest of my life. I didn't want or need anything more. I suddenly thought back to Amelia. She had been to my home. Had she liked what she saw? Did she want my house? I shook my head, telling myself to stop being ridiculous. Why would a young woman like Amelia want a tiny, remote cottage in the countryside? No, I thought she was more likely looking to get her hands on the big house or the money. I could feel my cheeks burn at the thought of some stranger trying to rob me of what is rightfully mine. Miles had wanted me to have the house and the money; Mr Connor had told me so, and I wasn't about to give anything away to a stranger. Not without a fight, at least.

By the time I got to the small town, I had managed to calm myself down. I parked the car and walked slowly along the high street towards the café I had suggested meeting Amelia in the day before. The streets were quiet, and there were several vacant tables outside the café. I was early, so I chose a table and settled down. I could see every direction from my chair, so I was confident that I would see Amelia before she spotted me. I picked up the menu. It was surprisingly good, with plenty of choices, and I could feel my mouth begin to water. I chastised myself. I wouldn't be eating. I wouldn't be staying long enough. A quick coffee and a chat were what I had promised myself, and that was all I was going to indulge in.

Despite my vantage point, Amelia still startled me when she approached. I had been looking in the opposite direction, and she had come around the corner.

'Mrs Jameson,' she gushed. I stood up to greet her, but I was unsure exactly how. Should I kiss her cheek, shake her hand, or hug her? I held out my hand, and she took it. We shook briefly.

'Please, call me Kate,' I said. Amelia smiled, a huge grin showing perfectly straight white teeth. She genuinely looked pleased to see me. 'Thank you for agreeing to see me again.' I started, but Amelia butted in.

'Not at all; it should be me thanking you. I realise now how inconsiderate I was to just call at your house. I should have telephoned or written first. Please accept my apology.' I returned the smile, although I knew it was nowhere near as warm or welcoming as the one that Amelia had offered me. I handed Amelia the menu.

'Oh, I already know what I want,' she squealed in an excited, childlike voice. I looked at her blankly. 'This is my favourite café. I always order the same!' she continued as if stating the obvious. I was relieved when the waitress came over. Amelia had only just arrived, and I was already feeling uncomfortable in her presence. The waitress looked at Amelia, who quickly reeled off her order. Without thinking, I turned to the waitress and said I would have the same.

'Really?' Amelia gushed, 'That's amazing; we even have the same preferences.' I smiled a hollow smile. I didn't even know what Amelia had ordered, let alone whether I liked it. It had just slipped off my tongue; it was easier that way, rather than study the menu again or just order a drink. I had already broken my first rule. A quick drink, I had said as I had sat here waiting for god knows what to arrive.

Amelia tried to converse politely while we waited for our order to arrive. I could see she was struggling, not really knowing what to say, and I wasn't being much help. We didn't have long to wait as the waitress re-emerged. She placed two lattes on the table. I sighed with relief; at least I could drink that. I had hoped and prayed that I hadn't succumbed to an order of black tea or something else just as peculiar and equally tasteless. I peered at the tray as the waitress laid down two plates, both of which contained generous slices of Victoria sponge cake oozing with jam and fresh cream. I felt myself soften ever so slightly to the young woman sitting opposite me. She might be here to try to take away my inheritance, but at least she ordered a decent coffee and cake.

The waitress smiled as she placed two forks on the table together with a couple of paper napkins and left us to our coffee and cake. I picked up a fork and looked across at Amelia, who was already diving into her cake. She looked to be in her mid-twenties, but she acted much younger, I thought, watching the icing sugar puff around her mouth. I sliced the moist cake with my fork and placed a small piece into my mouth. It was delicious. The delicate sponge was overpowered by the homemade strawberry jam and thick whipped cream, but the entire combination was very tasty, and I felt myself succumbing to its temptations.

We ate our cake in silence. Amelia managed to polish hers off in no time at all, and then she sat back, wiped her mouth on her paper napkin and reached for her coffee. I still had a sizeable chunk of cake on my plate, and I pushed it around with my fork. I could see Amelia eyeing it up. God, she wants my bloody cake as well as my house, I thought, as I quickly broke the cake up and put a huge piece into my mouth before Amelia could get at it. It was a mistake. The sponge stuck to the roof of my mouth, clogging as I tried to swallow it. I took a sip of coffee, hoping to dislodge things, but this just made it worse as I succumbed to a coughing fit. I held my paper napkin to my mouth as I coughed and spluttered, trying hard not to shower Amelia with cake crumbs and cream. She suddenly sprang to her feet and started patting me gently on the back, taking on the stance of a mother watching out for their child. Her thoughtfulness warmed me. When I finally stopped coughing, I dabbed my eyes with the soiled napkin and thanked Amelia for her intervention. I am not sure she actually did anything to help me, but the thought was there, and it was gracious of her to try to help. I wasn't sure I would have done the same if I had been in her position.

I was grateful that the café and pavement were quiet. The fewer people who witnessed my dying swan act, the better. Thank God I hadn't chosen the same eatery as before, I thought; otherwise, they would think I had a real problem eating food. I tried to pull myself together, feeling embarrassed and undignified. I considered now to be a good time to get the conversation going before I could do anything else stupid or embarrass myself further.

'So,' I began tentatively, 'What made you look for me?' I was unsure how to broach things with Amelia despite the fact that I had gone over and over things in my head last night. The bottle of wine clearly hadn't helped me to focus, as I was no nearer to finding a way of grilling her in a way that she wouldn't suspect anything. Amelia looked shocked, her face betraying her emotions.

'I'd have thought that was obvious,' she responded coldly. 'I'm Miles's daughter.' She continued as if stating the obvious might help me to understand why she was here. I laughed inwardly.

'You have been Miles's daughter for some time,' I reply defensively. 'What are you, twenty-five, twenty-six? What I mean is why now, why have you come looking for me now?'

'I'm twenty-five.' If she was offended that I had added an extra year to her age, she didn't show it. 'I didn't know you existed until after Miles had died.' I wasn't sure if I believed her or not. Had Miles kept our marriage a secret? Did he never tell anyone he was married, not even Amelia's mother? I had so many questions, but I didn't want to scare Amelia off, so I held back and let her speak. 'I saw Mr Connor at the funeral. He told me about you and gave me your address. I just had to look you up.'

She lowered her gaze so I couldn't see what her eyes were telling me, although I knew that her mouth was spouting nothing but lies. Mr Connor hadn't been at the funeral, had he? I certainly don't recall seeing him there, and even if he had been, he wouldn't have recognised Amelia. He said he didn't know her, that he had no information about Miles's child, and he certainly wouldn't have breached confidentiality by giving her my address. He was a solicitor; he knew the rules. Amelia looked up again, and I sensed she knew something was wrong. Could she see that I knew she was lying? Miles had always said my face was a dead giveaway. Whenever I tried to hide something from him, he had always been able to see through me; my face, he had said, always belied my voice.

Without warning, Amelia started to cry. This time, all eyes were on her rather than watching my coughing fit, and I felt the urge to run before we could draw any further attention to ourselves. I mentally added up how much two coffees and two cakes would have cost, and adding an extra fiver for a tip, I left the money on the table and ushered Amelia out of her seat. It was a bad idea to meet here. It was too public, and whilst that was my initial intention, I could see now that emotions would be raw and privacy was what we needed, not a public place.

'Let's go back to my house,' I suggested, taking Amelia by the arm. The waitress appeared from nowhere, obviously thinking we were about to run off without paying. She glanced at the table, saw the notes I had left and waved us off.

I led Amelia to my car and helped her in. She was crying softly by now, and her face was streaked with mascara. We drove back to my house in silence, other than the muffled sobs coming from Amelia. I thought it best to let her cry, get it out into the open, as my mother would say when I was a child. When she was all cried out, we reached my garden gate, and I opened it and allowed her to enter first. I ushered her to the patio, and she sat in one of the chairs around the table while I went indoors to get a bottle of wine and a couple of glasses. I figured if she was going to open up properly and not tell me any more lies, she might need a little help to loosen her up. The wine was also to help settle my nerves, as I was still very uncertain about what Amelia might reveal. I took the wine and glasses out and sat down opposite Amelia. She had pulled the chair out next to her, but I couldn't bring myself to sit so close to her. I didn't know why. It just felt strange. She was Miles's daughter, but she wasn't mine, although I could feel myself slowly starting to warm towards her.

'I'm so sorry for crying,' she began. I shook my head so that she knew it was fine. I poured two glasses of wine and handed one to her. Amelia continued. 'It all just hit me again. The funeral, dad dying, the whole mess, everything...' She wavered, and I could see her eyes glistening as the tears threatened to spill over again.

'Why don't you tell me everything? Start at the beginning,' I urged. She nodded as I added, 'Oh, and Amelia, I only want the truth.'

She took a deep breath and then began her story. She took me literally and started at the very beginning. It took her a long time as she recalled her childhood, living in the big house before her mother had insisted that they move to the south coast to be near her grandparents as they were ill and needed someone to care for them. Amelia recalled the arguments between her mother and father about the move. Her father insisted they stay here, and her mother was distraught because her own parents needed her. In the end, her mother had issued an ultimatum. She was going, and she was taking Amelia with her. If her father wanted a relationship with her, then he would have to come, too. He relented, of course, in the end. She was his daughter; he loved her, and of course, he wanted to see her growing up.

Amelia spilt her heart out. Her story rang true, albeit well-rehearsed and clear-cut. She seemed to remember many things, things I am not sure I would have remembered from my own childhood, but Amelia's childhood wasn't like mine. My father didn't have a secret wife, for starters. I learned much about Amelia that afternoon as she poured out her heart and soul to me. She told me how she had hated living on the south coast; all her friends were here, and she desperately wanted to come back home. Her mother had been happy, though. She was back where she belonged, with her parents and family in the place that had been familiar to her, and so Amelia and her father had tried their best to fit in and start again.

Eventually, after about six or seven years, Amelia's grandparents passed away, and Miles tried again to move his family back here. Amelia recalled the conversations she overheard her parents having and how her mother had flatly refused to leave the south coast. She had heard her mother tell her father that she would die there, and he had responded by saying something along the lines of how that could be arranged. Amelia shivered when she recounted that, and I felt my hand fly to my mouth in horror. Amelia shot me a pathetic smile as if trying to lighten the mood.

'It's OK,' she said, 'He didn't kill her, she died of cancer.' This last statement took me by surprise as I hadn't realised that Amelia had lost both her parents. 'That's why I came back here. It's where I remember being the happiest,' she said matter-of-factly. I felt myself warming a little more to Amelia. She was twenty-five and had lost both her parents, so it made sense for her to return to the place where she had once been happy. I chastised myself for thinking she had come back for money.

She continued speaking as if she were talking to herself rather than to me; her stance made me feel like she had zoned out and wasn't even aware of my presence. She just seemed to pick up on my unspoken questions and answered them all without me having to say a word. Her mother had been ill for a long time and suffered a lot at the hands of the deadly disease of lung cancer. Her father had left them and gone to live in a rented apartment close by, near enough to have a relationship with Amelia still but far enough to be reasonably excused from having to care for her mother. Amelia and her mother sold the house, with Miles's consent, and moved in with an elderly aunt. After her mother died, Amelia inherited the money from the house and made the decision to move back here and look for a house of her own. She was renting at the moment but had a decent deposit to put down when the right house came up. I listened intently as Amelia told me her life story. She never said why Miles had moved out of the house he had shared with her and her mother, and I just had to ask.

'Why did Miles leave you and your mother?' I

immediately regretted the question as Amelia stared at me, the trance suddenly broken. A look of sheer hatred washed over her face momentarily as she spat the words.

'Well, that's obvious, isn't it?'

'It is?' I asked.

'He left because of you.' I felt as if Amelia had slapped me across the face. Her words stung.

'Me?' I said incredulously.

'He never stopped loving you, Kate. He told my mother at every opportunity that it was you he loved and that he wanted to go back to you. I think that was what killed her in the end. Without any hope of Miles coming back, she had no reason to fight the cancer, and she gave up and let the disease take hold. She didn't want to live if she couldn't have my father. She had begged him to divorce you so that they could get married, but he had always refused. I think once I came along, my mother thought things would change, and he would finally divorce you, but he didn't; in fact, if anything, it made him more adamant. You were never allowed to find out about me. He said it would hurt you too much, and he didn't want to hurt you any more than he already had.'

This was indeed a declaration I hadn't seen coming. I was stunned. Miles loved me and wanted to come back to me, but he couldn't because of this young woman sitting in front of me. Did he think her birth was the ultimate betrayal and that I would never have forgiven him? Would I? Who knows? Too much time had passed, too many emotions spilt over, and too many lives destroyed.

At that moment, I decided I wasn't going to destroy any more lives. Miles was dead, and so was Amelia's mother. They couldn't hurt me. The past was buried. It was time to think about the future. I wasn't a mother, so I had no real idea about how a mother would feel towards her daughter, but I did have some kindred feelings towards this young lady sitting on my patio, drinking my wine. We could be friends. I was sure of that. She had just told me that my husband had refrained from divorcing me and marrying his mistress because his heart had always belonged to me. That must have been a difficult thing to admit to, but she had. I at least owed her some kindness, even if I couldn't extend it to friendship just yet.

If Amelia was hoping to buy a house around here, we might, in time, get to know each other better; who knows, maybe we will become friends, I thought. Time is a good healer, and even today, in these few hours, I felt Amelia helped heal a part of me. Without speaking, I leant over and topped up our glasses. Amelia took a sip and continued to speak, although by now, I am not sure I was even listening. I was not interested in the mundane facts about how the cancer took hold of her mother and how she watched her die a slow agonising death. I am sure it took its toll on them both, but it simply didn't concern me. Although I was starting to feel something towards Amelia, I was not sure what; I felt nothing for her mother. The woman who had prevented Miles from returning to me. The woman who had lured him away. Miles had been my husband, and she had tricked him into getting her pregnant, all so he couldn't come back home.

I knew these thoughts were ludicrous. Miles didn't leave me for her. We had already grown apart. She just made the leaving easier for him. Harder for me. Amelia is her daughter; I thought as the hatred threatened to consume me. I took a mouthful of the chilled wine. She is also Miles's daughter I reasoned, as I looked over to the young woman who was still blabbing about her happy childhood. I tried to block her words out. I didn't want to hear how Miles had built her a Wendy house in the garden of the big house. The *big* house. My ears pricked up. That was how I referred to it, and now Amelia was calling it the *big* house. I tried to focus on what she was saying, my ears ringing with all the words.

'Where did you live as a child?' I blurted out, interrupting Amelia's childhood rendition.

'Wentworth Drive,' she replied without hesitation. So, Jean was telling the truth. Miles had lived in the house with his family. Mr Connor had been lying; he said that Miles had bought the house as an investment and hadn't lived in it.

Despite eating the cake earlier that morning, my stomach was beginning to growl at me. It was past lunchtime, and the wine had made me hungry. I wanted to stop Amelia from prattling on about her childhood.

'Do you fancy something to eat,' I asked quickly, whilst there was a slight lull in the conversation.

'That would be nice if it's no trouble.'

I stood, and Amelia did the same. She followed me to the kitchen. The same room I had ordered her to leave only days before. She saw the note she had written that I had left on the kitchen table and smiled. I busied myself fixing a cheese salad and reached for another bottle of wine in the fridge.

'Oh, no more for me, thanks. I have to get back home, and I think I'm already a bit tipsy,' Amelia said.

'You can stay here if you like; give us a chance to get to know each other a bit better,' I blurted out before I could stop myself. I could have bitten my tongue off when Amelia accepted my invitation without hesitating. Hadn't Miles always berated me for not putting my brain in gear before opening my mouth, and here I was inviting his daughter to stay over? His daughter, whom I didn't know existed a few weeks ago. His daughter, whom I didn't even know if I liked.

I reached into the cupboard for a tray and placed the cheese salad, plates, cutlery, and condiments on it. Amelia reached for the bottle of wine and tucked it under her arm so she could carry both glasses in her hands. We retraced our steps to the patio and tucked into a healthy salad washed down with copious amounts of white wine. The rest of the afternoon and evening went quickly. We chatted and laughed. I allowed Amelia to reminisce as much as I could, and then, when the conversation became too painful, I changed the subject or altered the course of the conversation. The hours flashed by, and I surprised myself by enjoying Amelia's company.

Late into the night, after consuming several bottles of wine, I showed Amelia to the spare bedroom and lent her one of my nightdresses. She thanked me sincerely and bid me good night. I climbed into bed exhausted. It had been a pleasant encounter, but now I wish that Amelia had gone home. We talked about everything and anything, but I still didn't know this woman who was sleeping in the bedroom next to me. She was still a stranger, albeit one who had told me her life story. My body ached, and my head spun. I needed to sleep, but my mind remained active and alert. I had left the bedroom window open, but the air was still warm and stifling. I heard the hoot of an owl as I closed my eyes and drifted off to sleep.

# Chapter Thirteen

When I woke the next morning, I could smell bacon wafting upstairs. I leaned over and checked my phone on the bedside table, it was eight fifty-three. I leapt out of bed and pulled on my dressing gown. I rushed downstairs, my head still woozy from drinking the night before. As I entered the kitchen, the radio was on quietly playing *The Gambler* by Kenny Rodgers, and Amelia was singing along softly, seemingly aware of all the words. Was the song trying to tell me something? I wondered as I entered the kitchen.

'Just in time!' Amelia shrilled, full of the joys of spring and with the same childish voice she had used in the café. Then sheepishly, she continued, 'I hope you don't mind; I took the liberty of making us breakfast as a thank you for your hospitality yesterday.' It seemed lost on Amelia that she was thanking me by preparing my own food in my own kitchen, but as the act was out of kindness, I chose to let it go.

'It smells marvellous,' I said, pulling out a chair and sitting at the island in the middle of the kitchen. Amelia poured me a cup of coffee and plated up a hearty breakfast of bacon, eggs, mushrooms, tomatoes, baked beans, hash browns, and toast, both brown and white. She certainly hadn't been shy about searching my cupboards, fridge, and freezer, I thought, as I took the plate from her. We tucked into the breakfast in silence before Amelia spoke.

'Did you sleep well?' she asked. I was surprised at her question because, as she was my guest, surely this should be something I should be asking her. I smiled and nodded, still chewing on my bacon. I felt uncomfortable having Amelia here in my kitchen, clearly feeling very much at home. The idea of her staying over last night seemed sensible as we had both been drinking, but now, in the cold light of day, I wanted her gone. It was too much too soon, and I could feel the panic in my chest. I hurriedly ate my breakfast and stacked the dishes in the dishwasher.

'I need to go into town this morning,' I said hastily, 'So I can drop you off. I will be leaving in about ten minutes.' Amelia blushed. It was obvious to us both that I was trying to rush her out, and I felt guilty, but I needed her to go. She excused herself and headed back upstairs. I followed her and quickly dressed and brushed my hair. I took a quick look in the mirror and hated what I saw: tired, bloodshot eyes, dry, dull skin, and pale lips. I needed to be alone. I needed to think.

I ushered Amelia into the car the second she descended the stairs, completely oblivious to how my actions might look. The truth be known is that right now, I didn't care what Amelia thought. My thoughts were completely irrational. I knew that, but I felt she had tricked herself into my house. Stupid, I know that; I had invited her, but had she somehow convinced me to do so? Coerced me into bringing her back here. I wanted her to leave now. As she climbed into the car, she took a look around. Surveying the remoteness of the countryside in which I live.

'It really is beautiful here,' she said. I slammed my car door, indicating that she should get in and do the same. We drove in silence for about twenty minutes.

'I'm really sorry if I have upset you in any way,' she said. I glanced across at her sitting in the passenger seat, looking small and frail.

'You haven't,' I replied, 'I'm fine.'

'I shouldn't have cooked breakfast. It wasn't my place to make myself at home in your house without permission.' *No, it bloody well wasn't.* My thoughts screamed back at her. My home, my kitchen, my sanctuary – she had no right to search through my cupboards at all.

'Honestly, it's fine,' I said again through gritted teeth. 'I just have a busy day, and I need to crack on,' I lied, pulling up on a side street on the outskirts of the town. I should have asked if this was a convenient place to drop her off or if she wanted a lift home, but I didn't. Truth be known, I didn't much care whether this was convenient or not; I just wanted to get rid of her.

Amelia climbed out of the car and stood on the pavement. Before she could say anything, I put my car into gear and sped off. I glanced through the rear-view mirror and watched as she got smaller and smaller before disappearing completely. The sudden feeling of relief washed over me, and I relaxed. I headed straight back home, my head pounding and my heart thudding; I needed to get back home and get rid of all traces of Amelia from my house.

I unlocked the back door and immediately ran upstairs. The bed in the spare room had been made; nothing was out of place. If I hadn't known she had been here last night, I could never have guessed, she had left it so neat. But I had known. I pulled the duvet from the bed, along with the sheets and pillowcases and went into the en-suite, collecting all the towels. A couple hadn't even been used, but these were also scooped up and dragged downstairs.

I loaded the washing machine and set it going, relaxing more and more as I watched the white sheets going round and round in the machine, washing away the smell of Amelia. I emptied the dishwasher and replaced the contents in the cupboards. I smiled as I took out the wine glasses. I couldn't keep throwing them away. I would have none left soon. I contented myself with the fact that the glasses had been fully sterilised and that all traces of Amelia had been eradicated. I chastised myself for being irrational. What did I think she would give me, for god's sake? She wasn't a leper. She was Miles's daughter, my husband's child.

A chill ran down my spine as I pulled out the cleaning products from under the sink and took the stairs, two at a time. I was on a mission. I re-entered the bedroom that Amelia had slept in last night and polished the room to within an inch of its life. When I was satisfied that everything was spick and span, I remade the bed with fresh linen and opened the window to allow the room to fill with fresh air; I could still smell the faint scent of her perfume over the lemony zest of the disinfectant and lavender of the polish. I then turned my attention to the adjoining bathroom, noticing the nightdress on the towel holder. My nightdress, the one I had lent to Amelia last night. I snatched it up; I could smell her perfume on the fabric.

Back downstairs, I flicked the switch on the kettle. I desperately wanted a glass of wine, but I wouldn't allow myself to get drunk again. I had had far too much last night, and look where that had got me. Whilst the kettle was boiling, I went outside and dumped the nightdress in the dustbin. No amount of washing would ever make me want to wear that again.

I made myself a cup of strong coffee and took it out to the patio. I sat down just as my phone pinged, indicating I had a message. I unlocked my phone. 'Sorry.' That was it, just one single word from Amelia. I wondered what she was sorry for and whether her intention had been for me to guess. Was it for tricking me into allowing her to stay here last night or for helping herself to my food, cooking breakfast in my kitchen as if she owned the place, or was it simply for being herself, turning up, and telling me her life story? I didn't know, and right now, neither did I care. I put my phone on the table, face down and hoped she would give me the space I needed to process what she had told me last night. I didn't need her badgering me. I wanted her to leave me alone.

I hoped that she would.

## Chapter Fourteen

Just over a week had passed, and I hadn't heard anything from Amelia. I hadn't replied to her message when she said she was sorry, and she hadn't elaborated. I had had a call from the estate agent following another viewing, and I had received another offer for the house. It was for the full asking price, but the prospective purchasers didn't want the furniture. I didn't blame them. I didn't want it either. It wouldn't be a problem getting someone to clear the house out, and maybe someone could make use of the contents. I accepted the offer and felt instantly cheered. I decided to pay Jean a visit as it was Wednesday and I knew she would be at the big house. I wasn't sure that I wanted to tell her about the offer on the house. I still hadn't decided whether she had something to do with the previous sale falling through, and part of me didn't want to take the chance of anything going wrong again.

Pulling into the driveway, I noticed two cars parked outside the house rather than just Jean's. I parked my car and got out of the car cautiously. I felt like an intruder on my own property. Pulling myself together, I stepped quietly into the hallway. I could hear muffled voices coming from the kitchen. They sounded angry, but because the kitchen door was closed, I struggled to make out what was being said. It was definitely two female voices, and they sounded as if they were arguing. I hurried up the stairs and hid on the landing. I held my breath as I waited for the kitchen door to open, revealing who was arguing in the kitchen. *My kitchen*, I thought, anger rising in my chest. I didn't have long to wait. I don't know what I was expecting or who I thought might be arguing with Jean, but I was certainly taken by surprise when the door flung open, and Amelia strode out. I struggled to breathe as Jean followed her. Her face flushed as she grabbed Amelia by the shoulders and spun her around. I was rooted to the spot. I wanted to confront them, but I was too shocked to do anything. This didn't seem right. The whole situation was wrong, very wrong, and I needed time to think things through. Neither Jean nor Amelia knew I was here, so I could stay where I was on the landing until Amelia left. I could then pretend to Jean that I didn't know Amelia had been there. I wanted to see if Jean admitted to seeing Amelia. Then I remembered my car! I had parked my car outside, next to Jean's. They would see it and know I was here! My mind raced. I needed to think of an excuse for not going straight into the kitchen when I arrived. Why hadn't I recognised Amelia's car? I pulled out my phone and put it to my ear.

'I'm really sorry, but I am going to have to find the housekeeper and ask her,' I said loudly, pretending to be conversing about the house. Both Amelia and Jean looked up at me, a look of horror mirrored between them. I waved and smiled whilst I continued with my imaginary conversation. I never took my eyes off Jean or Amelia, and I could see the panic in both their eyes. They hadn't expected me to call, obviously, and now they had been caught red-handed, they were like deer caught in headlights. I felt a surprising rush of satisfaction, having caught them out. 'I will call you back as soon as I find out.' I ended the call and headed down the stairs.

'Jean, Amelia, how are you both?' I asked in the most pleasant tone I could muster, given my mood. Jean opened her mouth to speak, but Amelia beat her to it.

'I just wanted to take one last look at my childhood home before you sell it,' she said, trying her best to seem wistful.

'You should have asked me,' I shot back. 'I could have brought you, and then you wouldn't have had to disturb Jean while she was working.' Jean lowered her gaze. I reached the bottom of the stairs and stood my ground, staring at them both. I would not be made to feel like a trespasser in my house by a housekeeper and a stranger. I could see how uncomfortable Jean was becoming, having been found arguing with Amelia, and she looked as if she wanted the ground to swallow her up.

'I will get back to my work,' she said. Then she turned and scuttled back to the kitchen like the lying rat that she was. I turned my attention to Amelia.

'Have you seen everything, or would you like another look?' I asked. Amelia seemed slightly taken aback at not being thrown out of the house immediately.

'I'd love a tour, please.' I thought this was a strange thing to say as surely she already knew the house, having lived here during the happiest part of her childhood. I was intrigued by her reaction to my suggestion, so I stepped aside and allowed her to climb the stairs before me. I followed her, wondering what fantasies she would share with me. I wanted to know which bedroom she had slept in as a child and where Miles had slept with her mother. I wanted to know everything about this house. Amelia climbed the stairs in silence.

'It's a good job you decided to drop by when you did,' I said. 'Another buyer has been found.' Amelia turned and stared at me. Her eyes were cold and distant, and I couldn't decide whether it was sadness or anger that was written on her face.

'That's good,' she replied, without showing any signs of emotion.

'Yes, it is. It will mean I can draw a line under things here and get on with my life. The buyer doesn't want any of the furniture, so if you would like anything for your new house, please let me know, and I can arrange for you to have it.' Amelia looked confused. 'I thought you said you were looking for a property around here – that you had sold up and moved back?' I questioned.

'Oh, yes, yes,' Amelia said, suddenly seeming to remember what her intentions were.

'Is there anything that you particularly treasure from your childhood that you would like?' I pressed her further, watching her squirm. And squirm she did. It seemed she had no idea what to say. Was she even aware of what was in the house? I knew there were no family heirlooms or personal possessions in the house because, according to Jean, Miles had already shipped these down to the south coast, but I wanted to see what Amelia's reaction was. She was quick off the mark. Thinking on her feet seemed to come easily to Amelia.

'I doubt there will be anything sentimental,' she said wistfully. 'I didn't come to see if there was anything I wanted; honestly, I just wanted to have one last look around for old times' sake.' I might have been inclined to believe her had I not heard her arguing in the kitchen with

Jean when I arrived, and I was intrigued by why neither of them had mentioned this. I decided to bide my time; now wasn't the right time to ask about the argument. I was convinced that if I broached the subject now, Amelia would just lie to me.

'Which bedroom was yours?' I asked. Amelia's eyes darted around the landing as if she was looking for answers. She pointed to the door at the far end, on the right-hand side.

'My parents had the room next to me.' She stated that before I could ask her.

*Liar!* I wanted to scream in her face. I knew this wasn't right because Jean had shown me which room had been Miles's and his mistress's, and it hadn't been the one that Amelia pointed out. I tried to calm myself down. There were several explanations; Amelia could simply be mistaken; she hadn't lived here for a long time, but even then, I can remember the bedrooms of the houses I had slept in as a child, and I am much older than Amelia. She could, of course, be lying, but why? Then, of course, it might be Jean that is lying, and again, I had to ask myself why. I was confused, and by the look on Amelia's face, so was she. It was as if she had never been in the house before. I don't know why, but I had a niggling doubt in the back of my mind. She wandered around the house and seemed surprised by what she saw. She just didn't give the impression that this was familiar ground and that she was reminiscing. Then again, it could have all been in my imagination. I was aware of how irrational my thoughts were becoming.

We went downstairs and wandered through the rooms. Again, it felt like I was showing Amelia around the property for the first time. She didn't comment on anything. I thought she might have told me about her childhood, where she had played, what her doll's house had been like, how she and her mother had baked cakes, all the simple things that children enjoyed. I don't know whether the memories were too painful for her to voice or if they simply didn't exist, in this house at least. After the tour, she thanked me and headed for the door. Strangely, I didn't want her to leave. I had questions I wanted to ask her.

'Coffee?' I asked. Amelia turned and smiled.

'That would be lovely. The same café as before?'

I nodded, and we both got into our respective cars. I glanced at the house as I adjusted my rear-view mirror and saw Jean watching us leave, a scowl on her face. I realised then that I hadn't even spoken to Jean. I wasn't sure that I wanted her to know that I had a buyer for the house anyway, so I decided to leave it for now. Amelia arrived at the café slightly ahead of me, and I was taken aback when she said she had ordered something for us both. It felt like she was taking liberties again, although maybe this was just her way of being kind and friendly. To be honest, it was a little too friendly. I might have ordered for a lover or a husband, someone I knew intimately, but not for a stranger. She might be a stranger, I thought, but she is my husband's child. I had anticipated what she had ordered before it arrived, and I wasn't wrong. A latte and a huge wedge of Victoria sandwich.

'You know me too well,' I said, trying to keep the sarcasm out of my voice. *You don't know me at all, you stupid girl,* I thought as she smiled and handed me a fork.

'Did you come here as a child?' I asked as Amelia

popped a piece of cake into her mouth. She smiled and nodded. She swallowed her cake.

'My mum used to bring me on Saturday morning after dance class.'

'That's nice, tell me more about your childhood. What was your mother like?' I regretted the words immediately. I didn't care about Amelia's childhood, and I cared even less about the woman who had taken my husband from me, borne him a child and prevented him from returning home.

'She was beautiful,' genuine tears sprang to her eyes.

'Do you have a picture of her?' I asked. Amelia reached into her handbag and took out a photograph. It was a crumbled Polaroid showing a young woman with jet-black hair, piercing blue eyes and ruby-red lips. The child on her lap couldn't have been more than five or six years old. They were both smiling into the camera.

'My father took this picture of me and my mother.' I studied the photograph, but I was not really sure what I was looking for. There was no indication of where they were; the background showed a lawned area with a flowerbed. It could have been any garden, anywhere. I returned the picture to Amelia, and she put it back in her handbag.

I was beginning to wonder why Amelia had accepted my offer of coffee as she didn't seem to be in a rush to open up and chat about anything. It had been weeks since our last encounter, and, to be fair to her, I had practically thrown her out of my house. Still, I was intrigued as to why she had accepted my offer of another visit to the café. I didn't believe her story of visiting the house for old times' sake. She had been arguing with Jean when I arrived, and I had no doubt about that. I just needed to know why. I decided to broach the subject.

'I noticed you seemed a little upset with Jean earlier.' It was a statement rather than a question. I didn't think I could stomach another blatant lie from her if she tried to deny she and Jean had been arguing. Amelia stopped chewing, weighing me up before she answered. I could see in her eyes she was trying to figure out how much I had heard. Unfortunately, besides the raised voices, I had heard nothing of the conversation, but I wasn't going to let Amelia know this. 'I heard you arguing with her,' I finished, adding a little more weight to my accusation. Amelia waved her fork in the air dismissively.

'She can be so annoying at times,' she said, pushing another piece of cake into her mouth. I was convinced she liked Victoria sandwich cake because it did not allow you to speak once your mouth was full. She seemed to use the cake to gain precious time to think before answering my questions.

'Maybe, but that doesn't answer my question,' I offered, determined to get an answer.

'She expressed her disgust that you were selling the house, and I was trying to argue your point,' Amelia said with conviction while staring me straight in the eyes. Again, I didn't believe a word she said. I didn't believe Jean would comment on the house sale, and even if she did, why would Amelia stand up for me?

'Do you think I should keep the house?' I asked, knocking Amelia momentarily off guard.

'I think you should do what is right for you. As I said to Jean, the house might hold happy memories for us, but why would it hold anything but unhappy thoughts for you?'

She had a point. The house was simply a reminder to me of Miles's other life. His life without me. I had no reason to keep this house, and if Jean couldn't accept that, then that was her problem, not mine. I felt grateful to Amelia for arguing my corner when I wasn't there to defend myself, but something still didn't sit right with me.

I chatted away with Amelia for another half an hour or so before making my excuses to leave. I caught the attention of the waitress and paid the bill. Amelia had tried to pay in a non-committal sort of way, but I told her it was fine. I wondered what her reaction would have been if I had allowed her to settle the bill this time. Before leaving, I invited Amelia over for lunch the following Sunday. She accepted, and we said our goodbyes. I glanced back at Amelia as I rounded the corner, heading towards the car park. She was deep in conversation on her phone and didn't look up.

# Chapter Fifteen

Although I still couldn't quite put my finger on it, there was something strangely at odds about Amelia. Her behaviour simply didn't strike me as being genuine. I did think she was doing a very good job of *performing* for me. She tried to say the things that I presume she expected I wanted to hear, but that was just it; they weren't what I expected to hear. I appreciate her loss; she had lost both her parents, so it was understandable that she would be sad; however, this wasn't the side I had seen of her. Even when she was walking around the big house with me, she didn't show any emotion. I don't believe she visited the house to reminisce as she had told me; I firmly believe she had gone only to see Jean, and they were in the middle of a heated argument when I turned up. If I could find out what they were arguing about, then I might be able to get a handle on things; find out what Amelia really wanted.

I had to play it cool and bide my time if I had any hope of getting Amelia on board. I had to get her to trust me and open up. Only then would I be able to discover what was going on. Much as it irked me to invite her back to my home, it seemed the easiest way to talk to her. We couldn't keep going to the café for coffee and cake. My waistline would have something to say about that, as would my finances. I laughed to myself as I remembered I was a wealthy woman now, a multi-millionaire. Isn't that what I am?

Sunday came around quickly. I had prepared tuna steaks with new potatoes and a large salad. I knew Amelia wasn't a vegetarian, as she had cooked bacon in my kitchen, but I was unsure if she liked fish. I figured even if she didn't eat the tuna, she could pick at the salad and potatoes. I had put a bottle of wine in the fridge to cool but told myself there would be no second bottle this time and the invitation would not be extended to bed and breakfast. I needed to keep a clear head and find out what I wanted to know. I would probably have to keep repeating the invitations and maybe throw in a couple more café visits if I were to get Amelia to really open up, but chipping away little by little seemed like a plan.

Amelia rang my doorbell at exactly one o'clock. I glanced at the clock on the kitchen wall and smiled as I went to answer the door. The familiar waft of perfume preceded her as Amelia walked into the hall. She handed me a small bunch of roses hand-tied with a pink bow and a bottle of rosé wine. She certainly has a fondness for pink, I thought as I took the offerings, thanked her, and led the way through to the kitchen.

'Smells divine,' Amelia said, as she dumped her handbag on one of the chairs positioned around the island in the kitchen.

I could feel my nerves begin to stand on end as she made herself at home. There was just something a little too familiar about Amelia that I didn't like. She always seemed too comfortable, acting like she owned the place rather than the guest that she was. I hid my annoyance.

'I've got tuna steaks. I hope that's OK,' I asked. 'I wasn't sure what type of meat you liked, so I opted for fish.'

Amelia smiled broadly.

'I love tuna!' she almost sang the words. 'Is there anything I can do?'

'No,' I stated a little too abruptly. Amelia stepped back laughing, holding her hands out in surrender. 'Sorry, I am a bit overprotective of my kitchen,' I said, laughing with her. 'You can take the cutlery through to the conservatory, along with the condiments on the counter and glasses if you like,' I suggested, trying to give Amelia something to do so that she would get from under my feet.

I began to sear the tuna; the smell filled the kitchen, making me feel a little queasy. I wasn't sure if it was the smell of the tuna or the company that had suddenly turned my stomach, but I concentrated hard on the cooking to take my mind off it. I don't know why I felt apprehensive when Amelia was around. I suppose it is because I have only just met her and don't know her very well, but I don't recall having feelings like these before when meeting new people. Perhaps it is because, although Amelia is a stranger, she is somehow connected to me, albeit only through Miles.

I served the tuna steaks on plates with a garnish and carried the plates to the conservatory, where Amelia had set the table. She followed me with the bowl of salad. I retreated to the kitchen for the bowl of new potatoes and plucked the bottle of wine from the fridge.

'This looks lovely,' Amelia said with sincerity, as she added a glug of balsamic vinegar to her salad, followed by a huge knob of butter to her potatoes. I smiled as I watched her. She seemed to enjoy her food. Despite the fact that she was quite slim, she didn't hold back on potatoes, butter or cake, so at least I didn't have to worry about her having any hang-ups as far as food was concerned. Why should I be concerned about anything? I suddenly thought. She isn't my daughter. Was I beginning to have motherly thoughts towards this young lady? How ridiculous. She wasn't my flesh and blood, and I needed to get a grip. Still, she didn't have any parents, and she was only twenty-five; maybe I needed to show her more compassion.

'Any luck with the house-hunting?' I asked her as I sliced into my tuna steak.

'Yes, I have a viewing tomorrow at eleven,' she said. 'It's not far from here, actually. A little cottage at the other end of the dale.' I wasn't quite sure how I felt about the revelation. It didn't bother me that Amelia had a house viewing, but I hadn't expected her to look so close to where I lived, and I didn't know how this made me feel. 'You can come with me if you like?' Her invitation surprised me. I figured this would have been something she would have probably done with her mother, but as her mother was dead, maybe she saw me as the next best thing. 'I would really value your opinion,' she concluded.

'Well, in that case, I would love to,' I said, pushing my concern aside.

The afternoon was a pleasant one. We chatted easily about things of little importance, but I felt that I had learned a lot about my husband's child by the time she left at just after five. I don't know if she had hoped for an invitation to stay over, but when she felt it wasn't forthcoming, she refused a second glass of wine and stuck to drinking water. I didn't relent. This time, I wanted us both to keep a clear head and, when Amelia had left, there had still been almost a third of the bottle of wine left. Amelia divulged information about her favourite colour, pink, and there were no surprises there. Her favourite food was pasta, in addition to Victoria sandwich cake, and she would love to own a dog. I asked her if she had been allowed any pets as a child, and she said she hadn't.

Although she was happy to talk to me about the inconsequential things, she gave little away about her actual childhood. She skirted around the questions I asked about her schooling, her friends, her upbringing, and anything that might have given me an insight into her background and how she grew up. I longed to know what her relationship with Miles had been like. I supposed it hadn't been a good one. Otherwise, he would have remembered her in his will, but what had caused the rift?

After Amelia left, I cleared away the plates and tidied the kitchen before topping up my wine glass and retreating to the garden. The garden was my special place, particularly on a warm sunny evening like tonight. It had always been where I retreated to when Miles had first left me, and I had felt so alone. It was quiet and peaceful whilst also being full of life. The birds, rabbits, hedgehogs, and deer had all kept me company on those dark, lonely days. I kicked my sandals off and sat on the grass, feeling the slight prickle of the blades through my dress and the coolness of the ground. I breathed deeply. The scent of the roses wafting in the air, along with the heady fragrance of the lavender, calmed my frazzled nerves. Despite the fact that it had been a pleasant afternoon, the nagging doubts I had about Amelia wouldn't go away. I seemed to swing from feeling something for her; I wasn't sure what; I doubted it was love, but it was some kind of affection, to something which resembled utter despair. Not knowing what she wanted or who she was threw me into a state of panic that

I wasn't used to and didn't like.

I finished my wine and lay back on the grass, staring into the now-darkening sky. The air was still warm with the heady feel of summer. I could stay here all night like this; I thought as I let my mind drift back to the early days of my marriage. The days when Miles and I had been happy. We had been happy; I was sure of that. Although it was a long time ago and so many things had happened since those early days, I loved Miles deeply, and, according to Mr Connor, Jean, and Amelia, Miles had felt the same way.

I thought about Amelia's mother. Had Miles compared her to me? Had she been fun to my boring? Had she excited him? Had she been good in bed? Better than me? More alluring? Had he loved her?

I woke with a start and glanced at my watch. It was dark, the moon illuminating the face of watch. It was just past midnight. I shivered as I pushed my aching body to a sitting position. The grass had dampened my dress, and my back and arms ached. I pulled myself up and went inside, closing the door behind me and locking it as I went.

I made my way upstairs to bed, climbed under the duvet and slept like a baby until the sun rose.

## Chapter Sixteen

The next morning, I woke surprisingly refreshed. I had arranged to meet Amelia at the house she had booked to view at eleven. She had scribbled the address down on a piece of paper, and I glanced at it whilst waiting for the kettle to boil. I poured some muesli into a bowl and added some milk.

I knew exactly where the property was; it was less than ten minutes from my own house, and I felt uncomfortable at the thought of having Amelia live so close to me. I asked myself why, but I couldn't put my finger on anything in particular. I just wasn't keen on having her so close by all the time. Would she make a habit of popping in to see me when I didn't want company? I was so used to being on my own, and I had spent years keeping myself to myself. I simply didn't want my privacy invaded. I told myself I was being silly. Amelia was a young woman; she would soon make friends, or she might rekindle her old friendships; she wouldn't be looking to hang out with me on a regular basis. I felt relieved at the thought.

I finished my muesli, tidied the kitchen and then retrieved my laptop from the bureau in the living room. I wanted to research the property before I met Amelia, see what it was like, and, to be honest, find out how much it was on the market for. The house was very similar to my own in that it was a two-bedroom cottage in the countryside, but that was where the similarities stopped. My house is a traditional cottage with beams, deep window sills, and window seats. This house was, in my opinion, characterless and sterile. Just like Amelia, I thought with just a hint of sarcasm. Even the garden was an overgrown mess with cracked paving stones and weeds that were waist-high. There was nothing cottagey about the place at all. I hated it before we had even stepped inside. Well, at least it won't be hard for me to give her my honest opinion, I thought wistfully, and I didn't have to lie to try to put her off buying it. If she valued my opinion, then she would run a mile.

At just after ten-thirty, I decided to set off for the house. It wouldn't take me long to arrive, but I wanted to get there before Amelia and the estate agent. I snatched my handbag from the chair and locked the door behind me. I started the engine and drove slowly up the lane to the public road, listening to the presenter on the radio informing me that today's weather would be scorching. I checked the thermometer in the car, which was already showing 28 degrees. I didn't bother to press the air con button as the journey would be over before the car had cooled down, so I opened the window instead, instantly feeling the whoosh of fresh air as I did so.

I pulled up outside the house and, parking my car on the pavement, I climbed out and headed up the garden path. The front of the house was all paved. I presumed to allow the owner to park off the road, but I would have much preferred a country cottage garden with hollyhocks, poppies, peonies, lupins, and delphiniums. The lack of colour was depressing. The original wooden door had been replaced with a plastic one, albeit in a muted sage green colour. It was plastic nonetheless, and again, it did nothing to inspire me. I tried the handle. It was locked, of course, so I went around the back, hoping to see something that resembled a garden. The space was small and overgrown. A greenhouse in the far corner was almost buried under brambles and weeds. The lawn, if you could call it that, was a mass of dandelions and buttercups, and the trees by the fence were overgrown, with branches so heavy that they almost touched the ground. Well, at least it wasn't paved, I thought wistfully. Although it would take an awful lot of hard work to get it to resemble a garden again. I was beginning to understand why the online particulars of the house had very few photographs. If the inside was anything like the exterior, it would make for depressing viewing. The sound of a car engine brought me to my senses, and I retraced my steps to the front of the house.

As I reached the front door, the estate agent was climbing out of his car. He looked as if he was fresh out of school and was dressed casually in a white open-necked shirt and navy-blue linen trousers, which had creased terribly while he had been sitting in the car. He walked towards me with his hand outstretched.

'Pleased to meet you, Miss Jameson,' he said.

'Mrs,' I corrected, shaking his hand. 'I'm Kate.'

'Ah, you must be Amelia's mother, pleased to meet you.' Before I could correct him, Amelia pulled up in her car and jumped out.

'Hi,' she squealed in the childish voice I had now come to associate her with. 'I'm so excited!'

'Well then, let's not waste any time and get inside,' the agent said, unlocking the door and stepping aside so that Amelia and I could enter.

The house was small and I was grateful that the agent had decided to remain outside. Actually, once I had entered the property, I envied him being able to stay in the sunshine. The house smelt awful, and I felt myself trying hard not to gag. Judging by the expression on Amelia's face, she felt the same. Her excitement, it seemed, had been short-lived. We looked at the kitchen first, which was very basic with rickety old units that had certainly seen better days.

'You would have to replace everything here,' I said, trying hard to hide my satisfaction. I didn't want the house to be nice or in good repair because I didn't want Amelia to buy it, and it seemed like I was in luck. Amelia said nothing as she moved into the living room. Where my own cottage had a wood burner, in keeping with the age and style of the property, this cottage had an ugly gas fire surrounded by dark brown cracked tiles. I could sense the disappointment Amelia was feeling. Every ounce of her dismay simply added to my own feeling of contentment. There was no way Amelia would buy this house.

We wandered upstairs, trying not to touch the grubby handrail that was thick with white paint that had yellowed over time. Layer after layer had been added without anyone seemingly having tried to remove the old paint before adding another layer. There were two bedrooms, one on each side of the landing and a tiny bathroom at the top of the stairs. I popped my head around the bathroom door. The toilet was stained yellow, and the enamel on the bath had worn away, leaving rusty stains, the plug hung from a tarnished chain. I moved into the first bedroom whilst Amelia took the second. The beams had been painted over, again with thick layers reminiscent of the handrail.

I peered out of the window. The views were the only pretty thing about the house, but I was absolutely horrified to see that, across the dale, my own house was within view. There was no way I wanted Amelia to buy this house. Of course, she wouldn't be able to see me from this distance, but the very thought that my house was within eyesight of what might be her house filled me with horror.

I crossed the landing into the bedroom that Amelia was looking at. She, too, was staring out of the window, and I wondered if she had noticed my own cottage in the distance. If she had, she said nothing.

'What do you think?' she asked, turning to face me. I was incredulous. Was she seriously contemplating buying this wreck? I wasn't sure how to respond.

'Why don't we go for a coffee and discuss it properly,' I offered, buying myself some time.

'Good idea,' she agreed, smiling for the first time since we had entered the house. We thanked the agent, and Amelia said she would be in touch with her decision after we had discussed things properly.

'No problem at all,' the agent said, as he locked up the house and drove away.

'Meet you at *the* café?' Amelia shouted, as she climbed into her own car. She didn't have to elaborate; it was as if the café was our meeting place and the only one in the town, which, of course, it wasn't. She didn't wait for me to reply as she drove off, her sunroof open and her hair flying about.

I looked up at the house one last time before getting into my car, following Amelia at a much slower pace. Amelia was sitting in a chair, looking at her phone, when I arrived. Once again, to my annoyance, she had ordered for me. She seemed to think it was some kind of unspoken rule between us that we both had to have a latte and a piece of Victoria sandwich cake when we visited *our* café, and it was starting to irk me. I felt like telling her that, actually, today, I didn't want a bloody huge piece of stodgy cake, but I kept my mouth shut and smiled. As we waited for the waitress, Amelia began to talk about the house.

'Of course, it needs a lot of work, but well, I don't suppose your own house was as beautiful as it is now when you first bought it. I bet you've made it like that.' I wanted to tell her that the house was, in fact, very endearing from the outset, which is why we purchased it, and that any changes that were made were done when Miles was by my side. I didn't voice my thoughts as I didn't want to offend Amelia. She was trying to compliment me on my home, and I didn't need to be rude to her.

'Well, I guess it all depends on how much money you've got to spend,' I said diplomatically. Amelia screwed her nose up.

'Not that much!' she said, laughing.

I laughed with her, relieved that she sounded as if she wasn't going to buy the place.

'Then again, if I put in a cheeky offer, they might accept it, which would then give me spare cash to do some of the work.'

The waitress arrived with our order before I could reply. It was the same waitress we had seen before, and she smiled broadly when she recognised me. As the waitress left, I turned my attention back to Amelia. I had to get her to reconsider buying the house.

'What do you think of the house?' she said, taking me by surprise.

'Well, I wouldn't be buying it, would I?' I replied, unsure of how to tell her I would run a mile.

'No, but I value your opinion, which is why I asked you to come with me.'

'Well, in that case, I would say keep looking. I think the house is over-priced in its current state, and it will take a lot of cash to get it habitable.' Amelia looked downhearted, and I felt a little mean. In fact, the property could be made really nice. It's true it was overpriced, but if the vendor was willing to negotiate on the price, a good deal could well be done. However, I wasn't going to tell Amelia that. We ate our cake and drank our coffee. Suddenly Amelia made her excuses and said she had to go. We said our goodbyes, and I watched as she hurried off, wondering where she was heading. The waitress came to collect our empty plates.

'Can I get you anything else?' she asked.

'Just the bill, please,' I said, suddenly realising that, once again, I had been left to pay. 'Can I ask you something?' I said, looking up at the waitress. She stopped loading the tray and smiled at me, anticipating my question. 'Can you tell me how long this café has been open?'

'Yes, I can. It has been open for just over three years. My sister and I bought it just after Covid. It was a risk, but we've both worked hard, and it has been successful.' She said proudly. I was confused.

'Could it have been a café before you bought it?' I asked.

'Oh, no, it had been a bank for about 70 years, I think.'

I thanked her, and she continued stacking the tray before leaving to retrieve my bill. Amelia had lied to me again. She said she had come here with her mother every

Saturday as a child, but she couldn't have. This café would have been a bank when Amelia was a child; in fact, it had probably been a bank when her mother was a child, too. I paid the bill, left a tip and headed back to my car, wondering again where Amelia had gone when she rushed off.

# Chapter Seventeen

I had just pulled up outside my house when the familiar ringtone of my mobile phone shrilled loudly. I reached over to my handbag on the passenger seat and plucked the phone out. It was the estate agent calling to tell me that the house sale had fallen through again. I was livid. Once was bad luck, but twice made me smell a rat. Someone, it seemed, was sabotaging the sale. I instructed the estate agent to get more detailed feedback and to call me again when he knew exactly why the buyers had pulled out. I just wasn't going to accept that two buyers would get so far down the line and then pull out. It didn't make sense. Neither had tried to renegotiate the price nor given a proper reason for withdrawing their offers. I couldn't blame Jean this time because she wasn't aware that I had found a new buyer; I hadn't told her. I was starting to feel very frustrated. The agent would think I was paranoid or downright stupid if I continued to pursue the possibility of foul play when, in fact, it made more sense to accept that I had just been unlucky twice.

I let myself into the house and poured a glass of ice-cold lemonade from the fridge. My phone pinged, indicating I had received a text message. I grabbed my glass and headed out into the garden, scrolling down to read the message. It was from Amelia.

'You'll never guess what?' I read, hearing the high-pitched, childish voice as if I was speaking to Amelia rather than reading her message. 'I've put in an offer for the house!' My heart sank. This can't be happening, I thought despairingly. I continued to read the message. 'It's a really cheeky offer, but, well, if you don't ask, you don't get, right? I will keep you informed on the progress. Thanks again for coming with me today xx.'

I read the message again before taking a long sip of the lemonade. The tartness of the lemons made me shiver as I swallowed. What was I going to do? I couldn't let Amelia buy the house, but I had no idea how to stop her. I felt an overwhelming sense of entrapment, and I simply couldn't think of a way out. I was on tenterhooks, waiting for Amelia to come back to me and let me know if her offer had been accepted. I prayed that it hadn't. I drained my glass and went back indoors to refill it, but once I opened the fridge and noticed the bottle of wine, I decided I needed something stronger than lemonade to get me through the day. How much bad news could I take in one day? First, the house sale falls through, and then Amelia declares she might be my new neighbour!

I began to consider the possibility of Amelia as my neighbour. I didn't like it, not one bit. I contemplated my options and deliberated over selling my own cottage and moving into the big house. This would prevent me from suffering Amelia as a neighbour, but it would also mean giving up my beautiful home and living in the soulless house Miles had once shared with his mistress and Amelia. I would still be reminded of Amelia daily, probably more so if I lived in her childhood home. Eventually, I came up with a plan and set to work making it happen.

More than three hours later, I received another text

from Amelia. I had just taken a cake from the oven and placed it on a wire rack to cool when I heard the familiar ping of a text coming through. I reached for my phone and read the message.

'My offer has been declined. Apparently, someone else has offered on the house, and it has been accepted.' She ended the text with a crying emoji, and despite the feeling of elation that washed over me, I also felt a little bit of sadness for Amelia. I smiled inwardly as I replied.

'Never mind, there will be other houses,' I said, ending my message with a smiling emoji, stopping short of adding a kiss.

I was putting the finishing touches to the Victoria sandwich cake I had just baked when my phone rang. I answered to the voice of the estate agent. He had nothing much more to tell me except that the prospective purchasers of the big house had pulled out because they feared the amount of work that needed doing to it would be too costly. I was baffled, but when I quizzed the agent further, he could shed no more light on matters.

I ended the call and thought about the conversation we had just had. I appreciated that the house was huge, but it wasn't dated and didn't need any major work done to it; I guess not everything would be to everyone's taste, but certainly, the expensive jobs such as a new kitchen or bathrooms didn't need tackling, everything was in perfect working order, in fact, it was more like a show home than a family home. I decided that when I next received an offer on the house, I wouldn't tell anyone. Not Amelia or Jean, and I would instruct the agent not to show anyone around the house on Wednesdays when Jean was around. I mistrusted that woman immensely, although I was pretty certain she had nothing to do with the last sale falling through, as she had been unaware of the offer. Or had she? I had told Amelia, and I knew that Jean and Amelia were in touch; I had heard them arguing in the kitchen. Maybe Amelia had told Jean about the offer? I shook my head to try to clear my thoughts. Nothing made sense, but I could at least console myself with the fact that Amelia wouldn't be buying the house across the valley from me. I smiled as I dusted my cake with icing sugar and stood back to admire my work.

I had been settled in my chair for less than half an hour when the doorbell rang. Reluctantly, I put down my book and headed towards the door. I could see Amelia's familiar face smiling back at me through the glass panel. I felt my heart sink. I had hoped for a nice peaceful afternoon, lost in my book, but as Amelia had already seen me, I couldn't pretend I wasn't at home. I opened the door, and she stepped inside, uninvited.

'Ooh, it smells lovely in here,' she said. 'Have you been baking?' She went into the kitchen without waiting for me to answer, squealing with delight as she saw the freshly baked Victoria sandwich cake on the kitchen counter.

'Coffee?' I asked, adding, 'And cake?' Amelia chuckled.

'I can never resist Victoria sandwich, you know that.' I flicked the switch on the kettle and added coffee granules and milk to a couple of mugs. I reached for a couple of plates and cut two modest slices of cake, annoyed that I had to spoil the look of the cake so soon after baking it. 'Sorry to call on you like this,' Amelia continued as she dug her fork into the cake. 'It's just that I feel so devastated about losing the cottage, and I needed someone to talk to.'

I nodded, waiting for her to continue. 'Do you think I ought to increase my offer?' Her question took me by surprise. I had expected her to take the news in her stride and accept that someone else had beaten her to it, but she didn't seem to want to give up that easily.

'Can you afford to increase your offer?' I asked cautiously, 'especially with all the work that needs to be done on it.'

'Well, no, not really, but then I wouldn't have to do the work immediately.'

I frowned, allowing Amelia to see my concern. The house wasn't habitable in its current state, so she would have to start working on it sooner rather than later.

'What if the other person increases their offer again? You are just asking to get into a bidding war, and then you might end up in a situation you can't get out of that will render you spending more money than you have.'

I tried to explain as gently as I could that Amelia needed to leave this well alone and accept that she would not be buying the house. I crossed my fingers that she would see sense. Amelia continued to eat her cake, making appreciative noises as she chewed. I could see her mulling things over and waited in anticipation to see what she decided.

'You're right,' she said eventually. 'Something else will come up; I will just have to be patient. I just hate throwing money away on rent, and it is so expensive to rent around here. I don't want to end up spending my deposit on renting.'

She paused, and I felt like she was waiting for me to say something. Was she expecting me to suggest she move in here with me whilst she looks for a house? The thought made my blood run cold. The silence between us was uncomfortable, but I stood my ground and refused to enter into this conversation. I would not allow myself to be talked into taking her in as a lodger. After another ten minutes or so, Amelia stood to leave. She thanked me for the coffee and cake and said she would be in touch.

'I believe it's my turn to pay next time,' she said, leaning over to kiss me on the cheek. I stiffened as the smell of her perfume engulfed me. She pulled away and headed for the door. I stood rooted to the spot, shocked that she had been so overly familiar.

'Bye,' I shouted, as she closed the door behind her. Had she come over to talk to me about her disappointment about the house, or was her sole intention to try to persuade me to take her in as my lodger? I felt certain it was the latter, and I shuddered as I realised that I would have to be on my guard from now on. No more sharing bottles of wine and waiting until I was drunk before trying to get me to relent.

I climbed back into my huge, comfortable armchair and turned my attention back to the book I was reading before Amelia interrupted me, but I found it hard to concentrate. My mind was spinning, going over and over the conversation I had just had with Amelia and thinking of all the possibilities she might have had for calling on me. Discussing her disappointment in losing the house suddenly seemed the least likely reason for her visit.

## Chapter Eighteen

A couple of weeks after Amelia had informed me that she had lost out to someone else over the cottage for sale, my own agent telephoned to say that they had found another buyer for the big house. Third time lucky! I thought, as I was informed of the offer, ten thousand pounds under the asking price, and again, they didn't want the contents. I mulled the offer over momentarily but knew it was a good price, and I was lucky to be getting so much interest. I told the agent I would accept but that I wanted to keep things quiet this time, so if the prospective purchasers required more visits to the property, they would have to avoid Wednesdays. I didn't elaborate, but I got the impression that the agent knew I had my concerns about the housekeeper and confirmed that follow-up viewings wouldn't be done when she was present. Whilst I had thought it only fair before to let Jean know of an impending sale so it didn't come as a shock when her services were no longer required, this time, I felt no such allegiance to her. My conscience was clear. If Jean hadn't sabotaged the previous sales, then she wouldn't be kept in the dark now. It was her own fault I felt, as I ended the call to the agent feeling a renewed spark of hope over the sale of the big house.

I was relieved that I had not had any contact from Amelia over the last couple of weeks. I had half expected her to badger me with her ideas of moving in and how it would solve both our problems. Well, it might well solve hers, but I didn't have any problems, and her moving in with me would only cause them. I chastised myself for assuming that this was what Amelia had planned. It was only an assumption, and I was making many of these recently, like blaming Jean for the house sales falling through; however, I had my reasons, and I still doubted both Jean and Amelia's motives. The more Amelia kept her distance, the more I thought about her. It had been almost five months since I first met her, and still I knew nothing about her. She was reluctant to open up about her childhood whenever we met up, and gave little away in relation to her relationship with Miles. I still didn't know why he hadn't provided for her in his will. She was his child, after all.

I decided to do some digging for myself. Find out once and for all about Miles's secret family. I wanted to know everything. However, the internet, though useful, doesn't always provide the answers you need, especially if, like me, you don't really know where to look, so I turned instead to a private investigator. He wasn't cheap, but I figured he could save me a lot of time if he knew what he was looking for and where to look. All I wanted was Amelia's mother's name and an address where they lived down south. Should be a walk in the park for someone used to digging for dirt. It turned out to be surprisingly difficult. The private investigator took weeks, and I began to lose confidence in him when he finally contacted me with some information.

'I've still been unable to find anything out about Amelia,' he told me over the telephone, 'Maybe she has changed her name; who knows. It's so easy nowadays to choose to assume a different identity; people do it all the time.'

Do they? I wondered, having never really thought about it before and unsure why Amelia would choose to do so.

'However, I have uncovered an address on the south coast where your late husband lived for a number of years.' I held my breath, my chest tight and my heart thumping in my ribcage. 'I will email you my report along with the address. Do you want me to continue looking for more information about Amelia?' I paused, unsure of what I wanted. Before I could answer, the private investigator continued, 'If I am honest, Mrs Jameson, I think I have unturned every stone on that front; I can't find anything about her at all and trust me, I have tried. It's your money, of course, and if you want me to, I will keep trying, but I doubt I will find anything.'

'Thank you. Send me the email, and I will visit the address and see what I can find out. Send me your bill, too. I will settle this and get in touch again if I need anything later.'

'Of course, Mrs Jameson. It has been a pleasure working for you, and I hope you get the answers you're looking for.' He continued with sincerity, which was evident in his voice.

So do I, I thought, as I ended the call.

Half an hour later, I was sitting at the dining room table with my laptop, reading the report the investigator had sent through. It was basic, considering how long he had spent on it, but he did say he had left no stone unturned, so even if he hadn't found out much, he had at least been thorough. I opened the second attachment, which proudly displayed the address where Miles had lived, presumably with his family, and a second address, an apartment where I imagined he had moved to when he had left Amelia and her mother. The third attachment was the private investigator's bill. I winced as I read it. It was very steep, but I knew I would never have found the addresses without his help. I certainly didn't think Amelia would have given them to me, and I would have struggled to explain to her why I needed them. *Why did I need them?* I thought, as I clicked on my banking app and paid the investigator's invoice. *Because I didn't trust Amelia, didn't believe anything she had told me, and because I felt something didn't quite add up about her,* my inner voice screamed back at me, as I pressed send and saw my bank balance diminish by thousands of pounds. I was glad that Miles had made me a very rich woman because, at this rate, I would need his money just to ease my mind.

Safe in the knowledge that I had a couple of addresses that would form the starting point of my search, I felt a little more relaxed. There was no rush to do anything immediately, so I decided to sit on the information the private investigator had given me and wait until the sale of the big house had gone through before considering my next steps. The last few weeks had been difficult. I had expected the estate agent to call at any time and inform me that the sale had fallen through for a third time. The buyers needed to sell their own house and get a mortgage, so because of the chain, there was more risk this time, but as there wasn't anything I could do about that, I decided to sit tight and just wait. I contemplated travelling down south to visit the addresses that Miles had lived in, but my mind constantly changed. I didn't want any more aggravation. One thing at a time, I told myself. I needed to deal with the house, and then, when I had all of that out of the way, I could concentrate on Amelia.

## Chapter Nineteen

It was a beautiful sunny day when I exited the office of my solicitor. I had signed several documents in readiness for the sale of the big house. Unlike the first two offers, this one seemed to be going through smoothly, and I wondered, not for the first time if it was because I hadn't told Jean or Amelia about the impending sale. Mr Connor had suggested I sign the contract in readiness for exchange as he was expecting a completion date to be set at any time. I was in good spirits as I left the dark office and stepped into the bright sunlight. I decided to treat myself to an early lunch in celebration and perhaps start to plan my trip down south to see what I could unearth about Amelia and her mother. As I left Mr Connor's office, I literally collided with a young woman and almost knocked her off balance.

'I'm so sorry,' I said with genuine concern as I grabbed the young lady's arm to try and steady her. 'Amelia!' I exclaimed, as I instantly recognised her once she was upright again. Amelia looked rather sheepish as she brushed herself down and plastered a smile on her face. Had she been following me? I thought irrationally.

'Hi,' Amelia said breathlessly. 'How are you?'

'I'm fine, you?' I asked warily. I was convinced that this meeting wasn't simply a coincidence. I felt certain that Amelia had followed me here. She looked up at the solicitor's office questioningly as if expecting me to explain why I was there. I stood my ground and said nothing. It was none of her business why I was seeing Mr Connor, and we were so close to completing the house sale that I had no intention of informing her of anything in case she had something up her sleeve to undermine things.

'Good,' she said. The silence between us was awkward, and before I could stop myself, I blurted out that I was about to go for an early lunch and did she want to join me.

'That would be lovely, thank you,' Amelia replied, falling into step beside me. I wanted to choose a different café this time, but Amelia propelled me towards the same one we had visited before.

'Do you mind if we sit inside?' I asked, as Amelia headed for a table outside. 'I've forgotten my sunglasses this morning, and the sun gives me a terrible headache when I can't shield my eyes.'

'Of course,' Amelia said with concern in her voice. She pushed open the door to the café. The familiar face of the waitress, who I now knew to be one of the owners, greeted us.

'Hi,' she said with a slight wave. Amelia grinned and waved back. We chose a table by the window, which was shaded from the sun, and settled into our seats. I snatched up a menu quickly, hoping to prevent Amelia from ordering for me. I really didn't want another piece of Victoria sandwich cake. Amelia did the same, although I could sense her watching me instead of reading the list of available food. A few minutes later, Jude, I had read her name badge which was displayed on her pretty red and white checked apron, came over to take our order. Amelia opened her mouth to speak, but before she could say anything, I spouted off my order.

'I'll have the Greek salad, please, and a cappuccino,' I said, smiling as I replaced the menu in the holder on the table. If Amelia was surprised by my choice, she didn't show it, and I half expected her to say she would have the same. She didn't. Instead, she ordered a cheese and pickle sandwich on brown bread and herbal tea. It seems we are both ready for a change today, I thought, studying Amelia as she, too, replaced her menu in the holder on the table.

'What have you been up to then?' I asked, trying to start a conversation in what I felt was a rather tetchy atmosphere.

'Oh, you know, this and that,' she replied, giving nothing away.

'Any more houses catch your eye?' Amelia shook her head, looking sad. Her disposition seemed in stark contrast to mine, and I felt a little guilty that things were going smoothly for me when Amelia seemed to be in turmoil. Still, I figured she would find a suitable house soon, just as long it wasn't near me. Jude returned after about fifteen minutes with our food and drinks and organised them on the table in her now familiar manner.

'It's so lovely to see you ladies again,' she said as she smiled and told us to enjoy our lunches. I tucked into my salad, savouring every mouthful. The feta was sprinkled on the salad in copious amounts, and the olives were rich and had a defined buttery texture. The dish was delicious. I glanced across at Amelia, who seemed to struggle with her sandwich. She took a couple of bird-like bites before placing the sandwich back on her plate.

'Are you OK?' I asked. It wasn't like Amelia to be slow

with her food. She had always struck me as someone who savoured her meals, but today, she seemed down-spirited, her appetite non-existent.

'Yeah, I'm good,' she replied unconvincingly. I didn't know what to say. I wished now that I hadn't invited her for lunch as she was beginning to put a dampener on my own good spirits. I pushed the thoughts aside, feeling mean.

'You don't sound very happy,' I pushed, not really wanting to know what the matter was but feeling obliged to make the effort to find out. Amelia opened the sandwich and picked at the cheese inside with her fingers. She popped a piece of Cheddar into her mouth and chewed slowly.

'My landlord has just said I have a month to find somewhere else to live because he is selling the place,' she said eventually. I was taken by surprise at this revelation and wasn't sure how to respond. Was she lying, trying to trick me into offering her a place to stay? I thought.

'I'm sure there will be other places to rent,' I said, trying to sound convincing.

'I've looked; they are either too expensive or too far away,' she replied, shaking her head in dismay.

'What about buying the place you're in now?' Amelia looked confused. I continued, 'You said the landlord wanted to sell it, so why don't you make him an offer?' The solution sounded perfect to me, so I was a little bewildered as to why she hadn't thought of this herself.

'I don't know,' she said unconvinced.

'You like the place, don't you? So why not make him an offer?' Amelia looked uncomfortable, as if she didn't know how to respond. I continued to eat my lunch and drink my coffee whilst I studied Amelia sitting opposite me. I had convinced myself now that Amelia was lying. I didn't believe for a minute that her landlord was selling the house she was renting. I believed this was a ploy to make me feel sorry for her and offer her my spare room. There was no way I was going to fall for it. After another long awkward silence, I made my excuses to leave. Instead of asking for the bill, I got up to pay at the counter, leaving Amelia lost in her thoughts. She made no attempt to pay, and I didn't expect her to. After paying, I returned to the table to collect my handbag and saw Amelia crying quietly. I sat back down.

'Don't worry, something will turn up,' I said, trying to console her. Without warning, she turned to me.

'Can I stay with you? Please, I can pay my way, help with the chores, anything. I promise you won't know I'm there. It will just be until I find somewhere to buy.' Her eyes were red and puffy from crying, and I felt a little bad for doubting her sincerity. She really did look as if she had the weight of the world on her shoulders. I almost relented. Almost.

'I'm sorry, Amelia, but the answer is no,' I said, as confidently and assertively as possible. Amelia's face turned red, and I wasn't entirely sure if it was out of embarrassment or anger. Without another word, I stood and left the café. Amelia remained where she was. I looked back a few minutes later, but she still hadn't left. I didn't feel cruel or unkind; I felt vaguely satisfied. I had felt for some time that Amelia was trying to wheedle her way into my home, and she had to be put straight. I wouldn't have my privacy invaded, not by her or anyone. She might be Miles's child, but she wasn't mine, and I owed her nothing.

For whatever reasons, Miles had chosen not to leave Amelia anything in his will; not the house, money, or even a simple family heirloom, but this had nothing to do with me. It wasn't my doing. I had nothing to make amends for.

I headed back to my car and got inside. My phone rang shrilly, and I reached over and retrieved it from my handbag lying on the passenger seat. It was Mr Connor.

'Exchange of contracts has taken place, Mrs Jameson, with completion due on Friday,' he said with a distinct air of satisfaction.

'That's excellent news, thank you,' I said as I pushed the button to end the call. I wanted to scream with excitement. It was Tuesday, and I had just three more days to empty the house before Friday. I pushed all thoughts of Amelia from my mind and concentrated on the sale of the house.

Driving home, I made a mental list of what I needed to do. I had already spoken to a removal firm, which was on standby to clear out the contents of the house as soon as the solicitors had set a date. I had arranged for everything to be put into storage. I thought it was only fair to ask Amelia again if she wanted anything before I decided to sell the lot.

As soon as I arrived home, I contacted the removal firm and the storage company and arranged for the house to be emptied on Thursday. I would go and see Jean tomorrow and tell her the house had been sold and that she and her sons would no longer be required to tend to the house and gardens. I knew she wouldn't be happy having this sprung on her, but I told myself again she had no one to blame but herself for the situation.

## Chapter Twenty

The next morning I rose early and cleaned and tidied the house before showering and getting changed. I glanced at my watch. It was ten minutes to ten. I decided to make myself a cup of coffee and some toast before venturing to the big house on Wentworth Drive to deliver the sale news to Jean. I was confident telling her about the sale now as there were only two more days to go before completion, and she couldn't disrupt things at this late stage of the negotiations. The buyers stood to lose a hefty deposit if they pulled out now that contracts had been exchanged.

I wasn't entirely sure how I was feeling. Despite the fact that I was relieved that the house had sold, I was also a little apprehensive about telling Jean that she and her sons no longer had jobs. There was something about Jean that unnerved me. I couldn't quite put my finger on it, but I sensed that if I got on the wrong side of her, things could turn nasty. I had seen her argue with Amelia, and she didn't strike me as someone to mess with.

I finished my coffee and toast and, deciding I couldn't put things off any longer, reached for my handbag and car keys and headed outside to my car.

I pulled up on the drive next to Jean's car and switched the engine off. I sat for a few minutes staring up at the house. Its façade was expressionless and drab to the point of being boring, and I wondered why anyone would want

## My Husband's Child

to live there. A slight tap on the driver's side window brought me quickly back to the present as I turned to see one of Jean's sons standing next to my car. I wound the window down, peering into his face questioningly.

'Hi,' he said. 'I was just wondering if there was anything in particular you might need doing this afternoon, as we are pretty much done with all the routine jobs.' I was a little unsure what to say. I had never had a conversation with either of Jean's sons before, and I didn't really know how to answer him. He was the gardener; surely, he knew what needed doing.

'No, I, I don't really know,' I stuttered. 'Whatever you think is necessary, I guess.' He smiled, turned, and went to join his brother, who was working on the flower beds on the far side of the house. I climbed out of the car and entered the hallway just as Jean came out of the drawing room. She smiled, but the expression didn't reach her eyes.

'Good morning, Mrs Jameson,' she said in a polite but very professional voice.

'Hello,' I replied. 'Jean, could I have a word with you, please?' Jean stopped and turned to face me. 'In here,' I suggested, retracing Jean's steps to the drawing room. Jean followed me in silence. I sat down and beckoned Jean to do the same. She took the seat opposite me. 'I have some news,' I began.

'You've found a buyer for the house?' it was a question, not a statement, so I knew Jean hadn't been aware before.

'Yes, that's right,' I replied.

'That's good; I am really pleased for you. I hope things turn out well this time.'

'They have,' I said without thinking. Jean eyed me

suspiciously as I continued. 'The sale completes on Friday.' Jean's mouth dropped open.

'This Friday?' she asked. I nodded. 'But how, how can it go through so quickly?' Jean was flustered now, her mouth twitching as she spoke.

'Well, it won't really be any quicker than usual,' I said, regretting my words as soon as I said them. A look of betrayal swept over Jean's eyes.

'You just didn't think to tell me sooner,' she said accusingly. I was amazed. This woman was my late husband's housekeeper, employed to keep the house clean, and yet she thought it was perfectly fine to grill me about things that were of no concern to her. She was rude and arrogant, and I was glad that I wouldn't have to see or speak to her again after today.

'I saw no reason to inform you of my business,' I replied curtly. 'My solicitor has looked over the contract you had with Miles, and as I will no longer require your services or your sons' services, you will be paid in lieu for the time stated on the contract. Thank you for your work. You can collect your things now and tell your sons I no longer need them.'

Jean looked ready to explode. Her eyes narrowed, and her brow furrowed. She really was very angry indeed. She stood, turned on her heels and headed for the door, fuming. 'Oh, just one thing, Jean,' I said, getting to my feet and holding out my hand, 'your keys, please.' Jean dived into her apron pocket and fished out a set of keys. She placed them on the coffee table set between us and left the room. I retrieved the keys and dropped them into my handbag before turning to see Jean striding across the gravel driveway, calling her sons. Within ten minutes, all three of them had departed, and I sighed a huge sigh of relief, glad that the confrontation was over and that things hadn't got any worse.

I walked around the house expecting to see something out of place, perhaps a leaving card from Jean, something to make me regret having made her redundant, but I saw nothing out of place. The house was, as always, spotless. Back in the hallway, I reset the alarm, putting in a new code. Although I had Jean's keys, I still didn't want to risk anyone entering the house without my knowledge and resetting the alarm seemed an obvious move. Collecting my handbag, I locked the door and returned to the car, half expecting my tyres to be slashed or the wing mirror broken. I laughed at the thought as I told myself to stop being paranoid. They might be disappointed at losing their jobs, but they weren't criminals. Jean hadn't asked me if I would pass her details on to the new owners, and I hadn't offered to do so. I figured she would probably call by after the sale had gone through and introduce herself if she wanted to keep her job. She would probably bad-mouth me at the same time, but who cares? My bank balance would be heaving and the sale completed, so there wasn't anything Jean could do to spoil things for me.

Driving home, I turned the radio up loud and sang along to the rock anthems blaring out. I was upbeat and happy. I had had a difficult conversation with Jean, but it had turned out surprisingly better than I anticipated. There were just two more days to go before the sale was completed, and I could now plan my little holiday on the south coast. My high spirits dampened when my house came into view, and I could see Amelia's car parked outside. What did she want? I asked myself, pulling my car into the driveway and turning off the engine. I got out of the car and looked around. She was nowhere to be seen. I walked over to her car and peered inside. Her handbag was on the passenger seat, but she had vacated the car. I wandered around the back of the house and saw Amelia in my garden. My blood began to boil.

'Amelia,' I said, opening the gate and walking through. 'What can I do for you?' Amelia turned, startled. She obviously hadn't heard my car pull up, and she looked like a deer caught in the headlights. She had her phone to her ear but switched it off immediately and put it in her pocket. She seemed cagey, and I wondered who she was speaking to.

'Why didn't you tell me you'd sold the house?' she demanded, and her voice was cold and harsh.

'I'm sorry—' I began.

'So you should be,' she spat, obviously mistaking my words for an apology.

I was livid, the anger rising in me by the second. First, I had the rudeness of Jean, and now Amelia thought she could make demands of me and speak to me with no respect whatsoever. Who the hell did they think they were?

'I wasn't apologising, Amelia,' I said curtly. 'What business is it of yours whether I have sold the house or not?' I demanded. Amelia's bravado suddenly diminished as she could see I was in no mood to argue with her.

'I thought we were friends.'

'We are, but I still don't see how any of this is your business.'

'Miles was my father!' she screamed at me.

'And he was my husband,' I yelled back, unable to

control my anger anymore. 'Long before you and your mother came along, he was my husband,' I continued. 'I don't owe you anything. Now get the hell off my property and leave me alone!' Amelia ran across the lawn, pushed past me through the gate and headed for her car.

I didn't relax until I heard her engine start and saw the car move slowly up the lane. I sat down on the lover's seat, my head in my hands and wept. I must have sat like that for an hour; my face was smeared with tears and snot as I stood up and let myself into the house. I was tired, angry and confused. I could understand why Jean had been annoyed with me, after all she had lost an income today, even though I had made generous provisions for her to be paid well after the date of the agreement she had with Miles ended. However, I couldn't understand why Amelia was so angry. It wasn't as if I had seen her a lot over the past few months when the sale was going through, and, on the few occasions we had met, she hadn't asked about the house, so it wasn't as if I had lied.

Obviously that was what she had wanted all along. The house. She had been trying to get the house off me. It had been Amelia who had sabotaged the other sales, preventing them from going through and now, because she hadn't been aware a new buyer had been found, she couldn't do anything to stop it. Yes, that must be it. It was the only feasible explanation. What really confused me, however, was how Amelia had found out about the new purchaser. I had only just returned from telling Jean, and I certainly hadn't made Amelia aware of it. Who could have told her? Was it Jean, one of her sons, or maybe the estate agent? What about Mr Connor? I was being ridiculous now, and I knew it. Doubting each and every person who was aware of the sale. Let's face it: I might as well blame the buyer, too, I thought, knowing how irrational my thoughts were and how helpless I was at finding the answers. I was starting to think that my trip down south was a necessity now rather than an option. Surely someone could shed some light on things?

# Chapter Twenty-One

At eight-thirty the following morning, I pulled up outside the big house on Wentworth Drive, leaving the gates open behind me for the removal firm to enter. I had arranged to meet them at nine to oversee the emptying of the property, ready for completion the next day. It was a lovely morning, and the sun began to lift my mood. I felt apprehensive. I had mixed feelings of emotions; one minute I was unnerved, and I couldn't quite figure out why; the next, I was elated; glad to be seeing the back of the big house. Today would be my last visit to Wentworth Drive. I would leave the keys at the estate agents so the new owners could collect them from there and inform them of the new code for the alarm. I didn't want to set foot in this house again, ever.

I unlocked the door and turned off the alarm. I wandered from room to room, looking around the house. It was stupid, I know; it wasn't as if the house held any memories for me. I had only owned it for a short time, and I had never lived in it. Still, I felt a part of me was being taken, and I felt a little wistful. Maybe it was because the house had belonged to Miles, I thought. It was another piece of him that someone else was having.

I was standing in the hallway when I heard the doorbell ring, and I rushed to answer it. There were three huge trucks on the drive and more than half a dozen burly young men, each cheerfully greeting me as they made their way inside the house. They moved swiftly and efficiently, and it wasn't long before the first truck pulled out of the drive, full to the brim with furniture from the bedrooms. The removal men had instructions of where to take the contents of the house so they could be stored until I found out if Amelia wanted to keep anything, after which I would either sell or donate the remaining items.

By lunchtime, the house was empty, and I stood waving the final truck off. I retreated into the house and did one more final tour. I had already checked that all the windows were closed and the taps were turned off properly, but I just had to check again to be certain. What if one of the removal men had left a tap running, and the house flooded before completion? I thought, as I checked each of the rooms thoroughly.

Without any furniture, the house took on an eerie feeling. It had been unoccupied for a long time, but without furniture, it seemed even more impersonal. I wondered what the new owners were like. I knew they were a married couple because of their names on the contract, but that was all I knew. I hadn't been present for any of the viewings or asked the agent any questions about them. I didn't know if they were young or old or if they had children. I didn't care. I did, however, wonder if they would be happy here. I hoped they would be. Miles had been happy here, hadn't he? With Amelia and her mother?

I reset the alarm and locked the door for the last time. I climbed into my car and headed back up the drive towards the electric gates. Once I had passed through them, I stopped and pressed the fob, watching the gates slide back into place in my rear-view mirror. That's when I noticed her. Out of the corner of my eye, I spotted Amelia's car parked further up the road. I couldn't see if she was watching me or even if she was in the car, but I was absolutely certain that it was her vehicle.

I drove slowly up the road and headed towards the town centre, continually checking my mirror to see if Amelia was following me. I parked my car and headed toward the estate agents on the High Street. I was becoming paranoid, constantly looking behind me, convinced that Amelia would spring out at any time. I dropped the keys at the estate agent's office and gave strict instructions that no one was to collect them except the new owners after completion the next day.

'Oh, you can be assured they won't go to anyone else, Mrs Jameson,' the receptionist said. 'The keys will only be released to the new owners after we have had confirmation from the solicitors that completion has taken place tomorrow. Reassured, I thanked her and left.

I wandered around the quiet streets, doing a little shopping in readiness for my trip to the south coast and generally passing time before I found myself outside the little café that Amelia and I had visited on numerous occasions for coffee and cake. I peered inside the window, half expecting Amelia to be waiting for me. She wasn't, but Jude saw me and waved. I felt obliged to enter now that I had been spotted, so I opened the door and stepped inside.

'On your own today?' Jude asked as she approached me, smiling broadly.

'Yes, I'm just doing a bit of shopping and thought I'd pop by for a coffee,' I said, 'Cappuccino, please,' without glancing at the menu.

'Coming right up,' Jude said, and approached the

coffee machine.

I listened to the coughing and spluttering of the machine as Jude heated the milk and ground the beans before placing a cup of hot frothy coffee in front of me. I smiled and thanked her as I stared out of the window, watching the few shoppers on the street. I searched for Amelia but didn't see her; maybe I had been mistaken, I wondered if the car I had seen on Wentworth Drive really had been hers. I drank my coffee, feeling a sudden rush as the caffeine started to work, lifting my mood.

I finished my coffee, left my money on the table and headed for the door, mouthing a silent goodbye to Jude as she served another customer. Jude smiled and waved. She didn't rush over to the table this time to see if I had paid. She trusted me now. I was a regular customer, and I never left without paying. It saddened me to think that some people would do this, but in the disrespectful world we live in, I guess it happens more often than I would like to imagine. The impact on small establishments like this could be ruinous if it happened regularly.

I returned to the sanctuary of my cottage. The place I had always felt safe and happy, although this time, as I neared the lane, I felt agitated. What if Amelia were waiting for me again? Her letting herself into my garden the other day had unnerved me, and I half expected her to turn up uninvited whenever she felt like it. I began to relax as I pulled down the lane and noticed that Amelia's car was nowhere to be seen. What if she's parked somewhere else and walked?' I thought, my breathing getting faster and ragged. I tried to calm myself down, telling myself to stop being ridiculous, but it wasn't until I was safely in the house with the door locked behind me that I felt I could relax. I was edgy and apprehensive. Amelia had made me like that by turning up here when I hadn't asked her to. I wouldn't let her take away my sanctuary, spoil the only place I really loved to be. I had to get a grip; otherwise, I would let her win.

Tomorrow, I will see the completion of the sale of the house, and then I can take my trip down south and see what I can find out about Amelia. Knowledge, I felt sure, would only serve as a tool. To be warned is to be armed, and my fear of Amelia was born through my lack of knowledge. I knew nothing about her, so making decisions wasn't easy. If she thought she could get anything out of me; the house, the money, whatever, she was sadly mistaken. Still, I wanted to know more about her. I felt she was hiding a lot, and it was time to uncover the truth.

# Chapter Twenty-Two

Completion day dawned, and I woke with mixed feelings, apprehension being the strongest. I wasn't sure why I had these feelings of unease, but I still anticipated that something might go wrong. My sensible head told me that it was impossible at this late stage, but my agitated conscience told me anything could happen, even on completion day. What if they didn't have the funds? What if their mortgage was refused?

I made my way downstairs, trying to calm my nerves. Glancing at the clock on the kitchen wall, I noticed that it wasn't even seven o'clock. It was too early to call the solicitor for an update; in fact, it was too early to do anything. I made myself a cup of coffee and headed back upstairs to bed. I settled back down, propped myself up with a mountain of pillows and reached for my book. I knew I wouldn't be able to go back to sleep as my mind was working in overdrive, but I also knew it would be a very long day if I got up too soon.

I flicked through the pages of my book, not really noticing the words in front of me. I shuffled further down in bed, feeling the morning chill before the sun had managed to stream through the window. I leaned over and took my coffee cup from the bedside table. I was like a child, restless and fidgety. I let the book fall from my grasp as I sipped my coffee slowly.

Soon, it would be over. The house would be transferred into someone else's ownership, and I would be free from its burden and reminders of the past that Miles shared with Amelia and her mother. I no longer had to see or speak with Jean, and all the difficult encounters I had with her would become a distant memory. Amelia, however, was another matter. I wasn't sure yet how I would tackle her. I didn't know if I wanted to unshackle myself from her hindrance or whether I could manage if I kept her at arm's length. I wasn't entirely sure someone like Amelia could be kept at arm's length. She was overwhelming and dominating, but above all, she was possessive, and I felt her desperate needfulness was born out of a longing to be loved. Had she desperately needed her father's love and reassurance, and Miles had failed her? I didn't know, but part of me wanted to find out. If I had any shred of decency, I would try to help Amelia. After all, she had lost both her parents and didn't seem to belong anywhere. I might not want her living on my doorstep, but surely, I could lend myself to being her friend and perhaps meet up with her once in a while for coffee.

Surprisingly, the time went quickly as I sat in bed huddled under my duvet, and the next time I glanced at the clock, it was almost eight. I jumped out of bed and climbed into the shower, eager to get the day started so I could put closure to the sale of the house. My stomach groaned with hunger pangs, but I didn't really think I could keep anything down; much was my feeling of anxiety and unease. I made another coffee and settled for a bowl of cereal and a splash of milk. I took my bowl and mug out to the patio, enjoying the early birdsong as I ate, still lost in thought. At nine o'clock I would call the solicitor for an update, make sure that everything was going according to plan, and get reassurance that completion would indeed go ahead today. My phone pinged, and I reached over to see a text from Amelia.

'Hope everything goes according to plan,' she had typed. All of a sudden, my concern seemed to increase. Did she know something I didn't? Was she taunting me? Had she done something to scupper the deal even at this late date?

My heart beat loudly in my chest, threatening to break free from my rib cage as the sour taste of milk from my cereal threatened to force its way back up my windpipe. I told myself to breathe slowly, calm down, and take things easy. I was reading far too much into an innocent message.

I took my bowl back to the kitchen, unable to eat any more of the cereal. I contemplated replying to Amelia's text but decided against it. I didn't want to engage in conversation with her today of all days. I wouldn't let her vex me. She isn't worth it, I told myself. I needed to find something to occupy my mind this morning; otherwise, I would go insane.

Completion was unlikely to take place early as there were all the last-minute things that solicitors had to do, or at least they say they had to do, in order to charge extortionate fees. Then, the bank would have to release the money, which would then need to be sent to me before the keys could be handed out. I needed to be patient. I decided I would spend the day making plans for my trip to the south coast. I could look online and find a nice hotel, research the distance I would have to drive, and look up the addresses the private investigator had given me. The internet was a marvellous tool, I concluded. It provided so many answers.

I found myself wishing I could simply put Amelia's name into a search engine and that it would reveal everything I needed to know about her. It would certainly be much quicker and would save me the bother of a long drive to the south coast, but I was actually looking forward to the trip. It would be an adventure.

After tidying the kitchen, I got my laptop out and sat at the kitchen table with my notepad and pen. A Google map of the area on the south coast revealed an array of small hotels and B&Bs. I opted for a hotel. It was less personal, which was exactly what I needed. It would be just my luck if I chose a B&B to stumble across one of Amelia's friends who would report back to her that I was snooping into her past. Yes, I thought, I really was becoming paranoid now. I wasn't sure whether I could find a hotel with vacancies. It was the height of the summer, and usually, good hotel rooms at this time of year were taken, but I found a couple that looked nice and enquired about availability for Monday through to Friday the following week. One got back to me almost immediately with a price that I considered reasonable, so I paid a deposit and booked it.

I spent a little time looking at the photographs of the hotel online. It was a small boutique hotel with just thirty rooms. Small enough to be quiet but large enough not to be too personal. The hotel looked stylish and fashionable, with pretty gardens at the rear and a superb restaurant with a renowned chef. I didn't want anyone asking me questions or poking about in my business; I had enough of that at home with Amelia. I felt surprisingly calm after I had booked my little jaunt. At last, I felt I had something to look forward to, and confirming the booking made it feel more real. I had thought about taking the trip for some time, but now it was really happening, I could allow myself to feel excited.

It was almost lunchtime, and I still hadn't heard anything from the solicitor. I had intended to call him as soon as the office opened, but I decided against it at the last minute, thinking it was perhaps a little too needy; even solicitors required time to focus on their jobs without someone pestering them the minute they opened. Now, though, I decided I could wait no longer, and I reached for my phone. I scrolled through the numbers, but just as I was about to press the call button, the screen lit up with an incoming call, and at the same time, a text message pinged. I laughed to myself. It's all or nothing, I thought as I ignored the text and answered the call.

'Mr Connor,' I exclaimed. 'I was just about to call you for an update,' I said truthfully.

'Well, then, I am glad I have some good news for you. Congratulations, Mrs Jameson. The house sale has just been completed, and the money will be in your account by the end of the day.' I felt the relief wash over me as I leaned on the kitchen table to steady myself.

'That's great news, thank you,' I said. I ended the call and danced around my kitchen, feeling completely free and happy. I wandered over to the fridge and took out a bottle of wine. I studied the label. This was a good bottle, an expensive wine that I had been saving for a celebration. Today was the day to celebrate, I thought as I hovered over the cutlery drawer, looking for the corkscrew. Inevitably, all good wines came corked, and whilst I hated uncorking bottles, I felt I could make an exception today. My bank balance would swell again by the close of business, and despite the fact that it wasn't yet lunchtime on a Friday, I was more than ready for a celebratory drink. As the cork popped, I remembered the text that had come in at the exact same time as Mr Connor's call, and I picked up my phone to read it. It was from Amelia. Just one single word, but it said so much.

'Congratulations!' I was stunned. How could one word provoke so many unanswered questions, the most important one being how she knew completion had occurred before I did?

I wasn't sure whether I was angry or annoyed or a mixture of both. Perhaps I was reading too much into the message; maybe Amelia was just lucky with her timing, not knowing whether the sale had been completed or not. She knew it was due to happen today, so maybe she just sent the text in anticipation. Or maybe someone had told her? I called Mr Connor back, and his secretary answered almost immediately. She informed me that Mr Connor was in a meeting, but she would do her best to help me if I told her the problem. The problem, I felt like shouting down the phone, was that someone in their office couldn't keep their mouth shut! Instead, I thanked her politely and said only Mr Connor could help and would she please ask him to call me back when he was free.

I hung up and read Amelia's message again, checking the time of the text and comparing it with the call from Mr Connor. They both occurred at exactly the same time. Coincidence, I told myself. It had to be. How could Amelia have possibly known? I poured myself another glass of wine and took it out to the garden. The heat of the midday sun warmed my face and began to soothe away my annoyance. Completion had happened; the money would be in my bank in a few hours. Amelia couldn't do anything now; it was over, finished, end of. My phone rang, and I literally jumped, spilling some of the wine. I cursed. The wine was expensive, and I didn't want to waste it even if I could afford to purchase as many bottles as I fancied.

'Hello,' I answered curtly, brushing the spilt wine from my dress.

'Mrs Jameson, hi,' I immediately recognised Mr Connor's voice.

'Oh, Mr Connor, thank you for calling me back,' I said.

'No problem. What can I do for you?' He sounded annoyed. Perhaps his patience was wearing thin with me now that he had earned his fee, I thought, feeling a little foolish.

'I just wanted to know if you have told anyone else apart from me about the completion of the house sale?' I said, recognising how ridiculous my question sounded.

'No, why should I have?' he sounded genuinely confused.

'No, no, it's just that someone has congratulated me, and I wondered how they knew,' I tried to explain, knowing how feeble my explanation sounded.

Mr Connor laughed. 'Lucky guess?' he offered as he said goodbye and hung up.

Either that or you are a liar, I thought, taking another swig from my glass.

At just after five o'clock I nervously opened the banking app on my phone to check the balance. I half expected the balance to be zero. This might all be a trick, I thought, Miles's way of getting to me from beyond the grave. With a beating heart, I held my breath and peered at the balance. I don't know whether it was the effects of the wine or the figures swimming in front of my eyes, but I felt myself going lightheaded, and the ground began to spin. Was this how it felt to be rich beyond my wildest dreams? I laughed, a high-pitched victorious laugh that sounded warped, and although it had come from my mouth, it was a sound I didn't recognise.

# Chapter Twenty-Three

I woke the next morning not having remembered even going to bed, although when I went downstairs, everything appeared to be normal and in order. The kitchen was tidy, and I had washed and dried my wine glass and put the bottle in the bin. I didn't remember doing any of these things. Maybe that was the beauty of expensive wine, I thought, smiling. I felt good. I had no hint of a hangover. I was ready to face the world. I intended to use the weekend to pack and plan my journey. I wanted to pop into town to open a couple of high-interest accounts and transfer some money over before venturing on my travels, and I figured this morning was a good time to do that. After showering and dressing, I decided to venture into town early. I could avoid the busy shopping times, stock up on what I needed for my travels and pop into the bank.

I reached the town and parked up just after nine o'clock. I decided to make the bank my first point of call, so I wouldn't have to carry my shopping around any longer than necessary. The bank was very quiet, with just one other customer before me. I spoke to a very efficient teller who explained the different accounts to me and advised me of my best options. Less than half an hour later, I was back on the street in the morning sunshine, feeling like a weight had been lifted from my shoulders. I had never had so much money in my entire life, and I didn't really know

## My Husband's Child

what to do for the best. I kept some of the money aside for a purchase I intended to make later; a purchase I couldn't wait to reveal to Amelia, knowing her reaction would be worth every penny. I then transferred the remaining amount into a couple of accounts that would earn me a healthy amount of interest. It seemed the sensible thing to do.

I traipsed around the shops, enjoying the peace and quiet before the onslaught of Saturday shoppers descended on the narrow streets. I enjoyed shopping when no one was around, and this was the perfect time. I stocked up on some essentials for my trip to the south coast and bought bottled water, fruit and snacks. I didn't want the plastic-wrapped prepared sandwiches that never looked or tasted anything like the wrappers announced they would, opting instead to buy fresh bread from the bakers and slices of ham from the delicatessen. I would be more than happy to make my own sandwiches for the journey, and at least then my ham sandwiches would taste like they should. I was quite partial to a freshly made sandwich, probably because of the accompaniments that went with them. I couldn't image a turkey sandwich without being slathered in stuffing or a ham sandwich without lashings of mustard. I tossed a couple of bags of crisps and some salad into my basket, along with a few apples and a couple of bananas and made my way to the counter to pay. In the corner of my eye, I spotted a familiar figure. I tried not to look too closely as I didn't want to be seen, but I was certain that it was Amelia. I paid for my shopping and hurriedly packed the goods into my bag, trying to avoid being seen. It was hopeless. The shop was so quiet and even trying to be inconspicuous was impossible, as I turned to leave the shop, Amelia was standing directly in my path.

'Amelia! Hi,' I said, trying to feign surprise. I wondered, not for the first time if she had been following me again.

'Hi, fancy seeing you here so early,' she replied. 'I always like to come into town early to avoid the crowds,' she continued smiling. Before I could reply, she added, 'Fancy a coffee?' I purposefully glanced at my watch.

'I'm so sorry, Amelia, I can't, not this morning; I have to be somewhere.' Amelia waited for me to elaborate. I didn't. I smiled broadly and walked out of the shop, leaving her looking, and probably feeling, a little foolish.

I hadn't meant to sound so brusque, but I felt convinced that she had followed me here, and it irked me that she thought I had nothing better to do than join her for coffee at the drop of a hat. Not only did she expect me to join her, but she also appeared to think it was acceptable to allow me to pay every time we met up. Not once has she put her hand in her pocket. I might be a multi-millionaire now, but I hadn't always had money to burn, and old habits die hard. I believe in being equal, taking turns, and sharing. Amelia, it seemed, didn't understand any of these things, and I wondered who had taught her manners; I doubt it had been Miles; he had been a stickler for good manners.

Back on the pavement, I breathed deeply and hurriedly returned to my car. I had bought everything I needed for my trip, and I didn't want to risk bumping into Amelia again if I remained in town. As I pulled my car out of the car park, I noticed Amelia hovering in the distance. She was following me! I felt certain that it hadn't been a coincidence that she was in town so early on a Saturday morning. She had been watching me. I drove back home, continuously checking my rear-view mirror, expecting to see Amelia's car come into my vision at any time, but I saw nothing. I pulled into the lane and then stopped. What if she followed me home? What if she came to see what was so pressing that I didn't have time for a coffee with her? I didn't want to speak to her. I couldn't risk her finding out that I was planning a trip down south.

I reversed my car back up the lane and continued to drive further along the road, stopping at another lane a few hundred yards along. I pulled my car down this lane and parked up. It was a short walk back to my house across the fields, and it meant my car wouldn't be parked outside my house if Amelia stopped by. I didn't want her to know I was home and the car would be a dead giveaway.

I heaved my bags out of the boot and lugged them over the stile to the field. It was a pleasant walk, made easier because the farmer had cut the grass recently, so I didn't have to weave my way in and out of the towering foliage. I was glad I hadn't purchased too many things as the shopping began to weigh me down a little, and by the time I reached my house, I was starting to flag in the morning heat. I unlocked the door and put my bags down, turning the key in the lock behind me. I didn't put anything past Amelia, and I am pretty certain if she did stop by, she wouldn't think twice about trying the door handle to see if I was in, whether I answered the door or not.

I moved swiftly from room to room, pulling the curtains. It was going to be a hot day, I told myself, and the curtains would prevent the sun from penetrating the house, making it even hotter inside. I knew the real reason I was pulling them was to prevent Amelia from peering through my windows and catching a glimpse of me, but I didn't want to admit this, not even to myself. I decided I would get to work packing and set off on my trip sooner than I had originally planned. I had a hotel booking on the south coast from Monday, but if I set off today, I could take my time, spread the journey out and have a couple of nights somewhere en route. It felt like I was running away.

I pushed the thoughts from my mind. I had lived here for years and always felt safe, but now I somehow felt unnerved. I needed to know more about Amelia to be sure of what I was dealing with, and I felt certain she wouldn't be forthcoming with any answers. The nagging doubt remained in my mind that I had no idea why Miles had disowned his daughter in the end and left her with nothing. There had to be a reason for it.

After putting my groceries in the fridge, I went upstairs and started packing for the week ahead. My mind was made up now. I would set off today and make the trip down south slowly. There was no rush; the big house had been sold, and all the other paperwork had been dealt with. I had put the money in high-interest-earning accounts, and I was ready for a break.

It was still only eleven, so there was plenty of time to pack and start the journey. Once I had sorted my clothes, I went downstairs and made a picnic of ham salad sandwiches. I packed these, along with fruit, crisps, and water, in a cool bag and left them, together with my case, by the back door. I would have to go back and retrieve my car, I wouldn't be able to carry both my suitcase and the cool bag through the fields, and I was beginning to feel rather foolish at having abandoned my car earlier, thinking that Amelia might call unannounced. However, I still peered cautiously around the curtain to check that she wasn't lurking on the doorstep before unlocking the door.

I retraced my steps across the field, the walk taking me much less time without the shopping bags, and climbed into my car. I drove back along the road to the lane leading to my own house. All I had to do now was pack my suitcase and cool bag into the car, lock up and set the wheels in motion, literally.

I began to feel excited. I hadn't taken a holiday in a long time, and although this trip was about researching Amelia, it also felt like an adventure for me. I pulled up outside the house and switched the engine off. I still expected Amelia to jump out at any time. I was hesitant as I walked around to the back of the house. Would she be sitting on the patio waiting for me, demanding to know where I was going? The patio came into view, and I felt relaxed when I saw that the coast was clear. She wasn't lurking in the garden or settled in the lover's seat on the lawn. I unlocked the door and did a quick check of the house, leaving all the downstairs curtains closed, before stowing my suitcase into the boot of the car. I put the cool bag on the passenger seat along with my handbag and climbed behind the wheel.

Taking a deep breath, I turned on the SatNav, reversed back up the lane and started on my journey. I didn't feel totally at ease until I had been driving for a few miles. I wanted to be absolutely certain that I wasn't being watched or followed, and the feeling of both didn't leave me until I had put some distance between myself and my home. How had things got so bad, I thought, that I wanted to run away? I brushed the thoughts aside, chastising myself for thinking I was running away. I was taking a well-needed break; I wasn't running away. The fact that I had brought the break forward by two nights, having seen Amelia this morning, wasn't something I wanted to dwell on.

After driving for several hours, I decided to pull over in a lay-by. The sun was hot, and my mouth felt dry. This seemed as good a place as any to have a bite to eat and take a little rest. I climbed out of the car to stretch my legs and walked around to the passenger door to retrieve the cool bag. I took a few gulps of water, which had been kept surprisingly cold in the bag, and then unwrapped one of the sandwiches. I walked around whilst eating, taking in the scenery and enjoying the sun's rays on my face. I felt completely relaxed.

I was pleased that I had decided to set off earlier than I had originally planned. I could take my time and enjoy the journey rather than having to put my foot down and get to my destination as quickly as possible so that I could check into the hotel. I thought about how people often didn't realise that the journey was part of the adventure. We miss so much in our hurry to get to a destination. I was lucky; I didn't have to rush. I had all the time in the world, and I felt surprisingly free of all encumbrances now that the big house had been sold and I wouldn't have to see Amelia for a while.

I couldn't understand why that young woman bothered me so much. I had tried to warm to her, I really had, but there was something about her demeanour that made me wary of her. At times, she seemed warm and friendly, but there was always a slight vein of narcissist behaviour running through her; the conceited, self-righteous ego oozed from her pores, and I couldn't shake off my apprehension when I was around her. Whenever I was in her company, I felt she was clandestine. She kept her cards close to her chest, never giving much away, and yet she seemed to think she had an automatic right to know everything about me. She questioned my actions, thoughts and movements, and she made me feel extremely uncomfortable. When I wasn't with her, I couldn't stop thinking about her. I didn't want to, but I had an unending fear that she might turn up uninvited at my house at any time. I constantly felt like I was being watched; my every movement being closely monitored, and I didn't like it one bit.

Out here on the open road, I was free. I wasn't sure what my thoughts were going. Was I trying to convince myself that perhaps now was the time for me to move away and start afresh? I could move anywhere. I had enough money to start again in a new part of the country; hell, I could even choose a new country if I wanted to. Although I had lived in my little cottage for decades, I didn't really have a network of people around me. I had no friends that I met up with on a regular basis and no hobbies, clubs or classes to attend. I liked it that way. I had made it that way. I enjoyed my own company and the peace and quiet it afforded me, which was why I resented Amelia so much. She was the epitome of everything I despised. Entitled, nosey, conceited and overbearing. Miles hadn't done a good job of bringing her up.

I finished my sandwich, swallowed a few more gulps of water, climbed back into my car and started the engine. It was almost four o'clock, and I was just a few miles from the next village. I decided I would head there and see if I could find somewhere to stay for the night.

# Chapter Twenty-Four

I pulled up in the car park of a very quaint country pub. It had a thatched roof and whitewashed stone walls. The sign outside stood proud, displaying its name: The King's Head. I went inside and immediately felt as if I was stepping back in time. The low ceilings and dark interior were a stark contrast to the bright sunshine outside, and I felt myself shiver as the drop in temperature suddenly hit me.

'Good afternoon,' a voice from behind the bar greeted me in a friendly manner.

'Hi,' I said, walking towards the bar, 'I don't suppose you have any rooms for the night, do you?'

'Just the one?' the bartender asked.

'Yes, it's just for me,' I answered hopefully. The bartender quickly scanned the book laid in front of him on the bar and then turned and plucked a key off the hook.

'This way, please,' he said, as he led the way through the bar towards a narrow staircase. I hadn't noticed any customers in the bar area, but then I suppose it was a bit early for the Saturday night drinkers to have descended – if indeed such a thing existed in a tiny village.

The stairs were steep and rickety. With every step we took, they creaked and groaned as if they were complaining about the weight they had had to bear over the centuries. At the top of the stairs, the bartender took me along a corridor and stopped outside the last door on the left. He unlocked the door and pushed it aside, allowing me to enter. He waited patiently as I peered inside. The double bed was set against the far wall and was dressed in a chintzy throw which matched the drapes at the window. The furniture was old and in keeping with the country pub, but the bathroom was modern and clean. It looked comfortable, and I nodded in appreciation.

'It's perfect,' I said. The bartender smiled and asked me if I would like any help with my bags. Despite the fact that the stairs were steep and narrow, I declined his offer without a second thought. I returned to my car and opened the boot. Unfastening my suitcase, I transferred the essentials I needed for the night into a holdall that I always keep in the car and made my way back to my room.

I would have struggled to lug my suitcase up the stairs. In fact, I think even the bartender would have struggled to heave a suitcase up these narrow stairs, I thought, as I headed back up the creaky staircase. Once I returned to my room, I took a closer inspection at what was on offer. I opened the drawer on the table by the bed to reveal a bible and a notepad. The towels in the bathroom were soft and fluffy, and the roll-top bath looked inviting. I decided to take a bath, and then I would venture downstairs to the bar to see what food was on offer. A menu on the dressing table revealed that food was served from seven o'clock, giving me ample time to have a soak first.

Just after seven, I ventured back down the archaic staircase to the bar. I had expected to see a few diners. However, the bar area was still deserted, and I wondered if I was the only person staying here tonight, which made me smile as I recalled the bartender studying his bookings before offering me a room. The bartender looked up from his newspaper as I approached.

'What can I get for you?' he asked, smiling cheerfully,

'A glass of white wine would be lovely, thanks,' I replied. I wasn't sure whether an establishment like this would have a selection. Still, I figured country pubs in the middle of nowhere would differentiate between red and white, even if they didn't offer wine from different regions. I watched him reach for a bottle of wine in a fridge stocked with half a dozen of the same bottles. He poured me a generous glass and handed it over.

'Food?' he asked, handing me a menu. I smiled and took the offering from him.

I headed to a table next to the window, which looked out onto the village green. There were a couple of elderly ladies sitting on a bench chatting away and an erstwhile dog walker wandering aimlessly around whilst the dog sniffed at bushes and undergrowth, occasionally lifting its leg to relieve itself. Although I had already looked at the menu in my room, I scanned it again. After a few minutes, the bartender wandered over and asked me if I was ready to order. I requested a ploughman's platter, and he nodded as he scribbled on his notepad. He disappeared momentarily, and I assumed he had gone to the kitchen to place my order. I sipped my wine, which, despite not being of any particular vintage, was surprisingly good.

A few minutes later, the door opened, and a couple of elderly gentlemen walked in. The bartender greeted them warmly using their names, so I assumed they were locals. One of the men glanced around the pub and, on seeing me, he tilted his hat.

'Good evening,' he said. I mumbled a response and returned my gaze to the window. I had been alone all day, driving. I was tired and hungry, and I didn't feel like conversing with a stranger. The old man seemed to sense this as he turned his attention back to the bartender. The two men sat on rickety stools at the bar, chatting about the day's events, and I was relieved that they didn't appear to want to engage in conversation with me.

The doors to the kitchen suddenly swung open, and a woman similar in age to the bartender stepped out carrying a tray. She stopped at my table and placed the ploughman's platter in front of me, along with condiments, a napkin and cutlery. I thanked her as she turned to leave.

The ploughman's platter was a sight to behold. The plate was enormous, and every inch of it was covered with food. I could feel my mouth begin to water as I eyed the pork pie, pickles, roast ham, and selection of cheeses. I got to work on the food immediately, feeling myself begin to unwind as my hunger pangs were satisfied. I took another sip of wine and leaned back in the chair, savouring every mouthful.

I glanced over at the bar where the two elderly men were engrossed in conversation, a couple of pints between them; the bartender had returned his attention to his newspaper. Where was everyone? I couldn't understand how on earth a place like this survived with hardly any customers. If I weren't here, I doubted the pub would take much money at all this evening; how much could two elderly gentlemen spend?

I continued to eat the rest of my meal, but feeling full before I could finish it all, I pushed the plate away from me. It had been worth every penny, and I was surprised that no one else was enjoying the food offered here. After I had finished my meal, the bartender put his newspaper down and came around the bar to clear my plate.

'Everything alright for you?' he stated rather than asked.

'Yes, thank you, it was lovely, just what I needed.'

'Can I get you anything else? Another glass of wine, perhaps?' he added, noticing my glass was empty.

'Why not?' I replied. I didn't have to be up at the crack of dawn tomorrow, and, as it was still relatively early, I didn't want to retire to bed just yet. Things might have been different if the bar had been busy and noisy, but it wasn't. In fact, it was a very pleasant atmosphere, and I found myself feeling quite liberated.

It had been a very long time since I had eaten in a pub and even longer since I had done so alone. I doubted I would have felt so relaxed had I been anywhere else. I liked the fact that I didn't know anyone here, and they didn't know me. I could relax without expecting Amelia to come through the door anytime.

I thanked the bartender as he brought over my second glass of wine. He smiled and nodded. I spent another half an hour sipping my wine and staring aimlessly out of the window, mentally making plans for the next step of my journey. I had read that breakfast was served from eight o'clock, so I was considering eating and then hitting the road again at around nine. I figured the traffic wouldn't be too bad as the next day was Sunday; no rush hour traffic, no dodging angry motorists who were late for work. I could go further south and then find somewhere, perhaps in the New Forest, to stay before venturing onto the hotel I had booked from Monday onwards. I drained my glass and stifled a yawn. The long drive, the heat of the summer sun and the alcohol had begun to take their toll, and I could feel myself feeling drowsy.

I pushed my chair back, conscious of the loud noise it made on the stone-flagged floor, and winced. The two old gentlemen at the bar shot me a look. I walked over to the bar and placed my empty glass on the counter. Before I could speak, the bartender reached for the bottle in the fridge, took it out and began refilling my glass! I opened my mouth to speak, but nothing came out. Oh, well, I thought, looks like I am having one for the road. I took the glass and thanked the bartender.

'I think I will take this one up with me if that's OK.' I said, 'I've had a long day, and I'm exhausted.'

'Sure, of course, you can,' he said politely. The two gentlemen at the bar, who were still hugging their first pints, bade me goodnight, and I retreated up the creaky staircase to my room.

Back in my room, I pulled the curtains, got undressed and climbed under the duvet. The white sheets were pristine, and the cool cotton enveloped me. I plumped up the cushions and scanned the breakfast menu. It catered to every taste, from vegetarian to continental. Do they really get that many customers here that a breakfast menu like this was needed? I doubted it, given that on a Saturday evening at the height of summer, there were just two elderly gentlemen at the bar, and they had even made an art out of hanging onto a pint of beer for two hours. Maybe the place used to be more popular, I thought. I guess many pubs have their day and, once the younger generation finds other newer more modern places to patronise, the old country pubs lose their appeal. It was just another example of how times were changing.

My mind skipped to Amelia. She wasn't the sort of

person who would stay in a place like this. It was because of people like Amelia that they were dying a death. Amelia was the kind of woman who would go to wine bars, not country inns. I swallowed the last mouthful of wine, put the glass on the table by my bed, and shuffled down under the duvet. Although the day had been exceptionally warm, the room had a slight chill due to the thick walls and small windows, and the duvet was a welcome relief. I closed my eyes and drifted off to sleep.

It was the best night's sleep I had had in months.

# Chapter Twenty-Five

I woke at seven o'clock to the sound of a cockerel crowing loudly across the green. I smiled to myself and pushed the duvet back. I felt better than I had done in a long time. I had enjoyed a good night's sleep, and despite consuming more wine than I had intended, I was surprisingly alert and ready for the day ahead. I jumped into the shower, washed and styled my hair, dressed and applied a little make-up. I folded my nightdress and the dirty clothes I had worn the day before and stuffed them into my holdall before pulling back the curtains. It was another beautiful day, and the sun was already beaming down. I made my way downstairs. It wasn't yet eight, but if no one was around, I would happily take a little stroll outside before breakfast.

The stairs creaked and groaned with every move I made, and I found myself cringing at the sounds. The bar was eerily quiet. I guess when you are the only person staying in an establishment, this is what greets you in the morning, I thought, as I made my way to the door leading out onto the village green. I half expected the door to be locked, in which case I wasn't sure what I would do; sit in the bar and wait or tackle the groaning staircase again. To my surprise, the door was not only unlocked; it was propped open by a wrought iron doorstop in the shape of a fox. I walked out into the sunshine, feeling the rise in temperature the minute I stepped onto the grass verge. I breathed deeply. I hadn't noticed how stuffy the air inside the pub was until venturing back outside. I looked around me. The village was tiny. In addition to the King's Head, there was just one shop that doubled up as a post office, a church, and a dozen or so houses, all with neat little gardens and picket fences. It didn't take me long to explore the hamlet, and I was heading back inside the pub before I knew it. On entering the bar, I almost bumped into the bartender from the night before.

'Morning,' he greeted me with a warm voice. 'Take a seat, and I will bring you a menu,' he continued, walking over to the bar and plucking a menu from the holder. He handed me the card and asked if I wanted tea or coffee. I placed my order for coffee and quickly scanned the menu again, although I had already decided what I wanted to have. It would be another long day with a lengthy drive, so I needed a sustainable breakfast to set me up for what lay ahead.

'I'll have the full English, please,' I said, as he returned with a mug of steaming, freshly brewed coffee. I sipped my coffee and waited for my breakfast to arrive, checking my phone for messages. I had expected to hear from Amelia by now, but when I checked my text messages, they revealed nothing. I was surprised but also pleased. Maybe she had been annoyed with me for not accepting her invitation for coffee, but it was a little over the top even for her to behave so childishly. Maybe she has given up and decided I'm not worth the trouble. The thought warmed me, but I wasn't convinced by it. People like Amelia didn't just give up. They had to be made to give up.

I replaced my phone on the table just as my breakfast arrived. Like the meal I had enjoyed last night, this one more than lived up to my expectations. The plate was laden with bacon, sausages, eggs, tomatoes, baked beans, and hash browns, along with a separate rack of both brown and white toast and a couple of minute jars of jam and marmalade. It was a breakfast fit for a king. Maybe that's where the name of the inn came from, I thought, as I shook a little salt and pepper onto my plate and dived in. The smell of the hot buttered toast and freshly grilled bacon made my stomach groan, and I hadn't realised how hungry I was.

I devoured the breakfast in record time, a little embarrassed by how much I had managed to eat and how quickly. I finished my coffee and sat back in the chair. It was a good fifteen minutes later when the bartender reappeared. I think he knew I had finished but thought it best to give me a reasonable amount of time before collecting my plate.

'Can I get you anything else?' he asked as he stacked the tray with the dirty crockery.

'No, thank you. That was amazing. I'm going to just collect my things from the room, and then I will be making a move,' I replied, as I stood and headed for the stairs.

Back in my room, I checked that I hadn't forgotten anything, collected my bags, and headed back down the rickety staircase to pay my bill. The bartender was already waiting for me. I settled my bill and made my way outside to the car park to continue my journey.

Once on the road, I turned the radio up loud and sang along to the tunes. It was going to be another glorious day, and I planned to reach the New Forest by the early afternoon, giving me ample time to find somewhere to stay for the night and do a little sightseeing. The roads were quiet, day trippers obviously hadn't gotten up early, and I made good headway.

It was a little after one-thirty when I arrived in a little village in the New Forest. If I had thought the last village I had stayed in was picturesque, then this one took the main prize. It was utterly breathtaking, with thatch-roofed cottages, open heathland and semi-wild ponies wandering around. It was idyllic, and I immediately fell in love with it all. I parked my car at the side of the village green, praying that the ponies, who were happily grazing, would not decide to give it a quick kick when no one was looking.

The sun was high in the sky, hot and blistering. I spotted the local inn and headed across the village green towards it. The interior was dark, cool and welcoming. There were a couple of occupied tables with people enjoying lunch. The young lady behind the bar smiled at me as I entered.

'Hi,' she said in a voice as warm as the midday sun.

'Hi,' I replied. 'Can I have a glass of white wine please?'

'Any in particular?' she asked, stepping back to allow me to scour the bottles on display. It was evident that this particular establishment catered for many more people than the last one I had been in, and the choice of wine confirmed this. I chose an Australian Sauvignon and reached for a menu. As the barmaid poured my wine, I perused the food on offer and decided on a prawn salad. Despite the enormous breakfast I had eaten, I was beginning to feel a little peckish, and a salad would hit the spot before I ate again that evening. I placed my food order and asked if there were any rooms available. Without having to check the diary, the young lady smiled and confirmed that they had.

'Would you like to eat before I show you your room?'

'Yes, that would be nice, thank you.' I wasn't in a rush.

I ate my lunch and enjoyed a second glass of wine before being shown to my room.

In keeping with the age of the inn, which was centuries old, the room was oak-panelled with bedding and drapes in a subtle floral design. Like the King's Head, the floorboards creaked and groaned, seemingly in protest of the unrelenting years of being walked over, but the stairs were wide, and I felt much more comfortable carrying my bag up than I had in the previous establishment.

After settling in, I decided to take a stroll around the village. It was now late afternoon, and the sun's heat was beginning to subside, making it more comfortable to walk around. The village was beautiful. I wandered around, gazing at the manicured lawns, colourful flower borders and delightful cottages, each one screaming wealth but also pride. I could see how the people who lived here took pride in their homes, obviously completely aware of how lucky they were to live in such a beautiful part of the country. Several people were sat on the village green trying to enjoy a picnic whilst warding off inquisitive ponies looking for their next treat. The village was bigger than the last one I had stayed in, and I enjoyed wandering along the side of the stream towards the forest and heathland.

Just outside the village, I came across a tiny church steeped in history. I pushed the freshly painted gate open, listening to it creak as I did so, as if it were singing a soft hymn of its own. I wandered up the winding path, looking at the gravestones as I did so; some were completely illegible given the number of years they had withstood the weather, whilst others were new with fresh flowers and framed photographs. I stopped to look at one that was adorned with teddy bears and other cuddly toys, feeling a shiver down my spine as I read that the deceased was a boy of just seven years old. Although I wasn't a mother, I couldn't image anything worse than losing a child. The pain and anguish must truly be unsurmountable, I thought, as I continued towards the heavy oak door to the church.

I pushed hard against the door, expecting it to be heavy and difficult to budge. In fact, it succumbed easily to my push, and I slipped quietly inside. The interior was cold, but the light penetrating the stained-glass windows made it feel bright and alive. The walls were painted plaster and covered with murals depicting saints and scenes from scriptures. The cold flagstones added to the chilly feeling, and the air smelt damp and musty. I wandered down the aisle towards the altar, marvelling at the peacefulness on offer. I wondered how many people had worshipped within these four walls over the centuries and how many hearts and minds had been soothed. I wasn't a religious person, but I felt remarkably calm while surrounded by the statues and art. Although I had never been a churchgoer, I could see how, in a place as beautiful as this, people with troubled minds would come seeking peace.

I sat down on the front pew and looked up at the statue of Jesus before the stained-glass window. It was a pretty remarkable story, however you looked at it. Whether you believed in God and all that he had to offer or you didn't, it was, like Father Christmas, one of the best-known stories of all time. I was surprised to find myself saying a silent prayer, and I wondered if this was how religion made its way into people's minds and lives. Was it the needy, those who sought answers, and those who were lost that believed? If so, then was I in that category, and that was why I found myself praying? I didn't know.

I felt a sudden urge to get back outside into the sunlight. The feeling of peace and tranquillity was quickly being taken over by one of fear and dread. I ran back up the aisle and pushed the door open, which revealed a sudden influx of sunlight. I stepped back outside and jogged down the path back towards the gate. Pushing it open, the creaking now sounded like a muffled scream rather than the soft hymn I heard on my way in. I was breathless by the time I had reached the village green again.

I willed myself to slow down, conscious that I was drawing attention to myself. I retraced my steps to the inn I had booked for the night. As the welcome sign depicting The Blacksmith's Arms came into view, I felt myself begin to calm down. I had absolutely no idea what had just come over me, but the sudden urge to run, to escape from who knows what prevailed, and I couldn't get my feelings of fear under control. Churches were supposed to be places of peace, and usually, whenever I visited one, this is exactly how I felt, but today something was different. Maybe it was because of my own predicament rather than the church itself. I wanted the day to end; I wanted it to be morning so I could be on my way. I suddenly felt like a fish out of water. The village was beautiful, picturesque and pretty, but I didn't belong there.

Entering the Blacksmith's Arms, I noticed the same young lady was still behind the bar serving drinks to the handful of customers. I decided to make my way up to my room and rest. My mind was in overdrive. It had been a long day, and the sun's heat had sapped my energy. Yes, that was it; I was just exhausted I told myself, as I waved to the barmaid and pushed the doors open leading to the staircase and the guest bedrooms. Once I was back in my room, I lay on the bed and closed my eyes. Within minutes, I was sound asleep, dreaming of Amelia.

I woke with a start, feeling cold and shivery. I glanced down at my arms and noticed goosebumps covering my skin, the hairs standing on end. I rubbed my arms to try to encourage them to warm up and felt the roughness of the skin under my touch. I fought the urge to climb under the duvet and pull it up around my neck. Instead, I walked to the bathroom, popped the plug in the bathtub and turned on the hot tap. Steam penetrated the room almost immediately, and I could feel my muscles beginning to relax, the coldness subsiding. I poured some of the complimentary bath oil into the water and swirled it around with my hand, feeling the welcome warmth as the hot water rose further up my arm. I breathed deeply, relishing the aroma of lavender from the oils. I stepped out of my clothes and climbed into the tub, allowing the water to wash over me and penetrate my cold, aching limbs. I thought, not for the first time that maybe I was coming down with something. A cold, a virus, maybe? I wasn't sure, but I certainly felt tired and lethargic, and despite the surging temperatures of the summer sun outside, I felt chilly without any apparent cause.

I lay in the bath until the water began to cool, and then, indulgently, I turned the hot water tap back on, relishing in the instant heat. I spent more than half an hour soaking my tired limbs until the skin on my hands and feet had turned wrinkly. Reluctantly, I climbed out of the bath and wrapped myself in an enormous, soft, fluffy towel. I instantly felt better. The hot water had warmed my body, but I still felt completely washed out. I wasn't just tired; I was exhausted. Despite having just woken up, I still needed more sleep.

I wandered back into the bedroom. I wasn't hungry, but I knew I needed to eat something; otherwise, the feeling of exhaustion wouldn't pass. I scanned the menu and decided to order room service. I climbed into the fluffy bathrobe hung in the wardrobe and phoned my food order downstairs. Whilst waiting for room service, I sat in a chair by the window, watching people come and go, laughing as they enjoyed the early evening sunshine.

The pub was beginning to get busy with what looked like both locals and holidaymakers, and I was glad that I had decided to eat in my room. I wasn't in the mood to converse politely with strangers, and a busy pub was the last thing I needed tonight.

Less than half an hour after I had placed my order, there was a light rap on the door. I opened it to find a young man standing in the hallway brandishing a tray laden with food. I stood aside and allowed him to enter. He quickly laid the tray down on the table by the window and left me in peace. The food smelt divine, although I still hadn't managed to work up much of an appetite. I had ordered a chicken pie with vegetables and mashed potatoes, but all I could do was pick at the crumbling pastry and push the vegetables around the plate with my fork. I forced myself to eat a few mouthfuls. I found the food tasteless and difficult to swallow, but I knew it wasn't a true representation of the meal before me.

I sighed, realising that I was indeed succumbing to something. Hopefully, it would pass quickly, perhaps a twenty-four-hour bug or maybe just tiredness. I felt myself crossing my fingers in hope whilst forcing down a couple more mouthfuls of vegetables. When I felt I couldn't stomach any more food, I climbed into bed and pulled the duvet close. I was still wearing the fluffy dressing gown, and despite the warmth of the evening, my body ached, and I shivered uncontrollably. Minutes later, I was sound asleep, and this time, I didn't dream about anything.

# Chapter Twenty-Six

I woke the next morning before dawn. Glancing at my watch, pleased that I didn't have to get up immediately, I turned over and went back to sleep. The next time I woke, it was just after seven. It was still too early to rise, but I desperately needed to pee, so I reluctantly climbed out of the warm bed and hurried to the bathroom, switching the kettle on as I skipped past the tea tray in my hurry to get to the toilet. I made myself a cup of coffee and returned to the comfort of the bed. I had slept for hours, and I felt much better than I had the evening before. I didn't have the sore throat that I had anticipated would be the next symptom; the aches and shivers abated, and my body felt more relaxed.

I was grateful that I hadn't succumbed to anything worse than tiredness. It was to be expected I thought, as I sipped my coffee. It hadn't just been a busy couple of days with some long hours of driving; it had been a stressful couple of months, what with selling the house and finding out about Amelia. Perhaps these few days away had just heightened my senses a little too much, and my body was telling me to slow down. I was determined to listen to my body. I didn't want to make myself ill. This was supposed to be a holiday.

I might be looking up where Miles, Amelia, and her mother had lived, but it needn't be a chore. I must take things easy, slow down, and enjoy the moment. I was done with rushing around. I had come to terms with many things recently, and this morning I decided that whatever this trip revealed, once I was back home, I was going to put Amelia out of my thoughts. She wasn't my daughter. I didn't owe her anything. All she had brought me was anxiety and stress. I had started on this journey now, so I would see it through, but once it was over, that was it. Amelia wouldn't take up any more of my thoughts or my time.

I finished my coffee and showered, enjoying the hot water as it bounced off my body. There were no more goosebumps; my aches had dissipated, and I felt much better. I pondered how much a good night's sleep was essential for the body and mind to recuperate, and once again, I felt thankful that I hadn't succumbed to anything more drastic than tiredness. I washed my hair, smelling the lemon scent of the shampoo as the steam burned the inside of my nostrils.

Once I was dressed, I dried my hair and applied a little make-up. I ventured downstairs for breakfast. The small restaurant was already a beacon of activity. Most of the tables were occupied, and I had to settle for a tiny table next to the door. I headed for the buffet table and helped myself to orange juice, muesli and yoghurt. A short time later, a young lady wandered over to take my order. I ordered a full English breakfast; my appetite had now returned with a vengeance, and coffee.

I glanced around the room at the other diners. There were a few young families, but the majority were couples who looked to be of retirement age. I smiled inwardly when I considered how this beautiful part of the country was genteel, so it didn't surprise me that it appealed to the more affluent people of a certain age. You wouldn't find young people getting drunk in these country inns, nor would you stumble across hen parties and stag dos. No, these places were meant for more discerning characters.

The young waitress arrived with my breakfast and coffee, and I tucked in earnestly. Pleased that my appetite had returned, I relished the crispy bacon and devoured the greasy fried egg and tasty field mushrooms. When I felt sated, I pushed my plate aside and drank my coffee whilst nibbling a piece of toast with zesty marmalade spread thickly over it.

I had already planned my journey. I googled the boutique hotel I had booked for the next five nights, and I figured I would be there in less than two hours. I contemplated hanging around the village until lunchtime, but I didn't relish another walk to the church, and as there was little else to do in such a compact place, I decided I would move on and perhaps stop en route if somewhere took my fancy.

After settling my bill, I headed back to my room to collect my belongings and then stepped out into what was promising to be yet another glorious day of sunshine. It had been a wonderful summer so far, with wall-to-wall sunshine and very little rain. I was pleased that I wouldn't have to spend too much time behind the wheel of the car today. I planned on driving for an hour and seeing where it took me. I could then stop off for a while before continuing the final leg to my destination in time to check-in.

The roads out of the village were narrow, surrounded by rolling countryside mixed with dense forest. Just short of an hour after I had set off, I stumbled across another quaint village. I decided to stop, stretch my legs and have a wander around. I parked my car at the side of the pavement and climbed out. The village wasn't much bigger than the one I had just left behind; however, this one seemed to have more in the way of amenities. In addition to the traditional country pub, it also had a couple of small shops, a post office and a café.

I wasn't ready for lunch; the breakfast I had consumed at the Blacksmith's Arms would probably set me up for the rest of the day, so I decided to wander around the village before taking a seat in the café for coffee. It was a pleasant stroll. The sun was hot, its rays relentless. I saw the wild ponies trying to shade under the trees on the village green. I noticed a signpost pointing to the church but decided to give this a miss. After yesterday's experience, I wasn't sure I was up for another word with God. For some reason, he didn't seem entirely happy with me at the moment, and I didn't want to tempt fate and annoy him twice in as many days.

I wandered off the main road through the village and spotted a tiny bookshop on the corner of the lane behind a couple of thatched cottages with picket fences and roses climbing around the door. The quintessential English country idyll, I thought, as I entered the bookshop. I was pleased to see that, besides myself, there was just one other customer; even then, the shop seemed cramped, and there was little room to turn around, let alone browse the shelves. A tiny wrinkled woman with white hair and wire spectacles peered over the wooden counter. She had a witch-like appearance, but a smile that radiated warmth, and I felt myself instantly smiling back at her.

Despite its size, the shop stocked a seemingly endless array of different titles on various subjects, and I was in awe of how many books could be shoehorned into such a small space. My eyes were instantly drawn to a shelf about horticulture, and I chose a couple of books to take with me on my travels. The old woman behind the counter seemed surprised that I wanted to purchase the books, and I wondered when she had last made a sale. She wrapped my books in brown paper and tied them neatly with a piece of string. This really was like stepping back in time, I marvelled, as I half expected her to want me to pay in shillings rather than with my card. Fortunately for me, card machines had also made their way to this part of the country.

I left the shop with my neatly packaged books and headed for the café I had spotted when I first entered the village. The café was quiet, but I chose a table outside, next to a flowing clematis draped over a fence. The huge plant was laden with heavy white flowers, and the strong almond fragrance was heady and overpowering. A middle-aged woman wearing a crisp white apron, tied with a neat bow at the back, wandered over to my table to take my order.

'Just a coffee, please, cappuccino,' I asked with a smile. The woman smiled back and popped her notepad into the pocket at the front of her apron.

'Be right back,' she said as she disappeared into the café, reappearing a few minutes later with a huge cup and saucer, which she placed before me on the table. I thanked her, and she left. A picture of a swan had been expertly traced in chocolate onto the frothy milk on top of my coffee, and a complimentary homemade square of flapjack was proudly displayed on the saucer. I popped the piece of flapjack into my mouth and savoured the buttery texture and sweet taste. The coffee was smooth and silky.

I reached into my pocket for my phone, and realising I had it on silent, checked my messages to see if I had missed anything. Amelia. The name sprang to the screen like a slap to the face. I didn't know if I wanted to read the messages, ignore them or simply delete them. I put my phone back on the table and drank another mouthful of coffee, savouring the hot sensation in my throat as I swallowed the liquid. I picked my phone up again and opened the messages.

'Hi,' I read. 'How are you?' Ten minutes later, she had sent another text.

'Do you fancy meeting up?' Another ten minutes later, another message.

'Have I done something to offend you?' The messages came thick and fast, every ten minutes until I saw that she had sent me eight messages in total, each getting a little more aggressive as she obviously thought I was ignoring her. I scrolled through all the messages until I got to the last one.

'I'm not going to keep contacting you if you haven't got the decency to respond; that's it, we're done!'

I laughed out loud when I read it, bringing unwanted attention to myself from a couple of other customers in the café garden. I felt my face redden in embarrassment and concentrated on my coffee. Was that really it? Was that the last time I would hear anything from Amelia? Had she finally got the message? I wanted to believe it, but I very much doubted that she would be so easy to get rid of. It had been just over an hour since Amelia's first message to her last, and in that time, she had turned cold and nasty. What on earth was going on in her head to make her snap like that? Did she not even consider that perhaps I had just been busy and didn't have a chance to reply to her messages, rather than suggesting I had simply ignored her?

I considered replying, telling her I had been in the car, driving and hadn't even seen her messages, but I thought better of it. She might ask me where I was and when I would be home. I didn't want her to know I wasn't at home. She might go snooping around, and I didn't want her anywhere near my house, especially when I wasn't there. I decided to ignore the messages. It was what I was being accused of, after all, so why bother replying? If Amelia really did mean what she had threatened, then it would be all the better; I could eradicate her from my life without actually having to do anything. She had done the hard work for me. All's well that ends well. I felt an air of satisfaction as I left the money for my coffee, along with a tip, on the table and headed back to my car to continue the final leg of my journey.

Just over an hour later, I pulled up outside what looked like a very luxurious boutique hotel. I parked my car in the private car park at the rear and ventured inside. On reaching the reception desk, I was greeted by a woman who looked to be in her late twenties, dressed smartly in a grey skirt and white blouse; her name badge introduced her as Maggie.

'Good afternoon,' she said politely, 'How can I help you?' I coughed quietly before replying.

'Hello, I have a reservation for five nights. My name is Jameson, Kate Jameson.' Maggie typed away on the keyboard in front of her and peered at the screen.

'Yes, I have that, Ms Jameson. Please follow me,' she said as she reached behind her, plucked a key off the board, and walked around the counter to greet me. I followed her to the lift. She pressed a button, and the doors opened immediately. We entered the lift together.

'Your room is on the second floor,' Maggie said as she deftly pressed the keypad and the lift doors closed. We rode in silence. The doors opened again, and Maggie stepped out into the corridor. I followed her. She walked a short distance down the hallway and stopped outside the second door on the right. She put the key in the lock, gave it a quick twist and stepped aside as the door sprung open, allowing me to enter.

Maggie remained at the door whilst I inspected the room. It looked perfect, and I was thrilled that I would be spending the next five nights in such beautiful surroundings. The room was elegant, and it was clear that it had been designed with luxury in mind. The huge king-size bed was adorned with crisp white bed linen and opulent cushions. There was a state-of-the-art coffee machine and a large selection of coffee and tea. I opened the fridge, which was stacked with bottles of fruit juice, wines, shorts and mixes. A basket next to the coffee machine revealed a selection of snacks and biscuits. I walked into the bathroom, which revealed a roll-top bath and abundant toiletries from a high-end luxury brand. There were fluffy towels, slippers and bathrobes. I turned to Maggie with a huge smile on my face.

'This is absolutely perfect,' I said, and I meant every word.

'I hope you have a wonderful stay with us, Ms Jameson, and if I can be of any assistance at all, please do not hesitate to let me know. Now, what about your cases? Do you need a hand with them?'

I nodded in acceptance, and we took the lift back to

the reception, where Maggie rang a bell, and a young man arrived to help me with my case almost immediately. He followed me to my car, extracted the case from the boot and duly delivered it to my room in record time. I unpacked my clothes and hung them in the wardrobe. If this was going to be my home for the next five days, I didn't want to be living out of a suitcase. I then decided to take a walk, get my bearings, and look around.

I ventured out into the bright sunshine and looked up and down the wonderful high street. The hotel, with its shiny plaque proudly displaying its name: Utopia, was smack bang in the middle of the cobbled street, surrounded by interesting shops, chic clothing outlets and trendy wine bars, cafés and restaurants. It was a welcome change from the sleepy villages I had spent the last two nights in, and it really was a little piece of heaven on earth. I was looking forward to spending time here and exploring what was on offer. So far, the town seemed to be the perfect mix of country, coast, and forest; it had something to please everyone, and it certainly pleased me. I could see why Amelia's mother had wanted to live here. The draw was obvious and instant. I spent a few hours wandering around, checking out what was on offer before heading back to my hotel to prepare for dinner.

I had decided I would eat in the restaurant tonight rather than take room service. I was feeling much better than I had the night before. I was looking forward to my meal. I took a long soak in the deep roll-top bath and carried out my usual routine of applying make-up and styling my hair before heading downstairs.

The restaurant wasn't large, but neither was it small. It was, like the rest of Utopia, simply perfect. It was intimate and personal. Tables were set far enough apart that people could have a conversation and not be overheard. There was no cramming in of tables in this establishment. I felt a little disheartened. I wouldn't be able to eavesdrop on anyone this evening, and as I only had myself for company, I wondered what else I might do. I walked over to the bar and studied the wine list. I ordered a bottle of Italian Pinot. I wasn't going to kid myself that a glass would do. The bartender duly obliged, placing a wine cooler and a sparkling crystal glass on the bar.

'Are you eating with us this evening?' he asked politely.

'Yes, if you have a table free.'

'All guests staying with us are accommodated; we only have a handful of tables open for non-residents. Please, let me show you to your table.' He picked up the wine cooler containing my bottle of wine along with the glass and led the way to a table at the far end of the restaurant. It gave me a perfect view of the room, and although positioned in the corner, it did not give the impression of being tucked away out of sight.

Much thought had been put into the restaurant's layout, and I marvelled at how well the space catered for everyone, be it couples, groups or single people like myself. I thanked the waiter as he poured me a glass of wine and placed the bottle back in the cooler. Before I could take a sip, a very efficient waitress descended on me, brandishing a menu. She smiled broadly as she methodically explained the day's catch and informed me what soup was being served that evening. I thanked her, and she left me to study the menu.

The waitress returned a short time later and took my

order. I decided on a wild mushroom risotto to begin with, followed by pan-fried sea bass. My stomach began to rumble, and I willed it to be quiet, conscious that other diners might hear it. I scanned the restaurant. It wasn't yet eight o'clock, but most of the tables were already taken, the majority were couples with one or two single gentlemen. I felt a little self-conscious, if not quite liberated, when I realised that I was the only female dining alone. I wondered what the others thought, but then I realised that no one was taking any notice of me, and I began to relax.

This was exactly the place I needed to spend the next few days. I felt certain it would help me to unwind after the exceptionally busy few months I had endured. It was small and intimate enough to be personal but not too small that I would stand out like a sore thumb.

My starter arrived, and I tucked in with relish. The risotto was perfectly cooked, the dish just enough to satisfy the initial hunger pangs, but it left me wanting more. The sea bass didn't disappoint either. It came with lobster tempura and wilted greens, and I gave the chef mental praise. The dish was absolutely delicious. The service was impeccable, with the waiter topping my wine up whenever it dropped to a certain level, often without me even knowing he was there; such was the professionalism and efficiency of the hospitality staff on duty. I really couldn't have asked for more. The waitress cleared my plates away and left the dessert menu. She was wise enough to give me some breathing space, allowing me to digest the sumptuous meal I had just eaten before returning to see if I had room for more.

I sat back in my chair, swirling the wine around in my glass while contemplating the list of desserts. I opted for a chilled chocolate fondant with hazelnut ice cream, praying that the richness wouldn't react with the wine and cause me to feel nauseous. It was a risk I was prepared to take.

After I had finished my meal, I allowed the waiter to top up my wine glass with the last of the wine, and I then made my way through to the resident's lounge. I wasn't ready to retire to bed. I didn't have to be up early in the morning; I had no long car journeys to endure; tonight, I could relax and enjoy the evening.

The residents' lounge was decorated in the same elegant way as the rest of the hotel. The walls were painted in a pleasing shade of muted green. Chairs were arranged to make the most of the space whilst dividing the room into sections that would appeal again to couples, singles or small groups. High-backed leather chairs, along with high-quality comfortable sofas featuring plump cushions, were arranged around tables in various shapes and sizes. The far wall was adorned with a huge mahogany bookshelf that reached from floor to ceiling; the shelves were packed with books, reminding me of the tiny bookshop I had visited earlier. I scanned the titles on offer, everything from the classic *Wuthering Heights* and *Pride and Prejudice* to autobiographies and cookery books written by today's popular chefs such as Gordon Ramsay and Jamie Oliver. My eyes took in the titles, dozens and dozens of them. I would enjoy reading some of these this week, I thought, as I plucked a local map from the rack on display that also featured top attractions and other places of interest that holidaymakers might enjoy.

The lounge was quiet. I assumed that most of the diners would have ventured outside to sample the local wine bars once they had eaten. I chose a leather wing-backed chair at the far end of the room and placed my glass on the table, smoothing out the map. Taking out my phone, I looked up the two addresses the private investigator I had hired had given me. I set to looking up where Miles, Amelia and her mother had lived when they had moved to this neck of the woods. The first address was on the coast, approximately five miles from the hotel I was staying in. This was the house that Miles's child had been brought up in. I found the location on the map easily. The second address was about ten miles away and further inland, in a village not unlike the ones I had spent the past weekend in but seemingly larger.

I drained my glass of wine and decided to retire to my room. I had a busy day ahead of me tomorrow, and I wanted to be refreshed and ready to explore this part of my dead husband's life. I felt an unnerving sense of excitement. I was expecting to feel apprehensive when I got to this stage of my search for the truth, but surprisingly, the only feelings I had were anticipation and enthusiasm. I folded the map back up and, keeping it tightly in my grasp, headed to the lift that would take me up to my room.

# Chapter Twenty-Seven

The sun was streaming through the bedroom window, and I squinted as I tried to catch a glimpse of the time on the clock on the table next to me: seven forty-five. I pushed the duvet back and climbed out of bed. Setting the coffee machine, I took a long hot shower whilst waiting for the machine to brew my coffee. I really must invest in one of these machines, I thought, as I studied the array of buttons. I could choose a flat white, cappuccino, Americano, latte, and goodness knows how many other drinks at the push of a button.

It was almost nine when I went to the dining room for breakfast. The buffet was a sight for sore eyes, and it literally took my breath away. Although I wasn't a seasoned traveller by any stretch of the imagination, I did recognise a decent spread when I saw one, and this surpassed just about anything I had seen recently. There was fruit of every variety on offer, from fresh strawberries, peaches, plums and kiwis to the more mundane apples, oranges and pears. At least a dozen cereals were displayed, along with cheeses and cooked meats galore. I poured myself a glass of grapefruit juice and opted for a bowl of fresh fruit and a plain yoghurt. I took my bowl and glass to a table by the window and settled into my seat. A waitress hurried over immediately and asked if I wanted tea or coffee. I opted for coffee and then mentally began to plan my day.

I would venture down to the coast after I had eaten breakfast. I wanted to check out the house where Amelia had lived with Miles and her mother. It wasn't far, and it would leave me with ample time to explore the area and see what else I could find out. The waitress returned with my coffee and took my order. I chose kippers. There are only so many full English breakfasts I can eat, and I didn't feel ready for three on the trot.

I finished my breakfast, collected what I would need from my room and headed out into the bright morning sunshine. The car was stifling, and I made a mental note to park it somewhere a little more shaded when I returned. I turned the air-con up high and reversed out of the car park onto the main street, following the signs to the coast. It took less than fifteen minutes to reach my destination.

The coastal town was picturesque and bustling, and I drove slowly up the main street, looking for somewhere to park. I found a space down a side street that didn't appear to have any parking restrictions and pulled over. Grabbing my handbag from the passenger seat and the map I had taken from the hotel, I climbed out of the car and stretched my legs. I had a basic idea of the direction I needed to head in, and I began walking up the high street towards the address the private investigator had found for me.

It took me about twenty minutes to locate the lane, and I took a deep breath before I ventured further. The houses were big, huge, in fact, and I hadn't expected Miles to have bought a house of such a size. I tried to recall what the private investigator had told me, or had it been Amelia? I felt certain Amelia had said that she and her mother and father had lived here initially; however, she had given the impression that things had been rocky between her parents, leading to Miles moving out into a rented apartment.

After Amelia's mother had got sick with cancer, they sold the house and moved in with an aunt. Hadn't Amelia said she inherited the money from the house sale after her mother had died? Surely then, she was quite a well-off young lady; the houses down here were worth a lot more than in my part of the country, and I had inherited a princely sum from Miles. Why, then, hadn't Amelia been able to buy the cottage next to mine outright? Surely, she had enough money not to need a mortgage and would have been able to afford to do the cottage up? It didn't make sense.

I wandered down the lane, looking up at the enormous houses with their sweeping driveways and huge electric gates. I counted the numbers and stopped outside number 20, or at least this is where number 20 should have been. A large plaque outside the gates displayed an array of letter boxes, each with a name across the top and each with a number followed by a letter: 20A, 20B, 20C and so on. I was a little perplexed until it suddenly dawned on me that number 20 was now a block of apartments, and from what I could see, it had been divided into at least ten separate units. I peered through the gate and saw an elderly lady pottering in the grounds.

'Excuse me,' I shouted through the gates. She looked up and gestured for me to enter the grounds. I pushed a side pedestrian gate open and walked over to her. She looked ancient. She had a full head of hair, but it was as white as snow. Her hands and face were wizened, and it was obvious that arthritis had taken hold of her fingers. She looked at me with piercing grey eyes – eyes of steel – and I felt myself shudder.

'What can I do for you?' she asked in a voice as clear as a bell.

'I was just wondering if you know when this house was converted into apartments,' I asked.

'Ooh, I can't be sure of the exact year, my dear. I'm sorry. My mind isn't quite what it used to be.'

'Approximately?' I added, hopefully.

'Well,' she said, a look of deep concentration falling across her face, 'I have lived here almost thirty years, and someone had the place before me, so I guess about thirty-five years ago, maybe more.' I felt my knees go weak. That can't be right. Amelia was only twenty-five, and she had lived here as a young child. The old woman must be confused. I smiled at her. I was about to thank her for her time when she added. 'I have some paperwork inside; if you have the time, I can make some tea and show you. I don't get much company nowadays.' A hopeful look sprang into the old woman's eyes.

'That would be very helpful if you're sure it's no trouble,' I said, as I followed her up the path to the door of her ground floor apartment with bated breath.

The apartment was large and airy, with enormous floor-to-ceiling windows. I followed the old lady into her kitchen and watched as she deftly moved around, setting a tea tray with cups, saucers, and a teapot adorned with an old-fashioned knitted cosy. I offered to help, but she refused until it was time to carry the tray to the living room.

'It's my arthritis,' she said apologetically. I can't seem to lift anything heavy these days.' I took hold of the tray and followed her into the living room, placing it on a coffee table in front of two huge comfy armchairs. Light flooded the room.

'What a beautiful home you have,' I said with complete honesty. I wasn't surprised she had lived here a long time, although I doubted it had been as long as she remembered.

'Yes, I insisted on having a ground floor apartment; I love the garden, you see; it's my happy place,' she smiled before continuing. 'I can't garden like I used to, and I have a young man who comes to help out a couple of times a week, but I still enjoy the outdoor space.' She moved over to a bureau standing on the far wall of the living room. The oak desk was intricately carved, and it had a drop-down leather-bound hinged writing space. The old lady opened one of three drawers underneath and pulled out a box file. She carried it over to me and carefully placed it on my lap.

'It's all in there,' she said. I opened the box to reveal contracts, deeds and solicitor's letters. I scanned the contract and read it out loud.

'Mr and Mrs Lowther,' I said. Glancing up, I noticed the old lady smiling broadly.

'That's my husband and me,' she said, a look of love in her eyes. 'He's been dead ten years now.' I looked at the date on the contract and was confused. I checked the address and then studied the date again. There was no mistaking it. The apartment I was sat in was signed over to Mr and Mrs Lowther twenty-nine years ago. Mrs Lowther's memory hadn't let her down after all. She was as sharp as a new pin. I didn't understand it. How could Amelia have lived here with Miles and her mother? Had they only lived in an apartment, not the whole house? Maybe the investigator I had hired had got things wrong?

'How many apartments are there here?' I asked.

'Just eight, my dear. They are all quite large. The developer could have got many more in, but I think he was aiming for the more elite clientele,' she laughed as if she had just cracked a joke, and I laughed with her. 'There is a list of all past and future residents,' she said, nodding at the box file on my knee.

I rummaged around a little more and plucked out the list she was referring to. I scanned the list quickly and then again, more slowly, making sure I hadn't missed anything. There was nothing on the list that indicated that Amelia, Miles or her mother had lived here. I was just about to replace the list in the box when something caught my eye. I glanced again, shocked, as the name Mr Jameson sprang up from the page. Miles had lived here! I checked the dates; something was amiss. Amelia was twenty-five, and she had moved down here with Miles and her mother when she was ten or thereabouts, but this document stated that Miles had lived here more than twenty years ago, which would have meant that Amelia was only five. That wasn't right.

'Something caught your eye?' Mrs Lowther asked. She was much more astute than I had given her credit for initially; nothing appeared to get past her.

'Yes, I have just recognised the name I was looking for, Mr Jameson.'

'Ah, Miles! What a lovely man!' My blood ran cold as I looked at the little old lady sitting opposite me. She had known Miles.

'You knew him?' I asked incredulously. She laughed.

'Yes, of course I did; those were the days when neighbours spoke to one another, not like now, when no one has the time to speak, always in a rush.' She said with sadness in her voice. I wanted to know more.

'Did he live here alone?' I asked optimistically.

'No,' my heart sank as she said the word. 'He had a lady living with him. Her name was Katrina. I don't think they were married, though,' she added a little wickedly as if this was something unheard of, but then I suppose in her day, it wasn't the given thing to do. I couldn't tell her I was Miles's wife. She wouldn't have understood. How could she when I didn't understand myself?

'What happened to him, do you know?' I asked.

'Well, let me see, I don't really know the ins and outs because it all happened quite quickly. There was some sort of tragedy, and Miles moved out.' The cancer, I thought, recalling that Amelia had said her mother had succumbed to cancer. 'Katrina left shortly afterwards, and the apartment was put on the market. I never saw either of them again.' Her voice was sad, and I saw tears in her eyes. 'A young married couple bought the apartment, but they didn't stay long. There have been many people in that particular apartment over the years, which is a bad sign, I think. Maybe it's an omen, an unhappy place; who knows?' she shrugged her shoulders.

I thanked Mrs Lowther for her time. I couldn't express my gratitude enough; she had been very helpful, but her words had raised many questions. The paperwork didn't lie. Miles had indeed lived here with his mistress, but it seems Amelia hadn't. My mind spun as I went over and over the things I had just learned. I headed back to my car. My plans had been to visit this place today and then go to the flat where Miles lived alone tomorrow, but after the information I had gleaned from Mrs Lowther, I felt a sudden urge to dig deeper. Things didn't add up, and I wasn't sure I could put off the urgency of finding out more until tomorrow.

I reached my car and climbed behind the wheel. I took a deep breath. Why was Amelia lying? What did she have to gain by pretending she had lived down here with Miles and her mother? I started the engine and headed inland to the address the private investigator had given me. The address Miles had rented after leaving Amelia and her mother. The drive was an easy one with little traffic.

I pulled up outside a sterile-looking building. A square block of bricks with tiny windows and absolutely no character. It looked completely out of place in the village. The apartments where Mrs Lowther lived were much more appealing than this, and I couldn't imagine Miles being happy living here. According to Amelia, Miles had moved here when her mother had got sick with cancer, but then I wasn't in any mood to believe anything that Amelia had said. After all, she had lied about living here herself, so who knows what other untruths she had told me. I glanced again at the address the private investigator had given me. I pushed the intercom button for apartment 3C and waited patiently. After what seemed like forever, I heard a crackle and then a soft, croaky voice.

'Hello,'

'Hello, I'm sorry to bother you. I'm afraid I have a rather strange request; I'm looking for some information about someone who used to live here, Miles Jameson.' I felt certain I heard a sharp intake of breath before a long silence. Had the person at the other end of the intercom gone away?

I was just about to press the button again when the

voice asked, 'Who are you?'

Without thinking, I said, 'Kate, my name is Kate Jameson.'

Another sharp intake of breath and then a long pause. This time, I waited patiently, allowing the person inside to digest what I had just said and praying that they knew Miles. After what felt like forever, the voice spoke again.

'Come in,' it was more a demand than a request, and I pushed the door open at the sound of the release button.

I walked slowly along the corridor, looking at the numbers on the apartment doors. It reminded me of a cheap motel, the ones you see on the second-rate American films on Netflix. It wasn't the kind of place I associated with Miles. I was beginning to wonder if I knew Miles at all. It had been a long time since I had seen him, decades. Had he really changed that much, or had I never known him at all? I reached the door of 3C, but before I could knock, the door swung open to reveal a lady as old, if not older than Mrs Lowther. She beckoned me inside, and I duly stepped forward, allowing her to close the door behind me.

The inside of the apartment was much more pleasant than the outside. It wasn't large, but it was comfortable and had a homely, if rather tired, feel to it.

'Can I get you anything?' the old lady asked, 'Tea? Coffee?' I felt sure this lady knew Miles, and if I was correct, I had a lot of questions for her, so I figured accepting her offer of a drink would be a wise move.

'Coffee would be lovely if it's not too much trouble,' I said as light-heartedly as possible.

'No trouble at all. I was just about to make one for myself anyway.' I watched as the old lady shuffled to the kitchen using a walking frame.

'Can I do anything to help?' I asked, following her.

'No, it's fine. There is still life in the old dog,' she chuckled as she reached for a couple of mugs. She filled a jug with milk from the fridge and popped it into the microwave. Once she heard the ping indicating the microwave had finished, she removed the jug and poured the milk, with surprisingly steady hands, onto the instant coffee granules she had added to each mug.

'Sugar?' she asked. I shook my head and took the mugs from her grasp. I followed her as she retraced her steps to the living room and settled into one of the armchairs facing the fire. Despite the temperature outside, the fire was lit, and I could feel myself becoming hot and sweaty before I had even started to ask any questions.

'So, Kate Jameson, you say,' she asked, beckoning me to sit down. I sat in the armchair opposite her and nodded. 'You're Miles's wife, then?' I was astounded that she knew who I was. I had never met this woman before, didn't know her name, and yet not only did she know who Miles was, but she also knew that I had been married to him despite the fact that he had left me a long time ago for another woman and he moved down here to live with her.

'Don't look so shocked. Of course, I knew Miles was married. I don't approve of what he did or how he did it, but well, there's not much point in dwelling on things now, is there?' I wasn't sure how to respond. This woman before me must be at least eighty years old; she was slow on her feet, but like Mrs Lowther, her mind was sharp. Maybe it's something in the air down here on the south coast that makes people live forever, I thought a little wistfully.

'How do you know Miles?' I asked. The woman

chuckled.

'He was my nephew, my dear.' She watched as the shock spread over my face. Was she telling the truth? Miles had never mentioned her, and she hadn't attended our wedding. I think she read my thoughts. 'We were never a close family; we all drifted apart when we were growing up, what with one thing and another. I moved abroad for the early years of my marriage and came back to England when my husband died. I wasn't in England when you and Miles married, and well, I'm afraid I'm too old and frail to travel far, so I couldn't attend his funeral. I was sorry about that. I'm the only one left, you see, all the family are dead now, there's no one to keep the family alive after me.

There was a true sadness in her voice, and I thought perhaps she had forgotten about Amelia. I appreciated that Amelia wasn't a boy, and many people, particularly of this generation, considered only males to be heirs, but well, things have changed now. Amelia might not be my daughter, but she is Miles's, so someone is left. I drank my coffee in silence, the milk hot against my tongue. The old lady continued to talk. I think she was enjoying reminiscing. She told me her name was Grace and that she and her husband had not been blessed with children. She explained how she had rekindled her relationship with Miles when he had contacted her after moving down here with Katrina.

'It was such a tragedy. Don't get me wrong, I don't condone what Miles did to you,' she said apologetically, 'but no one deserves that,' I nodded, remembering how Katrina had got cancer.

'Yes, it was dreadful,' I said. Grace looked at me aghast.

'You know?' she asked incredulously.

'About the cancer? Yes, Amelia told me,' I replied. Grace's face turned ashen, and I thought she was about to have a heart attack. She clutched her chest, and I got up to help her. She waved me away as if I were a small child being scalded.

'Cancer? No one had cancer; I'm talking about the child, Miles's child,' she said. Her words were confusing, and I had to think hard to understand what she was saying. What did she mean no one had cancer? Amelia's mother had cancer and died; Amelia had told me that herself. Maybe Grace wasn't aware of it, though, I thought, but then what did she mean when she said no one deserved that? If she wasn't talking about the cancer, what was she talking about?

'I didn't know Miles had fathered a child until after the funeral,' I told Grace. 'I admit it was a shock, meeting her like that, out of the blue. It would have been better if Miles had told me himself.'

This time, Grace's head flopped onto her chest, and her breathing took on a shallow rasping sound as she gulped for air. I was really worried. Her face had turned grey, her mouth drooping, as she motioned towards a packet of tablets on a shelf above the fireplace. I grabbed the box, quickly read the label, popped two tablets and handed them to Grace along with the now-cold coffee. She gulped them down, swallowing hard. It was some minutes before she had regained her composure enough to continue.

'I don't think you understand, my dear. Miles did father a child, yes, but he had a son, not a daughter.' Grace's voice was a whisper, but her words came out as a roar. This time, it was me who felt faint; my head spun, and

I thought I was about to collapse. I sat forward in the chair, taking deep breaths, trying to slow my breathing. I felt sick, unsure whether I could control the bile threatening to move up my throat. I swallowed hard; the vile, acrid taste lingered in my mouth, and I wished I still had some coffee left, even if it was stone cold. A son? Miles had a son? Then, who the hell was Amelia, and why had she told me that she was Miles's daughter? Could Miles have had two children, and Grace wasn't aware of the daughter?

The world seemed to slow down. It took me a good five minutes to refocus, and I appreciated how Grace allowed me to calm down before she continued.

'Henry would have been twenty-five this year,' Grace's words seemed to echo and slur. Would have been? What did she mean? She continued, 'He died when he was five years old, drowned swimming off the pier on the south shore; it was such a dreadful time for everyone. Katrina fell into a deep depression, and Miles could do nothing to help her. He had wanted to move back up north, away from where the tragedy had happened, but Katrina would have none of it. It was understandable that she wanted to remain down here where she felt close to her son, but Miles just couldn't handle it. He moved out and came to live here with me; he blamed himself for what happened to Katrina.'

I didn't dare ask what had happened; I didn't need to. Grace continued, her voice fuelled by necessity now. It was as if she had to tell the story in her own words, in her own time, to someone who would listen. 'We will never know whether he could have saved her, but I guess there would eventually come a time when she was left alone, and that would be when she would do it. She took her own life, you see,' the words hung in the air like a noose swinging from the rafters. I couldn't believe what I was hearing.

Miles had fathered a son, not a daughter. His son was dead; Amelia was very much alive. Katrina had taken her own life; she hadn't died of cancer. It didn't make sense; none of what I was hearing made any sense at all. If Amelia wasn't Miles's child, then who the hell was she, and what did she want?

After the initial shock of what Grace had told me had sunk in and I had calmed down, she offered to make us fresh coffee and answer any questions I had. I jumped at the chance of another coffee; the acidic taste of the bile still lingered in my mouth like an unwelcome visitor.

'I can tell this has been a huge shock to you, my dear, and I'm sorry things aren't as you thought, but I am telling you the truth; I don't know who this Amelia woman is, but I can assure you she is not Miles's child. Miles remained single after Henry died. He wanted to move back to be nearer to you. I think he always regretted leaving you. I think he thought losing Henry was God's way of punishing him for the way he treated you. I believe he bought a big house somewhere up north. He put it in trust for Henry, but then, after the accident, it reverted back to being his. He was a very wealthy man but also a very unhappy one.'

I carried the tea tray back to the lounge with fresh mugs of milky coffee and slices of shop-bought cake and chocolate biscuits.

Grace shuffled over to a sideboard and took out a couple of photograph albums. She plonked them on my lap, and I tentatively turned the pages, gazing at the smiling faces of my deceased husband and the little boy who had been so tragically robbed of his life. I felt the tears prick my eyes. My heart clenched as I gazed at Miles's handsome face and the smiling eyes of his young son. Page after page of happy memories of a short life. I turned the pages slowly, looking carefully at each photograph. Some were of family gatherings, and others were just of Henry or Henry and Miles. There was none of Henry with his mother.

'She took them all,' Grace said; this woman had a canny knack of reading my thoughts. I looked at her, my mouth open. 'Katrina, she took all the photos of herself and Henry; she left no trace of herself, and after she had killed herself, Miles found them all burned, just ashes left in the grate.'

I shivered at the thought of a mother ending her life so she could be forever with the son she had lost. I scrutinised the group photographs repeatedly, looking for a sign, anything to shed light on who Amelia might be, but there was nothing. The only child in any of the pictures was Henry. Had Henry lived, he would have been the same age as Amelia is now. Was that just a coincidence? I asked Grace if there were any other children of the same age as Henry, either relatives or friends, but she said there weren't. I asked her who Henry had been playing with on the fateful day he drowned, thinking maybe Amelia had been there too, but Grace told me Henry had been with a nanny who had fallen asleep on the beach when she should have been watching him. It was all so very sad, but it didn't answer the burning questions I had about Amelia.

It was late afternoon before I said my goodbyes and left Grace in peace. I consoled myself that she had been happy talking to me, and she confirmed this by saying that she felt a huge weight had been lifted from her shoulders.

'I somehow knew I had to tell the story to someone,

Kate. I just didn't know who to tell until today. Thank you for stopping by. Try to be happy; Miles wouldn't have wanted you to be sad. He loved you, he really did,' she touched me gently on the hand, and I felt a shiver run down my spine. Isn't this what Amelia and Jean told me?

I hurried back to my car and drove to the hotel. My head was spinning. I just couldn't process all the information I had been told today. I doubted I would ever be able to process it. It was a mixed-up, garbled mess, but in the centre of everything was Amelia and I had no idea where or how she fitted in, but I did know I couldn't ignore the fact that she had wheedled her way into my life pretending to be my dead husband's child.

# Chapter Twenty-Eight

A huge feeling of relief washed over me as I entered my hotel room and closed the door firmly. It had been a difficult day, one I hadn't anticipated, and the things I had discovered threatened my sanity. Miles did have a child, a son, who had died. The child's death had ripped his relationship with Katrina apart. It wasn't surprising. I wondered how any relationship, even the strongest, could survive the sudden death of a child. Had Miles intended to return to me after all, before death caught up with him too? Was he now at peace with Katrina and Henry? What about Amelia? Where did she fit into all of this? Who was she, and what did she want?

I was beginning to think I had opened a huge can of worms, one that I had no idea how to close again. The situation threatened to engulf me. I was terrified. The truths I had uncovered today were explosive. I couldn't just go back home and forget what I had learned. Even if I decided never to speak to Amelia again, it wouldn't alter the fact that she had purposely ingratiated herself into my life. She lied her way into my affections because, whether I wanted to admit it or not, I had started to warm to her a little; that was when I thought she was Miles's child, his flesh and blood. Now that I knew her for what she really was, a cold evil intruder hell-bent on turning my life upside down, all I felt was hatred. I should have trusted my initial instincts. I had known something wasn't right about her; things hadn't stacked up from the start, but as the months went by, I had pushed the thoughts to the back of my mind, blaming them on the grief I felt for the loss of a husband who had betrayed me but who still held a special place in my heart.

I lay down on the bed and closed my eyes; images of Amelia sprang up in front of my face. She was clawing at my hair, gripping my arms, pulling, scratching, tugging, lunging for me. Her nails were razor-sharp and painted blood red. My eyes flew open, and I could feel the sweat pooling on my skin. I glanced at my watch; I had been asleep for just over an hour. I tried to calm my beating heart; it's just a dream, I told myself, nothing more than an overtired imagination. I stripped off and climbed into the shower, knowing that Amelia wasn't just a dream, though; she was very real, and she had to be dealt with.

I stood in the shower for more than fifteen minutes, feeling the hot water pound my aching muscles, releasing the tension in my shoulders, back, and neck. I closed my eyes and let the water wash over me, trying to flood out the awful memories of the day. I was tired and hungry, but I knew I couldn't face going down to the restaurant tonight. I dried myself, slipped into the fluffy bathroom and ordered room service. I needed to make plans and get things straight in my mind, but first, I needed food and rest.

When my meal arrived, I ate it at the table by the window, looking out onto the cobbled street below at the people rushing about, laughing, shouting, enjoying the late evening sun. They didn't appear to have a care in the world whilst I sat in my room drowning in despair. Not knowing what to do next. Who could I speak to? Who could help me? I went over and over the day's events, always coming to the same conclusion. No one could help me. I had no one. I suddenly realised that I had been alone for a long time. Decades of looking out for myself. I had survived this long without anyone by my side, and I could survive much longer. I just needed to come up with a plan to deal with Amelia. I didn't have a clue what I would do at this point, but I did know that only I could deal with her.

I finished my meal and pushed the plate away from me. I hadn't tasted a single mouthful, but the food had satisfied my hunger, and for that, I was grateful. I could now concentrate on making plans for Amelia. Firstly, I had to find out who she was and then what she wanted. I had to know why she had targeted me. Did she hold a grudge against me for some reason, or was she simply a cold-hearted opportunist? I wondered if she was on to me. Did she know I was here looking for evidence against her? I hadn't received any more texts from her, and I wondered if she had visited my house and knew I wasn't at home. I figured she would have to have called on several occasions to come to the conclusion that I was away rather than just out, and as I had only been gone four days, I hoped that she wasn't too far ahead in her chain of thoughts.

I needed the upper hand. I wanted to take her by surprise, not give her the chance to think up answers to my questions. I didn't want to hear any more lies. I was booked into the hotel until Saturday morning, but I didn't intend to stay that long. Not now, not with everything I had found out today. I had to get back home, and the sooner I could confront Amelia, the better. I would probably have to pay for the room for the whole week, but that didn't matter; nothing mattered now except getting back home.

I climbed into bed. I needed a good night's sleep. Tomorrow, I had a long drive ahead of me, and I needed to be refreshed and ready.

It turned out to be a long night. I spent hours tossing and turning, unable to drift off to sleep. I went over and over the conversations I had had with Mrs Lowther and Miles's aunt, Grace. *Miles did father a child, yes, but he had a son, not a daughter.* I heard the words repeatedly. *A son, not a daughter.* Eventually, I succumbed to sleep. My body surrendered to exhaustion.

That was when the dream returned. The one where Amelia reached for me with outstretched blood-red fingernails. She grabbed my hair, pulling me close, the razor-sharp nails digging deep into my eye sockets, trying to gouge out my eyes. I felt her tear at my skin, clawing her way to my heart. I sat bolt upright in bed, stifling the scream rising in my throat. I was soaked in sweat. I could taste the saltiness on my upper lip and felt my hair plastered to my face. I pushed the pillows behind me, supporting my back in a sitting position. I would not go back to sleep tonight. I was too terrified to close my eyes.

I woke the next morning with a stiff neck and a pain in my back. I was still sitting up, supported by the pillows, but my head had tilted sideways, causing stiffness in my neck. I gently rolled my head from side to side, listening to the tendons crack. I forced myself to get out of bed and went to run a bath. A long soak would help ease the pain I was feeling. I added a generous dollop of oil to the bath and eased myself into the hot water. I instantly felt revived. The tension in my muscles relaxed, and I allowed the water to wash over me, soothing my aching limbs. I leaned back and immersed myself completely in the water. I felt as if I was floating. I closed my eyes.

Suddenly, from nowhere, the blood-red fingers grabbed my hair, pulling me down, deeper and deeper into the water. I couldn't breathe; my mouth and nostrils filled with the oily bath water as I thrashed about, trying in earnest to free myself. My heart pounded. My chest was heavy, and I could feel the life beginning to drain from my terrified body. Then, instantly, my eyes flicked open, and I blinked rapidly. I gasped for breath as my face burst through the water. I gulped in the air, my breath fast and uncontrolled. On shaking legs, I climbed out of the bath, almost slipping on the deluge of bath water I had splashed onto the floor. I grabbed a towel and sat on the tiled floor, shaking. Had I fallen asleep? Was that a dream? Did I imagine it, or was Amelia here? I sobbed silently into the towel. Was I going mad?

I must have sat on the bathroom floor for a long time. When I finally came to my senses, I was cold and shivering, my body covered with goosebumps, and my hair, oily from the bath water, had begun to dry in slick tendrils across my face. I stood up and caught a glimpse of myself in the mirror. My eyes were haunted, my face grey and gaunt. I had to get a grip. None of this was real. It was all in my imagination.

I mopped up the water on the bathroom floor, trying not to slip on the oily patches. I needed to wash my hair, but the thought of taking another bath terrified me, so I stepped into the shower and allowed the water to wash away the oils and warm up my body. I quickly washed my hair. Once I was dressed and had dried my hair, I felt a little better, but I wasn't sure I could face breakfast amongst the other guests, so I opted again for room service. I was becoming a recluse, I thought as I phoned my order to the kitchen. My food arrived within fifteen minutes, and I tucked in heartily, surprising myself how hungry I was. The smell of the bacon and eggs was a welcome relief to the bath oils that still lined my nostrils. I didn't think I would dare take a bath again after this morning.

I finished breakfast and packed my things in my suitcase before going downstairs to reception. A middle-aged gentleman was on duty this morning. He looked up as I approached and smiled broadly.

'I am afraid I am going to have to check out early,' I said without meeting his gaze. I didn't like lying, and I felt uneasy.

'Oh, that's a shame,' he said, sounding genuinely sorry, 'I hope it's not because of the accommodation?'

'No, not at all; the hotel is wonderful, and I really wish I could stay longer.' I spieled out my well-rehearsed excuse of how my mother had been taken ill and I had to get back to care for her. 'I am happy to pay until the end of the week,' I finished, hoping this would make up for me vacating the room early.

'Not at all, Mrs Jameson. We will just charge you for your actual stay, and we hope to see you again very soon.' I thanked him, feeling pleased that good customer service was still very much alive in this part of the country. This was how you got repeat customers, I thought. This establishment didn't need to rip people off. After dealing with the pressing matters at home, I made a mental note to return and finish my holiday.

I had settled my bill, packed my car and began the long journey back home. If I needed to, I could stop somewhere overnight; however, I intended to try to do the entire journey in one trip. I felt a sudden urge to get back to where I belonged. I wanted to sleep in my own bed, surrounded by familiar things, in the house I felt safe in.

The first hour of the journey was frustratingly slow. It seemed that everyone had suddenly decided to descend on the south coast, and I felt annoyed and disheartened. However, as I got further away from the tourist traps and approached the New Forest and beyond, the traffic eased off, and the journey became easier.

I reached the lane to my house at just after nine pm and immediately felt myself begin to relax. The sun was just beginning to set, and the place looked surreal. I had only been away for a few days, but I had missed it enormously. Nowhere was prettier than this, I thought, as I drove slowly down the lane, pulled up outside my house and climbed out of the car.

I walked around to the back door, unlocked it and pushed it open. I stepped inside, dragging my suitcase behind me. The house was warm and humid. It smelt like it had been shut up for months rather than a few days. I pulled back the curtains and threw open the windows and the patio doors, immediately feeling the cool night air whoosh inside, taking with it the stale warm air of the past few days. I was pleased to be home.

I headed for the kettle, then changed my mind, reaching inside the fridge instead and taking a bottle of wine from the top shelf. I plucked a glass from the cupboard and returned to the garden. I was exhausted, and my body ached, but I knew I wouldn't be able to sleep. I settled in the lover's seat and poured myself a glass of wine. I had earned this after the long drive. I took a deep gulp, holding the cold liquid in my mouth, savouring its fruity taste before swallowing. I looked around me. The grass had scorched in the short time that I had been away, a testament to the hot sun and lack of rain. A rustle in the hedgerow caught my attention, and I turned to see a couple of tiny rabbits running amongst the rose bushes. I smiled as I watched their antics, completely oblivious to my presence. I loved how nature felt at home in my garden, safe and secure knowing that no one would harm them under my watch.

The past four days had revealed so much, but I was still unsure how to begin unravelling things. I had wanted answers, but now that I had them, I wasn't at all sure what to do with the information. I felt the phone in my pocket buzz and remembered I had switched it to silent when I was driving. I glanced at the screen, and Amelia's name popped up. I read the text, almost dropping the device as I did so.

'Welcome home.' I frantically got to my feet, looking all around me like a terrified animal. Other than the rabbits who were still playing in the undergrowth, I could see or hear no one. I snatched up the bottle and headed back indoors. I no longer felt safe. Amelia knew I had been away, but more importantly, she knew I had returned home. She must be watching me. Had she followed me all the way to the south coast? Did she know I had met with Mrs Lowther and Grace? I felt my palms become sweaty as I quickly placed the bottle and glass on the counter. I wiped my hands on the side of my trousers.

Walking from room to room, I rapidly shut all the windows and locked the door. I won't let Amelia frighten me. This is my home. It had been my home for a long time before Amelia came here, and I will not allow her to drive me away. I glanced across at my suitcase, which I had abandoned on entering the house, and went over to unfasten it.

I busied myself, filling the washing machine with my dirty laundry and re-hanging the clean items in my wardrobe. I wanted to do something. I needed to take my mind off Amelia, but I couldn't help glancing at the screen occasionally, expecting another message. None came.

Just after midnight, I went upstairs and climbed into bed. I lay there for what seemed like hours. My eyes open, my mind racing. I couldn't sleep. I was too scared to close my eyes.

# Chapter Twenty-Nine

At some point during the night, I must have succumbed and finally fallen asleep. I hadn't dreamt of anything, and I woke the next morning feeling refreshed and wide awake. I yawned and on realising that I was now back home in my own bed, I allowed myself to sink back onto the pillow and snatch another ten minutes under the duvet. It was early, not quite seven, and I figured I deserved a little lie-in this morning after all the driving I had done yesterday. However, I have never been an idle person, and lying in bed wasn't easy for me.

There is always something to be done, and this morning, I wanted to tackle the garden. The borders needed weeding and some of the plants were crying out to be watered. I forfeited my shower, deciding to take one after I had tackled the garden. Instead, I made myself a coffee and, placing it on the patio table to cool, I set about with my fork and trowel, despite the fact that it was still early to be working in the garden.

The feeling of being watched that had crept over me last night still lingered as I went about my gardening; however, in the early morning sunshine, things seemed a lot less sinister and last night's fear had subsided. I knew this place like the back of my hand. I knew every field, tree and bush, every plant and blade of grass. Nothing and no one could hide from me here.

As I tended the flower beds, I considered my next move. Should I contact Amelia or wait until she gets in touch with me? Her text yesterday lay unanswered, a sort of veiled threat, tempting me to reply, initiating a response. Did she want me to turn on her? Was that her intention? Did she want to tease out an accusation so she could pounce on me and pull me to shreds?

I wouldn't allow her to control the situation. Whether she had knowledge of my trip or not was irrelevant. She wasn't privy to the conversations I had had with Mrs Lowther or with Grace. She may, in fact, be none the wiser, which is probably why she was goading me into a confession. No, I would take things slowly from now. Do things on my own terms and in my own time.

I would wait until Amelia contacted me again.

I wasn't expecting to have to wait long for Amelia to make her next move, and she proved this to me a couple of days later. I sensed the urgency in her text this time. I figured she had become unsettled when she couldn't contact me at home. I felt certain she knew I had been away for a few days; her welcome home text indicated as much, but I still wasn't convinced she knew where I had been or why. I was worried that if I continued to ignore her, she might put two and two together, and if she did suspect that I was onto her, she could become elusive. I didn't want her to retreat; I wanted her out in the open where I could see her, and then, when the time was right, I would make my move.

Life had dealt me a poor hand lately, but I could still win this game; I had to win it; I just needed to keep my cards close to my chest for just a little while longer. The familiar ping of a text message caught my attention as I pegged the last of my washing out on the line to dry. It was another beautiful morning, and the sun was already blisteringly hot. I returned to the kitchen and poured myself a glass of water before heading back out into the garden.

I read the text.

'Why are you ignoring me? I just want us to be friends.' The message was void of any kind of emotion. No friendly kisses, no requests to meet up, just a blunt question. I hadn't ignored her; I had simply not responded. In my mind, there was a difference. The messages she sent to me when I was on the south coast were angry and accusatory. She hadn't given me a chance to respond before unceremoniously dumping me. Then, on my return home, she had simply welcomed me back. That message hadn't warranted a reply.

I drank the water, allowing it to dampen the inside of my mouth, which had suddenly turned dry, my lips sticking to my teeth. I needed to respond to her this time, but I also had to be very careful about what I said. Should I admit I had been away? It seemed ridiculous not to when she clearly knew I had. Maybe I should ask her how she knew I had been away. I shook my head. No, that wouldn't be a good idea. I didn't want her to think I was accusing her of anything, not yet. I didn't want her on the defensive. I carefully typed my reply and then pressed send.

'Sorry,' I said. 'I had to go away for a few days, but I'm back home now.' *But you already know that, don't you?* I thought.

'Hope your trip went well? Let's meet up, and you can tell me all about it!' came the reply seconds after I had sent mine. *Yes, let's!* I thought wickedly. *I can tell you all about my little trip down south, and then you can tell me who you really are, you lying little bitch!*

'Sounds like a plan,' I texted back.

'Where? When?' She was eager to see me, that was clear. She was always probing, asking questions, wanting to know things that didn't concern her. I needed to have a logical plan in my mind before meeting with her, though, so I had to bide my time.

I had a final solicitor's appointment that afternoon, and then my diary was free. I texted Amelia back and suggested she come for lunch the following Sunday. That would give me three days to decide what I was going to do. Amelia accepted the invitation without hesitation. I smiled inwardly as I put my phone back in my pocket.

I finished the jobs around the house, showered and changed before heading into town for my meeting with Mr Connor.

The meeting went quickly, and I was back outside in the hot sunshine less than fifteen minutes later, clutching a brown envelope tightly. I deliberated whether to stop at the café for a bite to eat; however, not wanting to risk bumping into Amelia, who seemed to turn up like the proverbial bad penny every time I ventured into town, I decided against it. The contents of the envelope I had just received from the solicitor would be revealed to Amelia at the right time, but now wasn't that time so I got back into my car and drove home.

I made a couple of telephone calls and then concentrated on fixing myself a late lunch and a coffee. I checked my phone to see if Amelia had left any more messages, and after seeing that she hadn't, headed outside to enjoy my sandwich in the sunshine.

I spent the next couple of days reviewing things in my mind. I bought myself a notepad and jotted things down. It helped me to make notes of what I had learned. It enabled me to try to put things in order and get a perspective on what I needed to find out from Amelia. I knew she wasn't my dead husband's child, but I still didn't know who she was or what she wanted.

By Saturday, I had more or less perfected my plan. I knew what I was going to say and, more importantly, what I was going to ask, and I wasn't going to let Amelia lie her way out of anything. I had considered what her responses might be, the most obvious being that Mrs Lowther or Grace had been lying, but why on earth would they? They didn't know that I would visit them. They didn't have anything to gain by lying, whereas Amelia clearly did; I just had to find out what.

## Chapter Thirty

Sunday came around quicker than I had hoped. I woke early, a feeling of anxiousness deep in the pit of my stomach. It wasn't simply apprehension. It was fear. Today was the day that I planned to confront Amelia. It had to be done, and I didn't want or need any more time. I was ready for the confrontation, but I wasn't expecting to feel like this.

I had been running on adrenalin for the past few days. I had been excited, ready to take on Amelia and her lies. I had perfected my plan, rehearsed what I would say over and over again, and I was word perfect. This morning, however, things were different. My confidence had vanished, replaced with a feeling of dread. What if things didn't go according to plan? What if Amelia was on to me?

I wondered if this was how people felt before performing before a crowd. Wondering if they were indeed good enough to be put on a pedestal by an admiring audience. Did they anticipate that things might go wrong, that they would be ridiculed or heckled? Was it possible that nothing and no one was fool-proof; that anything could go wrong at any time, no matter how well-rehearsed things were?

I can do this, I thought, as I climbed out of bed and walked into the shower. The initial burst of water was ice cold and I screamed inwardly, gritting my teeth as the cold penetrated my skin. Then the hot water kicked in, taking the place of the cold, dousing my goosebumps and replacing them with a feeling of warm bliss. I stayed in the shower for a long time, allowing the steam to penetrate my pores and reach into my soul. I let the hot water calm my nerves as I told myself that everything would be alright. I had this. I knew exactly what I had to do, and I could do it perfectly. I turned the shower off and stepped onto the fluffy bathmat, which absorbed the droplets of water as they dripped from my body. I wrapped myself in a huge towel and walked over to the mirror, which was coated in steam. I wiped the mirror, glimpsing my reflection as I did so. I smiled back at the confident woman. Today was the day.

I dressed, dried my hair and applied some make-up before heading downstairs. I made myself a coffee and shoved some bread in the toaster. Lunch was going to be a roast. I still didn't know what Amelia preferred to eat, but today, I didn't care. It wouldn't matter if she ate it or not. I spent the morning preparing the meal, peeling and chopping vegetables, mixing batter for the Yorkshire puddings and perfecting my gravy.

Amelia arrived at exactly twelve-thirty. I imagined her sitting in her car or hovering outside the door so that she could knock at exactly the right time – not a minute early or a minute late. I could feel my hatred for her rising in my throat as I remembered the conversations I had had with Grace and Mrs Lowther. I plastered a smile on my face and flung open the door. It took all my strength not to smack her square in the face the minute I saw her sickly, sweet smile.

'Amelia, hi,' I said, forcing myself to lean forward and

air-kiss her on the cheek, the vile smell of her putrid perfume lingering close to my nostrils. I immediately threw her off guard, and she stepped backwards slightly. Calm down, I told myself. Don't overdo it.

Amelia held out her hands, a bottle of red wine in one and a bunch of flowers in the other. I thanked her and took the offerings, annoyed that she had brought red wine when she obviously knew that I only drank white. Was this her way of provoking me, or was she really just so thoughtless? I opted for the former as I opened a cupboard and took out a vase. I filled it with water and arranged the flowers. Taking them into the conservatory, I placed them in the centre of the table I had set for our lunch.

'Lunch smells lovely,' Amelia said.

'It will be ready in ten minutes,' I replied. 'I thought we could eat first and then have a catch-up.'

'Good idea,' Amelia smiled broadly, showing her perfectly straight and gleamingly white teeth. I busied myself cutting the beef, watching as the blood seeped onto the plate as I carefully glided the razor-sharp knife through the meat.

'Hope you like your beef rare?' I asked, not remotely caring whether she did or not. I glanced up and thought I saw a slight grimace on her otherwise smiling face. I dished the vegetables and potatoes straight onto the plate. Normally, I would have placed them in serving dishes and allowed my guests to serve themselves, but today was different. Amelia was here out of necessity rather than pleasure, and I really couldn't be bothered going to the additional effort of trying to make a good impression. I wasn't interested in the slightest about making a good impression; I was interested in extracting a confession from her. I was interested in finding out who she was and why she had ingratiated herself into my life through lies and deceit. Whether she ate her lunch or not was completely inconsequential. It wasn't as if I had poisoned it and, therefore, needed her to eat it. The very thought made me smirk, and I felt Amelia become tense and uncomfortable beside me.

'Why don't you take a seat?' I suggested. 'I can bring the plates through.' Amelia did as she was told without saying a word. She didn't ask if there was anything she could do; she simply obeyed. I took the plates through to the conservatory and laid them down on the table, putting one in front of Amelia before retreating to the kitchen to collect the gravy boat and a bottle of white wine that I had been chilling in the fridge. Then, quickly noticing the bottle of red that Amelia had brought with her, I tucked it under my arm. I sat down opposite Amelia. She looked a little pale, and I asked her if she was alright.

'Yes, I'm fine,' she said unconvincingly.

I could feel the apprehension in her voice. She was like a startled rabbit. Has she figured something out? Was she on to me? Did she realise I had an ulterior motive for inviting her here today?

Too late, my dear, I thought, as I splashed gravy onto my plate, allowing it to soak into the mashed potatoes and perfectly risen Yorkshire pudding. I had expected my own appetite to be somewhat subdued, knowing what I had in mind for Amelia, and I was surprised at how hungry I was. I tucked in, savouring every mouthful. The meat was cooked to perfection, even if I had to say it myself in the absence of any compliments from Amelia, who was sitting sulkily, pushing the food around her plate in a rather pitiful gesture.

'Are you not hungry?' I asked, feeling slightly annoyed that I had put so much effort in just to see Amelia sit like a petulant child across from me, having not even tasted one mouthful. Maybe I should have just baked a bloody Victoria sponge, I thought sarcastically.

'I'm sorry, you must think I am so ungrateful. You've gone to so much trouble.' Her apology was lost on me. I no longer believed a single word that fell from her perfectly formed mouth.

'Not at all. Don't eat it on my account,' I replied, stuffing another piece of rare beef into my mouth. I could taste the blood on my tongue. I licked my lips and stared across at Amelia, unblinking. She sat motionless, her eyes glazed. I had absolutely no idea what she was thinking, but her eyes were full of fear. She was frightened! Good, I thought, that was exactly how I wanted her to feel.

Gone was the self-assured, confident woman with her lying spiteful tongue. In its place sat someone who had reached the end of the road, someone who had been found out, and yet, so far, I hadn't said anything. I was a little disappointed. It all felt a little too easy. I wanted to confront her, get her to admit her deceit, listen to her apologise, and enjoy seeing her squirm. Yet here she was, already defeated, already given up, and the fight hadn't even started. What a let-down. I had given her more credit than this. All my preparation had been for nothing.

I pushed my plate to one side. My own appetite was now sated, and I stared at Amelia.

'So,' I said. 'Why don't you start at the beginning and tell me everything,' I suggested, my face poker straight. Amelia fidgeted in her chair. I couldn't see her hands as she had them in her lap, but I imagined she was wringing them tightly. She smiled nervously.

'I don't know what you mean,' she began.

I laughed. A long low guttural laugh, and I saw Amelia flinch as if I had slapped her sharply across the face. I raised my hands above the table and clapped slowly, loudly, and rhythmically. She was good. I had to give her that. Even now, she was trying to deny it.

'Well done, my dear,' I said, 'but you must do better than that. Now, tell me who you *really* are.'

'You know who I am,' she began looking more and more uneasy by the second. 'Amelia, Miles's daughter.'

'Amelia, Amelia, Amelia.' I said her name repeatedly as if hearing it for the first time and not quite sure what I thought of it. I spat her name at her a fourth time as I yelled, 'AMELIA.' She flinched. 'We both know that you are not Miles's child.'

Amelia suddenly pushed back her chair and stood up, her worst fears having been laid bare. She knew now that I was on to her. 'Sit down!' I shouted, my fist thumping the table as I did so. I heard the plates lift up before crashing back down again, the cutlery rattling like broken teeth. I expected her to fight, run, scream, cry, anything, but she simply sat back down in her chair, defeated.

'I'm sorry,' she said in a quiet voice. I glared at her, rage escalating in my blood.

'Is that it?' I screamed at her. 'You're bloody sorry?' I watched as she flinched and sank further back in the chair, trying earnestly to allow it to swallow her up. 'You ingratiate yourself into my life at a time when I have just lost my husband and pretend to be his child?' I spat the words at her, incredulous, once more as I listened to myself say out loud what she had done. 'What exactly is it that you want?' I asked, watching her carefully for any sign that she might decide to make a run for it now that she had been found out. She wouldn't be able to get far as I had locked the door when excusing myself to use the bathroom, but nonetheless, I didn't want to have to fight her physically. She was much younger than me, and I have no doubt that her strength, if needed, would be greater; however, I was fuelled by anger, and my anger wouldn't dissipate anytime soon. I was surprised at the sudden venom she showed. My questioning her about what she wanted seemed to spark something fresh inside her.

'You really don't know?' she asked suspiciously.

I shook my head. I knew she wasn't who she said she was, I knew she wasn't a relative of Miles's, and I knew she had lied to me for months, but no, I didn't have any idea what she actually wanted or who, in fact, she was.

'You talk about Miles as if he was your dearly beloved husband when you hadn't seen him for years. He didn't want you; he didn't love you; he despised you; that's why he left you, and yet here you are, accepting his house and his money as if you have a right to it all!'

This time, I felt the sharp sting of Amelia's words, but I held my head high in defiance. She didn't know anything about my relationship with Miles. She had no right to comment on something that didn't concern her. Something that was dear to me.

'He was still my husband, and he wanted me to have his possessions,' I said defiantly. 'I loved him.'

Amelia laughed, and I felt a sudden rush of alarm as she appeared to have found her credence once more. She was no longer coming across as meek and mild; she had taken the upper hand, and I couldn't allow her to take control of the situation. 'So, who the bloody hell are you?' I screamed at her. Amelia continued to stare at me, a blank expression on her face except for the smile. A twisted, evil smile that appeared to slice her face in half. I imagined her jaw hanging loose, unable to close, and I shuddered.

I waited for what seemed like a very long time, expecting Amelia to start explaining who she was and what she wanted, but she just sat there staring at me. Then, just as I thought she wouldn't tell me anything, she suddenly snapped out of her trance and began to speak. Her voice was slow and quiet, and despite the incredulous words flowing from her mouth, her tone was dull and monotonous.

I had to strain at times to hear what she was telling me, but I wasn't sure if that was because of the volume of her voice or simply because I was having difficulty processing her words. She was describing Miles, my dead husband, the man I had loved my entire life but I didn't recognise him. Had I painted an unreal picture of him over the years? Had I allowed my memory to dull and my thoughts to become egotistical? Isn't that what we do over time, replace the sad thoughts, the things that hurt us, with happy memories? Perhaps that was what I had done. Maybe that was how I survived. I had managed to paint a melodramatic picture of my time with Miles. One that was far from the truth, and now I was simply living a lie, having told myself that Miles had gone to the grave still loving me.

I tried to focus on what Amelia was telling me. Her voice was angry, and she intermittently stifled sobs as she told me her story.

# Chapter Thirty-One

Amelia had been a young child of perhaps seven or eight when her mother had first met Miles. Miles was living with Katrina at the time, but they had already lost their child in tragic circumstances, and their relationship wasn't so much strained as completely broken. Katrina was lost in a world of sadness and despair, grieving the loss of her son, and Miles simply couldn't cope. To be honest, Miles was never good at emotion. Wasn't that why we had drifted apart? I don't recall ever sitting down and discussing anything important with him; he was always vacant.

I berated myself for thinking about Miles and concentrated on what Amelia told me. She was sitting bolt upright on the dining room chair. She looked uncomfortable, and I thought that maybe she was close to leaning too far to the right, and that she might lose her balance and fall onto the floor. I watched her closely. She brought her hands up and clasped them neatly together in front of her on the table as if she were about to pray. She continued her story.

'My mother fell for Miles, hook, line and sinker,' she said, her face taking on a softer glow as she recalled the time fondly. 'Miles used to take us on day trips and treat me to new clothes and toys. It was fun and exciting, and I enjoyed seeing how happy my mother was. We never had much money and always struggled to make ends meet. My mother had been depressed for a long time. I don't recall my father being around, but my mother told me he wasn't a nice person and he hadn't wanted anything to do with me.' Amelia shuddered, her eyes darkening as she continued. 'Anyway, Miles seemed to be the knight in shining armour that we had been waiting for. He loved me; I know he did,' a tear trickled slowly down her cheek. 'Then everything went wrong. One day, we were fine; the next, my mother was a total wreck, crying all the time and screaming at me for no apparent reason. I never saw Miles again, and my mother refused to talk about him except to say that he had returned south. I guess he just dumped her, like my father had done. I don't suppose I will ever know what really happened.'

I waited with bated breath, but Amelia just sat there in silence. I prompted her to continue.

'Where is your mother now?' I asked, but I was almost certain I already knew the answer. This was a tragic situation in more ways than one.

'Dead,' Amelia said, staring straight at me. That was when I noticed how piercing her eyes were. They were the most vivid shade of blue I had ever seen, almost translucent. 'My mother took her own life shortly after Miles left her, and that was when I went to live with my aunt in the big house.'

Her words shocked me to the core, and I felt my heart begin to beat faster. Had I heard her correctly? Did she just say she went to live with her aunt? Is Jean her aunt?

Amelia laughed loudly, a shrill scream that pierced the silence. 'You didn't figure that one out, did you?' she spat at me. 'Not so bloody clever after all!'

I held my breath, trying to take in what Amelia was telling me. It was a mess, a complete fiasco; what had Miles done?

'Yes, my mother, the one your husband decided to have a bit of fun with and then discard like rubbish, was Jean's younger sister. I think Miles thought he could do what he wanted with her because she was just a hired hand like Jean, someone to pick up and throw down whenever the fancy took him. His marriage to you was a distant memory; his relationship with Katrina was in tatters, and his son was dead. He had nothing. But it didn't stop him from ruining more lives.'

I could hear Amelia ranting on; the vitriol in her voice was clearly audible, and her hatred for Miles was clear and apparent. She blamed him for her mother's death, of that there was no doubt, and maybe she was right. Certainly, Miles had messed things up big time. I had no idea what had gone on after he had left me; how could I? I didn't even question why he looked after me financially after he'd left; I was just grateful that he did. Maybe I should have asked questions and tried to help, but why should I? I was too busy trying to rebuild my own sad life; I didn't have time to think about what had happened to his mistress or consider whether they were happy or not.

I had wanted Miles to return to me so badly. I had waited for him, longed for him, and forgiven him for everything he had put me through. I was just collateral damage in Miles's increasingly erratic life. True, I wasn't dead like Katrina or Amelia's mother, but my life wasn't exactly rapturous either. I had no friends or family, and I had spent my entire life waiting for a man to return to me, who never did.

Amelia's tears were flowing fast now, and I could see her trying hard to stifle her sobs. Here was a young woman, robbed of her mother in her childhood, a woman who had harboured a grudge for many years trying to make sense of things that she simply didn't understand. Her grief had turned to hatred, and her hatred to revenge. She thought Miles owed her, and I was beginning to think that maybe she was right. Maybe she did deserve something, but why had she gone about it this way? Why couldn't she have been truthful and told me her story in the first place instead of lying about being Miles's daughter? She read my mind.

'You want to know why I lied to you, don't you?' she asked, wiping the snot from her face with the back of her hand. 'Well, if the truth be known, I didn't want to lie about any of it. I figured my own story, the real story, was evidence enough of how much a bastard Miles had been. He ruined lives, you see. Miles ruined lives. It was what he was good at. First, yours, then Katrina's and my mother's and finally, if I had allowed him to, he would have ruined mine.' Her voice trailed off again; she was lost in thought.

'She made me do it?' Amelia suddenly blurted out, the tone of her voice suddenly changing.

*She*? What did Amelia mean? I willed her to continue, but she remained silent.

'Who made you, Amelia,' I prompted in a hushed voice, frightened to hear the answer.

'Jean. She only wanted the money, and she figured she had a good chance of getting it too,' she said, the same smirk taking hold again. 'But she hadn't figured on him leaving everything to you,' she continued. 'That's when things started to go a bit pear-shaped; the will you see shocked my aunt. She honestly thought that Miles would have made provision for her not just because of the years of loyal service she had shown him but because of how he treated my mother and me. But she forgot what a bastard Miles really was,' she spat the words out as if the very taste of them in her mouth was vile and putrid, and the sympathy I had started to feel for her suddenly disappeared.

Even now, after everything I had heard, I still had feelings for Miles. He was still my husband, and I still loved him. If he were alive today, I instinctively knew we would be together. He had left me, yes that was true, but he had never been happy without me. We were meant to be together; we were destined to be together.

Was I deluded? No, he had shown how much he loved me by forsaking everyone in favour of me when he died. His entire estate, everything he owned, had been left to me. If he had any regrets, they were for me and me alone.

I wondered what plan Jean had mustered up after discovering that Miles hadn't left her anything in the will. I thought back to the occasions we met, and her dislike for me was obvious. Amelia had said that she lived in the house with Jean after her mother had died, but Jean hadn't mentioned any of this to me. Then again, she couldn't because that would give things away, wouldn't it? Jean wanted me to believe that Amelia was Miles's daughter.

'Miles felt guilty about the way he had treated my mother,' Amelia resumed her story, and my attention immediately snapped back to her. 'He let me live in the big house with Jean and her sons until I turned eighteen, and then that was it; on the day of my eighteenth birthday, he showed up and kicked us all out. He didn't ask if we had anywhere to go, and he didn't care. He simply said he had helped all he could. I think, in his own way, he thought he had kept his side of the bargain, provided for me until I was of age and then simply washed his hands of me. Jean hated him with a vengeance. I could never understand how she could continue to work for someone like Miles. Still, I guess she had her reasons, that was until she found out exactly how much of a ruthless bastard he was when he hadn't left her anything in the will, not even a few hundred measly quid,' Amelia shot me a look of loathing. 'And then you show up, all high and bloody mighty, selling the house from under us before we could contest the will or anything.'

Contest the will? Was she really that naïve, or had Jean planted the stupid ideas into her head? They would never be able to contest the will with the story they had concocted between them. Admittedly Miles had treated Amelia's mother badly, but then so have thousands of men the world over who commit adultery and then sod off when it suits them, but they don't end up having to share all their worldly goods with any woman who shares their bed.

It was my turn to speak now. I had listened to Amelia's story of self-pity and defeatism. I had satisfied her attempts at making me feel guilty and succumbed to her hatred, but whatever Miles had done, be it to her mother or her aunt, it did not excuse what they had tried to do to me.

Amelia had committed an offence by pretending to be my dead husband's daughter with the aim of conning me out of money. However, we both knew that this wouldn't stand up in a court of law. I had no evidence; it was my word against hers, and she would obviously deny everything I said, plus she hadn't actually gained anything. She hadn't contested the will or even tried to yet; not that I was aware of anyway.

'I'm prepared to let this go,' I began in all seriousness, 'Providing you pack up and disappear. I don't want to set eyes on you again, ever. I don't want you hanging around my house; I don't want you texting me or calling me, and I don't want to bump into you anywhere within a hundred miles of this place. I want you to disappear back where you came from before you learned of Miles's death.' I thought I was being generous, given what Amelia had told me, but I hadn't bargained on her twisted personality and the resentment she had for me. She laughed long and hard. I felt my cheeks flush; the joke was well and truly on me.

'You don't have the right to tell me what I can and cannot do,' she screamed across the table. 'I have spent my entire bloody life being bossed around, and I won't be ordered about any longer and certainly not by you. You are nothing more than a sad old woman who has wasted her entire life on a loser who has never loved or respected anyone except himself. I'm glad he's dead, I'm glad his son is dead, and I will rejoice when you die, too.'

I got to my feet, knocking the chair over in my haste. The woman before me was evil with a venomous tongue and no respect for anyone.

'Get out of my house, you nasty little bitch,' I screamed as I pulled her from her chair. She laughed louder. It was a wicked, villainous laugh, and I wondered just how damaged she actually was.

Despite my best efforts to remove her from the chair, she remained steadfast. My blood began to boil. I had heard enough; I wanted her out of my house now. I tried to calm myself down.

'Get out of my house now,' I repeated, 'or I will call

the police.'

'Why? You haven't heard the rest of my story yet,' she said, her voice cold and harsh. 'I haven't even got to the best bit.' She beckoned me to sit down, and I obliged, unable to think straight. I wasn't sure I wanted to hear anything else she had to say, but I felt compelled to listen. I had wanted answers, and she was pouring out her guts. Whether I liked what she had to say or not, I knew I had to hear everything.

'You see, just before Miles died, I looked him up again. He didn't recognise me, of course, why should he? I had only been a child when he had unceremoniously dumped my mother, and then when he threw me out of his house at eighteen, it had been all organised over the telephone. He didn't come to the house to speak to us. I don't think he had the courage to face my aunt.' She smirked.

'When I called on him a few months before he died, I could see he hadn't changed; he was still a charmer, a lady's man. He thought he still had it, but he was just a stupid old man. I let him do as he wanted with me; he made my skin crawl, but I let him think I had fallen for him. His arrogance and sheer stupidity made him an easy target. At first, he had no idea who I was, then after we had been sleeping together for a few months, I told him. I hadn't known at the time that he had a weak heart, but well, it all played wonderfully into my hands. The only problem was the old bastard snuffed it before I could get him to change his will. He had goaded me into telling him who I was. I wish now I had held off a little longer so that I could have told him that I was carrying his child.' Her words stung. She said them gloatingly as if she had just been awarded a Nobel Prize.

*She was pregnant with Miles's child.*

My mind raced; I didn't know whether to believe her or not.

'He died before I found out I was pregnant,' her hand touched her stomach instinctively. How long had Miles been dead, five or six months? Did she look pregnant? I stared at her, trying to see whether she was telling the truth. It was impossible. Pregnant women were all different. Some glowed and grew huge; others took it in their stride with only the slightest of bumps to show for it. If Amelia was pregnant, then she was one of those women who could slip straight back into their jeans a couple of days after having given birth. I couldn't tell if she looked any different from the last time I had seen her. 'So, you see,' she continued, 'Things are very different from how you expected them to be. You might be sitting on a nice little nest egg, but once this baby is born and the necessary tests are carried out, I will have a claim on Miles's money.'

'So why pretend to be his daughter,' I asked, trying to call her bluff. She smiled.

'Because *she* has no idea I am pregnant,' she said with such candour I knew instinctively that she was telling me the truth. '*She* thinks I am going to share what we get with her and those loser cousins of mine. This baby is a dead cert, and I will inherit some of Miles's money, but I have absolutely no intention of sharing any of it. Jean can kid herself all she likes, but as soon as I have the money, I'm out of here; she will have nothing, and I will be long gone. Miles has been very useful despite everything else he did. I will look after his child; I promise you that you just need to ensure I have enough money to do it properly.'

I closed my eyes tightly, willing her to shut up, needing

her to shut up. But she wouldn't. She continued to tell me what she had planned after the baby was born. Her voice gloated, revelling in what she was telling me.

Without a second thought, I reached for the bottle of red wine on the table, and I struck Amelia over the head with it hard. I heard it crash down on her skull; the loud thud sounded sickening and final. She fell silent, her chin lolled against her cheek, but somehow miraculously, she remained upright in her chair. I saw a trickle of blood begin to seep through her hair and down her forehead.

The reality of what I had just done suddenly hit me, and I felt myself retch. I glanced at the bottle in my hand and then back at Amelia. *Was she dead? God, what have I done?* Should I call an ambulance? How can I? What do I say? Oh, she was pissing me off, so I hit her over the head with a bottle of wine. And by the way, she is pregnant. Pregnant? Shit, if I have killed Amelia, then I have also killed her unborn child. Miles's child, my husband's child.

I began to cry. My entire body shook as the tears flowed. I was wracked with guilt. What had I done? What should I do next? I needed to calm down and think this through carefully. Who knew Amelia was here? I doubted she had told anyone. She wouldn't have told Jean because she was planning to double-cross her. No one knew she was here. I told myself that was good. That was how it had to stay. But then Jean would come looking for her once she knew she was missing, and she might even tell the police about the little plan they had cooked up, and then they would come here, asking questions, looking for evidence.

I tried to push the thoughts from my mind. I had read too many books where the killer eventually gets exposed. I didn't deserve this. Miles owed me; how could he have slept with Amelia and got her pregnant? For God's sake, she was young enough to be his granddaughter. I had loved that man more than life itself, and he had treated me in the worst way imaginable even now, after his death, he was still dishing out the crap like I needed it, piling on more and more.

I looked over at Amelia's body, still sitting on the chair. Her eyes were glazed over and expressionless. She was dead; I was certain of it.

My legs were weak and unsteady, but I forced myself to go upstairs and retrieve a blanket from the cupboard. I returned downstairs and heaved Amelia from the chair onto the floor; grabbing her under the arms, I pulled her through the conservatory into the living room, where I wrapped her in the blanket. I let my hand fall on the swell of her stomach, caressing the baby she was carrying, and a tear fell from my eyes, dropping with a splash on the perfect curve of her abdomen. I said a silent prayer. This baby, like me, didn't deserve any of this. I turned and left the room, abandoning Amelia's lifeless body, still protecting her unborn child.

I returned to the conservatory and cleared the table, stacking the dishwasher and tidying the plates from the meal I had just shared with Amelia. It all made sense now why Amelia had picked at her food. Don't they say appetites and tastes change in pregnancy? Maybe she had to eat little and often to stifle morning sickness, I thought.

I was a complete wreck going about my jobs, trying not to think about the dead body in the next room. The one I had put there.

# Chapter Thirty-Two

The next morning, I woke early. I had a lot to do, but also there was a dead body in my house, and I needed a plan of action. It couldn't stay there much longer. I needed to get rid of it and fast.

For obvious reasons, I had slept fitfully, but by early morning, I had come up with something that resembled a plan, at least in my disturbed state of mind. I tried to pass it off as being workable. It all hinged on Jean and just how greedy or desperate she was for money. I couldn't believe I was putting my future in the hands of a woman I hardly knew and absolutely loathed. She had planned, with Amelia, to cheat me out of my inheritance. Still, despite everything, Amelia had been about to double-cross her, and I was pinning my hopes on the fact that anything was better than nothing. When Jean discovered Amelia's betrayal, I figured she would probably have wanted to kill her anyway. This way, she would get what she wanted without dirtying her hands. It all sounded perfectly workable in my mind, but then things didn't always go according to plan; I knew that first hand and with conviction.

I telephoned Jean. It was so easy to find her number on Amelia's phone, and I was aghast that she only had face recognition rather than a passcode to unlock it. It hadn't been easy trying to tilt her head at the right angle for the phone to recognise her face, but I was grateful that technology wasn't clever enough to recognise whether the face was dead or alive, at least not yet it wasn't.

Jean didn't answer. I glanced at my watch. It was six-thirty, probably too early even for a gold digger like Jean to prise herself out of bed. I sent a text instead, but this time, I waited until after nine o'clock. I sent the text from Amelia's phone. Jean may well ignore me, but I doubted she would ignore Amelia, who she saw as her cash cow. Just as I predicted, Jean responded less than ten minutes later. I texted back again, this time arranging to meet Jean here at my house. Jean's reply asked why, so I typed, 'Just do it!' I figured this was how Amelia would speak to her aunt. After all, I had heard them having heated discussions on a couple of occasions, and I knew there was no love lost between the pair. They were in this for just one thing: money.

I sat at the kitchen table and waited. The message I had sent from Amelia's phone told Jean to come to my house at ten o'clock, which was just forty minutes away. It didn't give Jean long enough to think about things, nor did it give her a chance to speak to her sons. Amelia's car was still parked outside my house, so she wouldn't be suspicious when she drove up. She would think that Amelia was already here. She was, of course, just not in the capacity Jean would expect her to be.

The knock on the door brought me to my senses. I took a deep breath and opened it. Seeing Jean stand on the doorstep, her hair lank and greasy, her clothes tatty and dirty, made me want to slam the door in her face and run a mile, but I couldn't. I had lured her here now, and I had no option but to spell out my plan and hope for the best. I stood aside and allowed Jean to enter my hallway. She looked around suspiciously. I led the way into the kitchen, and she followed me, her eyes darting in every direction.

'Coffee?' I asked.

'Where's Amelia?' she replied bluntly.

'All will be revealed, but I just wanted a little chat with you first, alone.' I continued to make two cups of coffee, remembering how Jean took hers from the times I had taken a flask to the big house. I placed the mugs on the counter, pulled out a chair and sat down. Jean did the same.

I proceeded to tell my story. I left nothing out. I told Jean everything that had happened yesterday, right up to Amelia divulging that she was pregnant with Miles's child.

Jean inhaled sharply, a flicker of doubt in her eyes. She wasn't certain I was telling the truth, and that was exactly what I wanted her to think.

'Pregnant?' she repeated. 'That's not possible,' she said, shaking her head.

'No, and why is that, Jean?' I asked, studying her closely, watching her eyes narrow as she stared back at me. I breathed deeply; now was my chance. 'She was going to double-cross you,' I said slowly, clearly, allowing the statement to sink in.

Jean's expression turned from doubt to anger in the blink of an eye as my words hit home. 'Yes, she had every intention of contesting the will, but not until after the baby was born, when she had proof that she was the mother of Miles's child. If she did it this way, she could keep it all; she wouldn't have to share anything with you or her cousins. It appealed to her immensely, the thought of getting her hands on millions and then doing a runner, leaving you with nothing but your dreams.'

Jean pushed the chair back, scraping the stone flags on my kitchen floor, the noise setting my teeth on edge.

'Where is she? I will kill the little bitch,' she screamed, rushing from the kitchen into the hall, angry at being made to look a fool. I followed her and watched as she pushed open the door to the sitting room.

'Already done,' I stated ironically, as Jean stopped at the doorway, staring at the wrapped corpse of her niece on my living room floor.

I held my breath and prayed.

This was the moment of truth. It could go either way, and I was mentally prepared for both. Either Jean's overwhelming love for her niece would prevail. She would call the police and report the murder, or, and I very much hoped this would be the outcome, the hatred I had just mustered up in Jean by telling her of Amelia's plan to double-cross her would remain the overriding factor and she would listen to my plan.

'What happened?' Jean asked, the blood draining from her face. I still wasn't sure which way this situation would go.

'It doesn't matter. The less you know, the better,' I said coldly. 'Now I need to know if you want to earn that money you so desperately think you should have.' Jean leaned against the door and stared at me. Her eyes were blue, piercing blue, just like Amelia's, and I wondered why I had never recognised the similarities between the two before.

'I want your help to get rid of the body,' I said calmly. Jean snorted as if I had just told the funniest joke she had heard in a long time. 'The fee is one million pounds,' I continued, without taking my eyes off her face. Jean stopped laughing, her eyes twinkling. 'You don't have to kill anyone, you don't even have to think up a plan, you just have to do what I tell you.'

'I'm listening,' she said, and I sighed with relief. She was on board. She hadn't even heard what I was going to ask of her, but I could see I had set the wheels in motion; the pound signs were all it took. She was so easy to persuade. I would have increased the sum considerably, doubling or maybe even trebling it, if necessary, but the sheer greed of the woman was a godsend.

'I want you to get your lads to dig a hole, a deep one. Tell them I'm having a patio laid or a duck pond or something. I don't care; I just need a nice deep hole,' I glanced over at the body wrapped in the blanket. Jean didn't need me to explain further.

'You're going to bury her here?' she asked incredulously, 'in your garden?'

'Hell no, of course not,' I said, 'Don't be ridiculous.' I walked past Jean back into the hallway and plucked a set of keys from the hook by the door. I dangled them in front of Jean's face. How I wished at this moment in time that it was Amelia standing in Jean's shoes. I had been waiting for this moment; to see Amelia's face when she discovered that I too could be conniving and ruthless. Due to Amelia's untimely death, I had been robbed of this little victory, but the irony wasn't wasted.

'These are the keys to the property over the valley,' I nodded as Jean recognised what I was saying, 'Yes, the cottage Amelia had wanted to buy. I was the person who bought it from under her nose. I couldn't have that little bitch living on my doorstep, well, not in the way she intended anyway,' I said.

Jean watched me as I sat down in the living room. She seemed unable to enter the room, seemingly transfixed, still leaning against the door. 'The house needs a lot of work. I will get contractors in once the body has been buried. Your boys need not know about Amelia. In addition to the million, I will pay them to work in the garden. Once the hole is dug, you and I will dump the body and then get the lads to concrete over it.'

After laying out my plan, I waited for Jean's reaction. It was slow. She was carefully considering everything I had said. Mulling it over in her mind.

'Amelia was going to leave with the money and not even tell you where she was going,' I said, praying that Jean would be on board with me. 'This way, after the body has been disposed of, you and the boys can disappear with your money, split however you feel appropriate, and I will be left to continue with my life in peace.'

'What if someone finds the body in years to come?' Jean asked. I nodded. She deserved more credit than I had given her. It was a good question.

'I have every intention of renovating the property and renting it out,' I said. No one in my lifetime will ever have access to dig up the garden, and, as you are considerably older than me, then I strongly doubt you have anything to worry about.' Jean smiled and nodded in agreement. 'Do we have an agreement?' I asked cautiously, still expecting everything to explode in my face.

'We do,' Jean said, as she moved forward ever so slightly to shake my hand. 'I will get the boys started straight away, and hopefully we can dump the bitch when it gets dark tonight.'

I let Jean out of the house, relieved that the conversation was over and that it had gone in the right direction. I was ecstatic if anyone could actually feel so happy after having murdered someone. She had it coming, I told myself as I recalled the conversation we had yesterday when she had been so disrespectful towards Miles.

I closed the door to the living room, shutting the body out of sight, and I waited. It was a long day but eventually, after seven o'clock, Jean phoned me. I snatched the phone up immediately.

'It's done. The boys have dug the hole; we can move the body tonight. I will get to you for ten.' She ended the call without waiting for my response. Of course, I would be ready; she knew that she didn't need a reply.

The hours ticked by slowly. I couldn't eat. My stomach churned. We were so close yet so far. I needed this to end. I wanted that bitch out of my house and six feet under where she belonged. I could still hear her shrill laugh ringing in my head, the sting of her words as she harshly ridiculed my dead husband.

# Chapter Thirty-Three

At exactly ten o'clock Jean entered my house. She didn't knock; she simply pushed the door open and entered without being invited. I guess that's what a million-pound arrangement to dispose of a body does to a relationship.

She was dressed in waterproofs, wellington boots and gloves, and I wondered fleetingly whether she had done this kind of thing before. I shuddered as I reached for my own jacket, boots and gloves. Despite the late hour, the air was still warm, and I felt the sweat begin to pool in the small of my back as I zipped my jacket up.

Jean entered the living room and took hold of Amelia's body. She heaved it onto her shoulder and walked back out of the door to her car, carrying the body as if it were a small child rather than a grown woman, a pregnant woman. Jean's strength surprised me. For a woman of her age, she had a considerable amount of muscle. The boot of Jean's car was already open, and she dumped the body inside and slammed it shut.

'Get in,' she ordered, and it was very clear to me who was in charge. I did as I was told, and we drove to the cottage in silence.

True to her word, Jean had made sure that the boys had dug a deep hole. It was much deeper than I imagined, and I knew if either of us fell in, there would be no way of getting back out. My mind flicked over the opportunity. A quick shove would mean Jean would be gone in an instant. I could throw Amelia on top and fill the hole back in; kill two birds with one stone, so to speak.

Jean glared at me, and I felt she was reading my thoughts. I pushed the thought from my mind quickly and concentrated on the task at hand. I had promised a fair price for the job to be done, and so far, Jean was holding up to her side of the bargain; the least I could do was to go along with it.

Jean hoisted Amelia's body from the car and let it slide into the hole her sons had dug in the back garden of my house. It landed at the bottom with an unceremonious thud. I cringed. Jean returned to the car and snatched up two shovels. She had thought of everything. She handed one of the shovels to me and began heaping the earth back into the hole. We worked together until all the soil had been replaced. By now, the sweat was pouring off both of us. The plastic fabric of our waterproofs, whilst helping to keep off the mud and heaven knows what other fibres, served to generate body heat on a scale unimaginable, and I couldn't wait to strip off and climb into the shower. The hole was refilled, and we got into Jean's car. She drove back to my house.

'Drink?' I asked as Jean pulled up outside my door. She smiled and followed me inside. We left our boots, jackets, and gloves in a pile on the hall floor. I grabbed a couple of glasses from the kitchen cupboard and a bottle of wine and headed for the garden, Jean following closely in my footsteps.

'I don't usually drink red wine,' I said, as I opened the wine Amelia had brought the day before, 'but then I don't usually bury people in my back garden,' I finished, pulling a strand of hair from the bottom of the bottle and handing a glass to Jean. We clinked glasses.

'Cheers,' Jean said, and I responded, raising my glass high before taking a long, deep drink.

# Chapter Thirty-Four

Everything went surprisingly smoothly. Once we had dumped Amelia's body, Jean told her sons that I had changed my mind about the pond or patio or whatever it was she had told them I had wanted, and she got them to concrete over the entire garden. I don't know if they asked any questions about who had filled in the hole but if they did, I am sure Jean had thought of something and her sons knew not to question their mother. They had spent their life doing what they were told and I was grateful that Jean very much ruled the roost where her sons were concerned. It took only a few days before the concrete was dry enough to walk on. The hot summer weather had made it dry out quickly, but it had to be protected so that it didn't crumble and crack as the drying-out process took place. After all, we didn't want to have to dig it all up again and restart the process, did we? Who knows what we might find?

I inspected the boys' work, trying to keep a smile in place when, all along, I hated every inch of it. It was everything I despised, and for what it was worth, it hid everything I despised too. It was the epitome of ugliness. A cottage garden devoid of plants and vegetation smothered in cold, harsh concrete. I would get to work making it better once Jean and her boys had departed, I told myself.

The following day, I made my way into town to the bank, and, as promised, I transferred one million pounds over to Jean. It didn't bother me one iota. It was certainly a lot of money, but in my eyes, it was money well spent. Jean had kept her side of the bargain, and now, so had I.

Jean told me she was emigrating. She was going to live in France. It was a dream she had always harboured, and now she had the money to buy a little gite; she saw no reason to put it off any longer. She asked me if we could keep in touch. I declined. I told her it would be best if we never contacted each other again. She smiled and nodded in approval. She never told me how much of the money she gave to her sons, and I never asked her. The deal had been between Jean and me, and she could share or spend the money in any way she felt fit.

I enjoyed overseeing the renovation of the cottage. Despite its compact size, the work took a few months to complete, but by the end of autumn, the contractors had finally departed, and the house was ready to be advertised for tenants. I had spent much time in the garden, transforming it from a concrete jungle into an oasis of greenery. I had enlisted the help of a carpenter who had made me some raised beds, and I had planted standard rose trees and lavender. Their fragrance engulfed me as I arranged a lover's seat in the corner of the garden and sat down to admire my work. What was once an unloved, derelict cottage was now transformed.

I reached for my phone and scrolled down the numbers. I stopped, selected the number I wanted and waited for the call to be answered. I made my enquiry and gave my name.

'We can't wait to welcome you again, Mrs Jameson,' the young lady on the other end of the phone said, as I thanked her and hung up. I had promised I would return to

Utopia once things had been sorted, and now that they had, my holiday awaited.

Maybe I could visit Grace and Mrs Lowther again, I thought, smiling to myself.

There is a saying, *Never work with children or animals*. Allison Lee did both before venturing one step further and delving into the world of suspense and murder.

Allison sold her small chain of children's day nurseries in 2022 to concentrate on her other passions: writing and animals. She writes fiction and nonfiction and lives on a smallholding in the North Yorkshire countryside with her long-suffering husband of 38 years, four dogs, ponies, donkeys, sheep, goats, pigs, and chickens.

BAD PRESS iNK,

publishers of niche, alternative and cult fiction

Visit

www.BADPRESS.iNK

for details of all our books, and sign up to
be notified of future releases and offers

## Also from BAD PRESS iNK

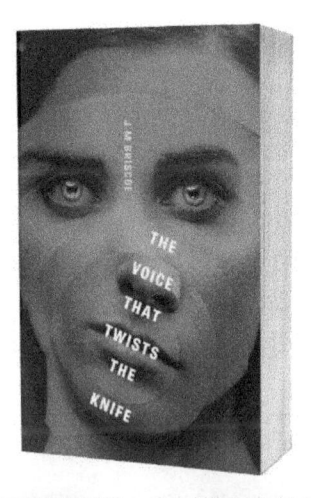

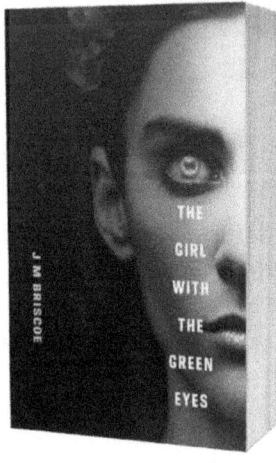

Bella is defective. You need to take her back.
Everyone tells her she is normal. Everyone is lying.
Eugenics, chimeras and the fierceness of a mother's love in a terrifying near future.
All three books in the Take Her Back Trilogy
by J M Briscoe

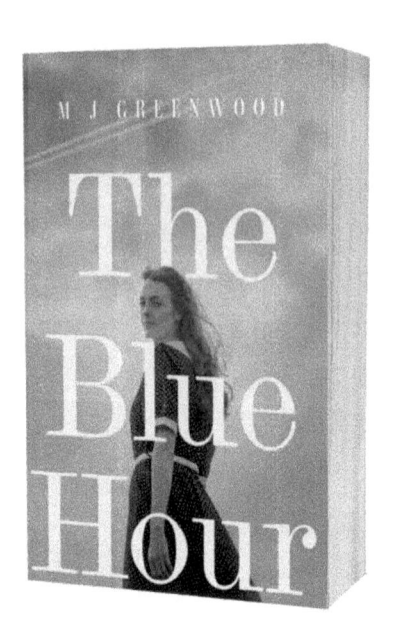

Two love affairs and two summers, 75 years apart.

Cantankerous Tilly is determined to grow old disgracefully.

Shy Ava is finding out looking after the elderly was never meant to be like this!

*The Blue Hour* by M J Greenwood

Evie Hepburn loves fairytales.

But fairytales can be dark –
particularly when you begin to live them…

*In Silence and Shadows* by Georgie St-Claire, the first in the *White Rose Witches* series

Welcome to The King George.

You know it. Your old local. Back in the day.

The stink of beer and piss, sticky carpets, nicotine stains on the ceiling, soggy bar towels, and the chance of a punch-up on a Saturday night – or anytime for that matter.

And in amongst it all an awkward 20-year-old, trapped behind the bar, with nothing to do but pull pints and wait for the next fag break.

Until he finds Amy. And life. And an escape – if he dares.

*The Sadness of The King George* by Shaun Hand

Get Carter meets Sons of Anarchy in this gritty British crime thriller series.

From being in a gang to becoming a gangster, the Heavy Duty trilogy invented Biker Noir.

Damage's club has had an offer it can't refuse, to patch over to join The Brethren MC. But as the bikes rumble and roar across the wild Northern fells, what does this mean for Damage and his brothers? What choices will they have to make as they ride through the wind? What bloody oil-stained history might it reawaken? And why are The Brethren making this offer? Loyalty to his club and his brothers has been Damage's life and route to wealth, but what happens when business becomes serious and brother starts killing brother?

The Heavy Duty trilogy by Iain Parke

# Important Notice – Please Read

BAD PRESS iNK Limited as the publisher of this book does not give permission for it to be used for the training of Large Language Models, Artificial Intelligence or any similar systems other than by prior written agreement of the publisher, or on the contractual terms below.

## Default training usage contract

By obtaining and using the contents of this book for the training of Large Language Models, Artificial Intelligence or any similar systems without the prior written agreement of BAD PRESS iNK Limited (the 'Publisher') you (the 'User') are deemed to accept these contractual terms and agree to pay the publisher a licence fee of £10,000.

This fee is deemed due and payable on the date the User acquires the book text.

The publisher gives notice of our right to add interest and collection costs for late payment under The Late Payment of Commercial Debts (Interest) Act 1998 Act as amended and supplemented by The Late Payment of Commercial Debts Regulations 2002 and Statutory interest will be charged at a rate of 8% over the Bank of England base rate.

The User agrees that the use of this book for the above training purposes is at the User's risk and the publisher offers no warranties and accepts no liability to the User for the use of the text of this book for the above purposes or any consequential losses that may arise.

This contract is governed by and to be construed in accordance with English law and the parties irrevocably submit to the non-exclusive jurisdiction of the Courts of England and Wales in respect of any claim, dispute or difference arising out of or in connection with this contract.

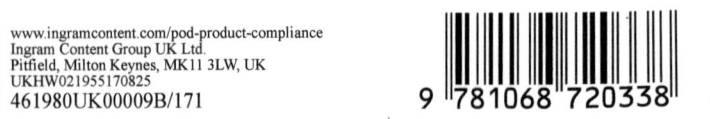